THE BIOGRAPHICAL EDITION
OF THE WORKS OF
ROBERT LOUIS STEVENSON

MORE NEW ARABIAN NIGHTS
THE DYNAMITER

BIOGRAPHICAL EDITION

MORE NEW ARABIAN NIGHTS

THE DYNAMITER

BY

ROBERT LOUIS STEVENSON

AND

FANNY VAN DE GRIFT STEVENSON

WITH A PREFACE BY MRS. STEVENSON

NEW YORK

CHARLES SCRIBNER'S SONS

1923

PREFACE

TO

THE BIOGRAPHICAL EDITION

THE little châlet La Solitude, where my husband spent, as he has said, the happiest period of his life, was curiously out of keeping with its surroundings. A châlet was an incongruous object in Hyères, and it was made more conspicuous by its position, clinging to a low cliff almost at the entrance of the old town. From this cliff the ground rose with a gentle gradient until just outside our garden gate, where it became more rugged and steep, breaking out near the summit into rocky crags that were crowned with the ruins of an ancient Saracen castle.

Our tiny châlet was the result of a visit of the owner to the Paris Exposition of 1878. There, amidst Chinese pagodas, Turkish mosques, and the like in miniature, stood a model Swiss châlet that so fascinated our landlord that he bought it outright and had it removed to be again erected on his property in Hyères. It was like a doll's house, with rooms so small that we could hardly turn round in them; but the view from the verandahs was extensive, the garden was large and wild, with winding paths and old grey olive trees where nightingales nested and sang. Looking in one direction we could see the Îles d'Or, and in another, the hills beyond Toulon. So quiet and secluded was our life here that we heard almost nothing of the outside world except through an occasional English correspondent. I remember, before we knew that cholera was raging in Toulon, only some three miles away, how we watched a cloud gathering over the town where it hung, heavy and lowering, day after day. We felt that it was somehow ominous, and were vaguely depressed. We were told afterwards that at that very time great fires were burning in the streets of Toulon by order of the mayor, and that the people gathered at night round these fires capering fantastically in a pagan dance, resurrected from the dark ages by no one knew whom or how.

But Toulon had another aspect than gloom. I shall never forget the day my husband and I drove there through lanes of roses from which the attar of commerce is made. On either side of us the rose hedges were in full bloom; the scent, mingled with the fragrance of innumerable violets, was truly intoxicating. When we alighted at a *place* dappled with sunlight that filtered through the trees, and cooled by a spouting fountain where girls in coloured gowns laughed and chattered as they plied their trade of lace-making, we felt that our lines had indeed fallen in pleasant places.

We made almost no new acquaintances in Hyères, with the exception of Dr. Vidal, our physician, and a local English chemist, Mr. Powell. We were divided from the new town by a series of wooden stairs running precipitously to the street below. Near the foot of one of these stairways was Mr. Powell's pharmacy, very conveniently placed for us, as was afterwards proved. The chemist himself became fired with the desire to write. One story, at least, of his, a little tale of considerable merit, was published in the *Cornhill Magazine*. I believe my husband was more interested in the success of this venture of Mr. Powell's than in that of *Prince Otto,* which he was then engaged upon.

Our life in the châlet was of the utmost simplicity. With the help of one untrained maid I did the cooking myself. The kitchen was so narrow that I was in continual danger of being scorched by the range on one side, and at the same time impaled by the saucepan hooks on the other, and when we had a guest at dinner our maid had to pass in the dishes over our heads, as our chairs touched the walls of the dining-room, leaving her no passage-way. The markets of Hyères were well supplied, and the wine both good and cheap, so we were able, for the first time, to live comfortably within our limited income.

My husband usually wrote from the very early morning until noon, while my household duties occupied the same time. In the afternoon the work of the morning was read aloud, and we talked it over, criticising and suggesting improvements. This finished, we walked in our garden, listened to the birds, and looked at our trees and flowers; or, accompanied by our Scotch terrier, wandered up the hill to the ruins of the castle. After dinner we talked or read aloud, and on rare occasions visited Mr. Powell or received a visit from him. The châlet was well named, as far as we were concerned, for it was almost a solitude *à deux*, but the days slipped by with amazing celerity.

One of the articles written by my husband at this time was entitled *Old Mortality*, and was afterwards printed with other papers in the book called *Memories and Portraits*. A friend of my husband's youth had died, and only his errors, which were many, were remembered, and the good in him forgotten. Injustice, and especially injustice to the helpless dead, always touched my husband very nearly. He wrote what was really a defence of his old friend, and then, realizing its personal nature, hesitated to publish it. Finally, he sent the proof sheets to his friend's sister, leaving it to her to say whether it should see the light or not. She responded with an urgent request for its publication. It is the irony of fate that the man who wrote *Old Mortality* and *The Defence of Father Damien* — in both instances because the person misjudged lay " in his resting grave " — should have had his own memory attacked, not by an enemy, nor even by a stranger, but by one he had had every reason to believe his loyal friend.

It happened, about this time, that an editor of a notorious London journal, who published scandalous stories concerning private individuals, was prosecuted for libel, found guilty, and punished by imprisonment. When the news came to us, my husband said this was an occasion that must be celebrated. In the evening we placed a candle in each window to serve as an illumination, and lighted a bonfire we had previously prepared in the afternoon for the purpose. My husband, our maid, and I clasped hands and danced round the fire, shouting and laughing. Nemesis followed. We did not notice, in our excitement, that the mistral was blowing, until we were chilled to the bone.

The next day my husband lay in the pangs of

a new malady — sciatica — and on the following evening he had a terrible hemorrhage. Had not the pharmacy been so near and Mr. Powell so quickly reached, I doubt if recovery would have been possible. Sciatica and a hemorrhage seemed enough for the endurance of any mortal; but there was more to follow.

The old town, with its crooked, narrow, foul lanes, its sunless, age-worn houses, was no better than a hotbed of disease. Typhus, smallpox, cholera, heaven knows what not — lurked there in its damp shadows. In the early morning we could hear the fast rolling of wheels under our windows, an indication that patients from the old town were being carried to the pest-house. A few weeks before his illness, my husband had written to the mayor of Hyères, pointing out to him the unsanitary condition of the old town, and the consequent menace to the whole community. A gratifying answer came to the effect that the place should be cleaned out immediately and thoroughly. The mayor kept his word so far as the old town was concerned, but the accumulated *débris* of ages was only carried a short distance away to be dumped, a huge unsavoury pile, just in front of a pretty cottage called Rosemount, whose English owner was absent from home. This was unendurable, and more dangerous than before, as all paths led past

Rosemount. Again the mayor was invoked, and
again he responded generously. My husband, in
his second letter, unfortunately mentioned the fact
that the road in front of La Solitude was in great
need of repair. We were assured that the odor-
iferous mound would be removed, and our road
mended and levelled. In the anxiety occasioned
by my husband's illness I had forgotten all about
the mayor's promises, but was reminded of them
by the unwonted activity of a gang of labourers
who were apparently spreading a thick layer of
some peculiar material over our road. To my
horror I realized that this was the contents of the
mound removed from Rosemount!

The mayor had reached the limit of his liberality,
and my impassioned appeals were ignored. In a
short time one or more out of every family living
in the vicinity of the road were infected with what
the doctor called contagious Egyptian ophthalmia.
My husband suffered with the rest, and was threatened with total blindness. Here was a predicament
for a literary man! Condemned to lie helpless on
his bed on account of the sciatica, his right arm
bound to his side lest an inadvertent movement
might bring on a recurrence of the hemorrhage,
speech denied him for the same reason, and now
a bandage over his eyes that precluded any attempt
to use them! Often, before, when I was near de-

spair, he would say to me, " Now if you would only
look at it in the right light, you would see that this
is the best thing that could have happened." When
I tried to read to him and found that I could not
make out a word in the darkened room, I said,
with forlorn irony, " I suppose *this* is one of the
best things that could have happened!" To my
shame, he took my remark seriously, replying,
" Why, how odd; that's just what I was about to
say." He was now, he continued, forced to take
a rest, which he would never do of his own free
will. " Don't you remember," he wrote (all this
was laboriously written in pencil on large sheets
of paper with his left hand), " don't you remember
Uncle George's [1] idea of what he called derivative treatment? His proposal to blister the soles
of my feet so I should be compelled to lie still?
Well, this is a form of nature's derivative treatment." He went on to say that there was something that he greatly wished me to do. I was to
go out for an hour's walk every afternoon, if it
were only back and forth in front of our door, and
invent a story to repeat when I came in — a sort
of Arabian Nights Entertainment where I was to
take the part of Scheherazade and he the sultan.
There had been several dynamite outrages in London about this time, the most of them turning out

[1] Dr. George Balfour.

fiascos. It occurred to me to take an impotent
dynamite intrigue as the thread to string my stories
on. I began with the Mormon tale, and followed
it with innumerable others, one for each afternoon.
As time passed, my husband gradually regained
his health to a degree, became again absorbed
in his work, and the stories of Scheherazade were
thought of no more.

After several migrations and changes of abode,
we finally settled in Bournemouth, in the South
of England. Our simple life of the châlet was
impossible here, and we found our expenses in-
creasing rather alarmingly. A theory of my husband's which he put into active practice was that
he who has must give. When he received a check
for a book or other work, he at once made a list
of those of his friends who needed money, and the
sum received was divided accordingly. This amiable and somewhat Quixotic proceeding often left
us with a lean purse. The money was given with
such freedom that the recipients would, I imagine,
have been surprised, and perhaps shocked, had they
known how little was left for ourselves. It is true
my father-in-law was always ready to come to our
aid, but we did not like to make him the vicarious
dispenser of these gifts.

On one of these occasions when money was abso-
lutely necessary, we cast about for something that

could be done quickly and without too much strain; the Scheherazade stories came to mind, and we both set to work to write out what we could remember of them. We could recall only enough to make a rather thin book, so my husband added one more to the list, *The Explosive Bomb*.

Thus *The Dynamiter* did double service; first, as an amusement for my husband during the tedious hours of his illness in 1883, and afterwards as a means of replenishing our depleted bank account. It was published in 1885 by Messrs. Longmans, Green & Co., and was as well received as we could have hoped.

F. V. DE G. S.

TO

MESSRS. COLE AND COX,

POLICE OFFICERS.

GENTLEMEN:

IN the volume now in your hands, the authors have touched upon the ugly devil of crime, with which it is your glory to have contended. It were a waste of ink to do so in a serious spirit. Let us dedicate our horror to acts of a more mingled strain, where crime preserves some features of nobility, and where reason and humanity can still relish the temptation. Horror, in this case, is due to Mr. Parnell: he sits before posterity silent, Mr. Forster's appeal echoing down the ages. Horror is due to ourselves, in that we have so long coquetted with political crime; not seriously weighing, not acutely following it from cause to consequence; but with a generous, unfounded heat of sentiment, like the schoolboy with the penny tale, applauding what was specious. When it touched ourselves (truly in a vile shape) we proved false to these imaginations; discovered, in a clap, that crime was no less cruel and no less ugly under sounding names: and recoiled from our false deities.

But seriousness comes most in place when we are to speak of our defenders. Whoever be in the right in this great and confused war of politics; whatever elements of greed, whatever traits of the bully, dishonour both parties in this inhuman contest; — your side, your part, is at least pure of doubt. Yours is the side of the child, of the breeding woman, of individual pity and public trust. If our society were the mere kingdom of the devil (as indeed it wears some of its colours) it yet embraces many precious elements and many innocent persons whom it is a glory to defend. Courage and devotion, so common in the ranks of the police, so little recognised, so meagerly rewarded, have at length found their commemoration in an historical act. History, which will represent Mr. Parnell sitting silent under the appeal of Mr. Forster, and Gordon setting forth upon his tragic enterprise, will not forget Mr. Cole carrying the dynamite in his defenceless hands, nor Mr. Cox coming coolly to his aid.

ROBERT LOUIS STEVENSON.
FANNY VAN DE GRIFT STEVENSON.

A NOTE FOR THE READER

IT is within the bounds of possibility that you may take up this volume, and yet be unacquainted with its predecessor, the first series of NEW ARABIAN NIGHTS. The loss is yours — and mine; or to be more exact, my publisher's. But if you are thus unlucky, the least I can do is to pass you a hint. When you shall find a reference in the following pages to one Theophilus Godall of the Bohemian Cigar Divan in Rupert Street, Soho, you must be prepared to recognise, under his features, no less a person than Prince Florizel of Bohemia, formerly one of the magnates of Europe, now de-throned, exiled, impoverished, and embarked in the tobacco trade.

R. L. S.

CONTENTS

THE DYNAMITER

MORE NEW ARABIAN NIGHTS

PROLOGUE OF THE CIGAR DIVAN

IN the city of encounters, the Bagdad of the West, and, to be more precise, on the broad northern pavement of Leicester Square, two young men of five- or six-and-twenty met after years of separation. The first, who was of a very smooth address and clothed in the best fashion, hesitated to recognise the pinched and shabby air of his companion.

"What!" he cried, "Paul Somerset?"

"I am indeed Paul Somerset," returned the other, "or what remains of him after a well-deserved experience of poverty and law. But in you, Challoner, I can perceive no change; and time may be said, without hyperbole, to write no wrinkle on your azure brow."

"All," replied Challoner, "is not gold that glitters. But we are here in an ill posture for confidences, and interrupt the movement of these ladies. Let us, if you please, find a more private corner."

"If you will allow me to guide you," replied Somerset, "I will offer you the best cigar in London."

1

And taking the arm of his companion, he led him in silence and at a brisk pace to the door of a quiet establishment in Rupert Street, Soho. The entrance was adorned with one of those gigantic Highlanders of wood which have almost risen to the standing of antiquities; and across the window-glass, which sheltered the usual display of pipes, tobacco, and cigars, there ran the gilded legend: " Bohemian Cigar Divan, by T. Godall." The interior of the shop was small, but commodious and ornate: the salesman grave, smiling, and urbane; and the two young men, each puffing a select regalia, had soon taken their places on a sofa of mouse-coloured plush and proceeded to exchange their stories.

" I am now," said Somerset, " a barrister; but Providence and the attorneys have hitherto denied me the opportunity to shine. A select society at the Cheshire Cheese engaged my evenings; my afternoons, as Mr. Godall could testify, have been generally passed in this divan; and my mornings, I have taken the precaution to abbreviate by not rising before twelve. At this rate, my little patrimony was very rapidly, and I am proud to remember, most agreeably expended. Since then a gentleman, who has really nothing else to recommend him beyond the fact of being my maternal uncle, deals me the small sum of ten shillings a week; and if you behold me once more revisiting the glimpses of the street lamps in my favourite quarter, you will readily divine that I have come into a fortune."

"I should not have supposed so," replied Challoner. "But doubtless I met you on the way to your tailor's."

"It is a visit I purpose to delay," returned Somerset, with a smile. "My fortune has definite limits. It consists, or rather this morning it consisted, of one hundred pounds."

"That is certainly odd," said Challoner; "yes, certainly the coincidence is strange. I am myself reduced to the same margin."

"You!" cried Somerset. "And yet Solomon in all his glory —— "

"Such is the fact. I am, dear boy, on my last legs," said Challoner. "Besides the clothes in which you see me, I have scarcely a decent trouser in my wardrobe; and if I knew how, I would this instant set about some sort of work or commerce. With a hundred pounds for capital, a man should push his way."

"It may be," returned Somerset; "but what to do with mine is more than I can fancy. Mr. Godall," he added, addressing the salesman, "you are a man who knows the world: what can a young fellow of reasonable education do with a hundred pounds?"

"It depends," replied the salesman, withdrawing his cheroot. "The power of money is an article of faith in which I profess myself a sceptic. A hundred pounds will with difficulty support you for a year; with somewhat more difficulty you may spend it in a night; and without any difficulty at all you may lose it in five minutes on the Stock

Exchange. If you are of that stamp of man that
rises, a penny would be as useful; if you belong
to those that fall, a penny would be no more use-
less. When I was myself thrown unexpectedly
upon the world, it was my fortune to possess an
art: I knew a good cigar. Do you know nothing,
Mr. Somerset?"

"Not even law," was the reply.

"The answer is worthy of a sage," returned
Mr. Godall. "And you, sir," he continued, turning to Challoner, "as the friend of Mr. Somerset, may I be allowed to address you the same
question?"

"Well," replied Challoner, "I play a fair hand
at whist."

"How many persons are there in London," returned the salesman, "who have two-and-thirty
teeth? Believe me, young gentleman, there are
more still who play a fair hand at whist. Whist,
sir, is wide as the world; 't is an accomplishment
like breathing. I once knew a youth who announced, that he was studying to be Chancellor of
England; the design was certainly ambitious; but
I find it less excessive than that of the man who
aspires to make a livelihood by whist."

"Dear me," said Challoner, "I am afraid I shall
have to fall to be a working man."

"Fall to be a working man?" echoed Mr.
Godall. "Suppose a rural dean to be unfrocked,
does he fall to be a major? suppose a captain were
cashiered, would he fall to be a puisne judge?
The ignorance of your middle class surprises me.

Outside itself, it thinks the world to lie quite ignorant and equal, sunk in a common degradation;
but to the eye of the observer, all ranks are seen
to stand in ordered hierarchies, and each adorned
with its particular aptitudes and knowledge. By
the defects of your education you are more dis-
qualified to be a working man than to be the ruler
of an empire. The gulf, sir, is below; and the
true learned arts — those which alone are safe
from the competition of insurgent laymen — are
those which give his title to the artisan."

"This is a very pompous fellow," said Challoner in the ear of his companion.

"He is immense," said Somerset.

Just then the door of the divan opened, and a
third young fellow made his appearance, and
rather bashfully requested some tobacco. He was
younger that the others; and, in a somewhat
meaningless and altogether English way, he was
a handsome lad. When he had been served, and
had lighted his pipe and taken his place upon the
sofa, he recalled himself to Challoner by the name
of Desborough.

"Desborough, to be sure," cried Challoner.
"Well, Desborough, and what do you do?"

"The fact is," said Desborough, "that I am
doing nothing."

"A private fortune possibly?" inquired the
other.

"Well, no," replied Desborough, rather sulkily.
"The fact is that I am waiting for something to
turn up."

" All in the same boat ! " cried Somerset. " **And**
have you, too, one hundred pounds ? "

" Worse luck," said Mr. Desborough.

" This is a very pathetic sight, Mr. Godall," said
Somerset : " three futiles."

" A character of this crowded age," returned
the salesman.

" Sir," said Somerset, " I deny that the age is
crowded ; I will admit one fact, and that one fact
only : that I am futile, that he is futile, and that
we are all three as futile as the devil. What am
I ? I have smattered law, smattered letters, smattered geography, smattered mathematics ; I have
even a working knowledge of judicial astrology ;
and here I stand, all London roaring by at the
street's end, as impotent as any baby. I have a
prodigious contempt for my maternal uncle ; but
without him, it is idle to deny it, I should simply
resolve into my elements like an unstable mixture.
I begin to perceive that it is necessary to know
some one thing to the bottom — were it only liter-
ature. And yet, sir, the man of the world is a
great feature of this age ; he is possessed of an
extraordinary mass and variety of knowledge ; he
is everywhere at home ; he has seen life in all its
phases ; and it is impossible but that this great
habit of existence should bear fruit. I count
myself a man of the world, accomplished, *cap-
à-pie*. So do you, Challoner. And you, Mr.
Desborough ? "

" Oh, yes," returned the young man.

" Well, then, Mr. Godall, here we stand, three

men of the world, without a trade to cover us, but planted at the strategic centre of the universe (for so you will allow me to call Rupert Street), in the midst of the chief mass of people, and within ear-shot of the most continuous chink of money on the surface of the globe. Sir, as civilised men, what do we do? I will show you. You take in a paper?"

"I take," said Mr. Godall, solemnly, "the best paper in the world, the *Standard*."

"Good," resumed Somerset. "I now hold it in my hand, the voice of the world, a telephone repeating all men's wants. I open it, and where my eye first falls — well, no, not Morrison's Pills — but here, sure enough, and but a little above, I find the joint that I was seeking; here is the weak spot in the armour of society. Here is a want, a plaint, an offer of substantial gratitude: *'Two Hundred Pounds Reward.* — The above reward will be paid to any person giving information as to the identity and whereabouts of a man observed yesterday in the neighbourhood of the Green Park. He was over six feet in height, with shoulders dis-proportionately broad, close shaved, with black moustaches, and wearing a sealskin great-coat.' There, gentlemen, our fortune, if not made, is founded."

"Do you then propose, dear boy, that we should turn detectives?" inquired Challoner.

"Do I propose it? No, sir," cried Somerset. "It is reason, destiny, the plain face of the world, that commands and imposes it. Here all our merits tell; our manners, habit of the world, powers of conversation, vast stores of unconnected knowledge, all that we are and have builds up the character of the complete detective. It is, in short, the only profession for a gentleman."

"The proposition is perhaps excessive," said Challoner; "for hitherto I own I have regarded it as of all dirty, sneaking and ungentlemanly trades, the least and lowest."

"To defend society?" asked Somerset; "to stake one's life for others? to deracinate occult and powerful evil? I appeal to Mr. Godall. He, at least, as a philosophic looker-on at life, will spit upon such philistine opinions. He knows that the policeman, as he is called upon continually to face greater odds, and that both worse equipped and for a better cause, is in form and essence a more noble hero than the soldier. Do you, by any chance, deceive yourself, by supposing that a general would either ask or expect, from the best army ever marshalled, and on the most momentous battlefield, the conduct of a common constable at Peckham Rye." [1]

"I did not understand we were to join the force," said Challoner.

"Nor shall we. These are the hands; but

[1] Hereupon the Arabian author enters on one of his digressions. Fearing, apparently, that the somewhat eccentric views of Mr. Somerset should throw discredit on a part of truth, he calls upon the English People to remember with more gratitude the services of the police; to what unobserved and solitary acts of heroism they are called; against what odds of numbers and of arms, and for how small a reward, either in fame or money; matter, it has appeared to the translators, too serious for this place.

here — here, sir, is the head," cried Somerset. "Enough; it is decreed. We shall hunt down this miscreant in the sealskin coat."

"Suppose that we agreed," retorted Challoner, "you have no plan, no knowledge; you know not where to seek for a beginning."

"Challoner!" cried Somerset, "is it possible that you hold the doctrine of Free Will? And are you devoid of any tincture of philosophy, that you should harp on such exploded fallacies? Chance, the blind Madonna of the Pagan, rules this terrestrial bustle; and in Chance I place my sole reliance. Chance has brought us three together; when we next separate and go forth our several ways, Chance will continually drag before our careless eyes a thousand eloquent clues, not to this mystery only, but to the countless mysteries by which we live surrounded. Then comes the part of the man of the world, of the detective born and bred. This clue, which the whole town beholds without comprehension, swift as a cat, he leaps upon it, makes it his, follows it with craft and passion, and from one trifling circumstance divines a world."

"Just so," said Challoner; "and I am delighted that you should recognise these virtues in yourself. But in the meanwhile, dear boy, I own myself incapable of joining. I was neither born nor bred as a detective, but as a placable and very thirsty gentleman; and, for my part, I begin to weary for a drink. As for clues and adventures, the only adventure that is ever likely to occur to me will be an adventure with a bailiff."

"Now there is the fallacy," cried Somerset.
"There I catch the secret of your futility in life.
The world teems and bubbles with adventure; it
besieges you along the street: hands waving out
of windows, swindlers coming up and swearing
they knew you when you were abroad, affable and
doubtful people of all sorts and conditions begging
and truckling for your notice. But not you: you
turn away, you walk your seedy mill round, you
must go the dullest way. Now here, I beg of you,
the next adventure that offers itself, embrace it in
with both your arms; whatever it looks, grimy or
romantic, grasp it. I will do the like; the devil
is in it, but at least we shall have fun; and each
in turn we shall narrate the story of our fortunes
to my philosophic friend of the divan, the great
Godall, now hearing me with inward joy. Come,
is it a bargain? Will you, indeed, both promise
to welcome every chance that offers, to plunge
boldly into every opening, and, keeping the eye
wary and the head composed, to study and piece
together all that happens? Come, promise: let me
open to you the doors of the great profession of
intrigue."

"It is not much in my way," said Challoner,
"but, since you make a point of it, amen."

"I don't mind promising," said Desborough,
"but nothing will happen to me."

"Oh, faithless ones!" cried Somerset. "But at
least I have your promises; and Godall, I perceive, is transported with delight."

"I promise myself at least much pleasure from

your various narratives," said the salesman, with
the customary calm polish of his manner.

"And now, gentlemen," concluded Somerset,
"let us separate. I hasten to put myself in fortune's way. Hark how, in this quiet corner, London roars like the noise of battle; four million
destinies are here concentred; and in the strong
panoply of one hundred pounds, payable to the
bearer, I am about to plunge into that web."

CHALLONER'S ADVENTURE: THE SQUIRE OF DAMES

MR. EDWARD CHALLONER had set up lodgings in the suburb of Putney, where he enjoyed a parlour and bedroom and the sincere esteem of the people of the house. To this remote home he found himself, at a very early hour in the morning of the next day, condemned to set forth on foot. He was a young man of portly habit; no lover of the exercises of the body; bland, sedentary, patient of delay, a prop of omnibuses. In happier days he would have chartered a cab; but these luxuries were now denied him; and with what courage he could muster he addressed himself to walk.

It was then the height of the season and the summer; the weather was serene and cloudless; and as he paced under the blinded houses and along the vacant streets, the chill of the dawn had fled, and some of the warmth and all the brightness of the July day already shone upon the city. He walked at first in a profound abstraction, bitterly reviewing and repenting his performances at whist; but as he advanced into the labyrinth of the south-west, his ear was gradually mastered by the silence. Street after street looked down upon his solitary figure, house after house echoed upon his passage with a ghostly jar, shop after shop displayed its shuttered front and its commercial legend; and meanwhile he steered his course, under day's effulgent dome and through this encampment of diurnal sleepers, lonely as a ship.

"Here," he reflected, "if I were like my scatter-brained companion, here were indeed the scene where I might look for an adventure. Here, in broad day, the streets are secret as in the blackest night of January, and in the midst of some four million sleepers, solitary as the woods of Yucatan. If I but raise my voice I could summon up the number of an army, and yet the grave is not more silent than this city of sleep."

He was still following these quaint and serious musings when he came into a street of more mingled ingredients than was common in the quarter. Here, on the one hand, framed in the walls and the green tops of trees, were several of those discreet, *bijou* residences on which propriety is apt to look askance. Here, too, were many of the brick-fronted barracks of the poor; a plaster cow, perhaps, serving as ensign to a dairy, or a ticket announcing the business of the mangler. Before one such house, that stood a little separate among walled gardens, a cat was playing with a straw, and Challoner paused a moment, looking on this sleek and solitary creature, who seemed an emblem of the neighbouring peace. With the cessation of the sound of his own steps the silence fell dead; the house stood smokeless: the blinds down, the whole machinery of life arrested; and it seemed to Challoner that he should hear the breathing of the sleepers.

As he so stood, he was startled by a dull and jarring detonation from within. This was followed by a monstrous hissing and simmering as from a kettle of the bigness of St. Paul's; and at the same time from every chink of door and window spirted an ill-smelling vapour. The cat disappeared with a cry. Within the lodging-house feet pounded on the stairs; the door flew back emitting clouds of smoke; and two men and an elegantly dressed young lady tumbled forth into the street and fled without a word. The hissing had already ceased, the smoke was melting in the air, the whole event had come and gone as in a dream, and still Challoner was rooted to the spot. At last his reason and his fear awoke together, and with the most unwonted energy he fell to running.

Little by little this first dash relaxed, and presently he had resumed his sober gait and begun to piece together, out of the confused report of his senses, some theory of the occurrence. But the occasion of the sounds and stench that had so suddenly assailed him, and the strange conjunction of fugitives whom he had seen to issue from the house, were mysteries beyond his plummet. With an obscure awe he considered them in his mind, continuing, meanwhile, to thread the web of streets, and once more alone in morning sunshine.

In his first retreat he had entirely wandered; and now, steering vaguely west, it was his luck to light upon an unpretending street, which presently widened so as to admit a strip of gardens in the midst. Here was quite a stir of birds; even at that hour, the shadow of the leaves was grateful; instead of the burned atmosphere of cities, there was something brisk and rural in the air; and Challoner paced forward, his eyes upon the pavement and his mind running upon distant scenes, till he was recalled, upon a sudden, by a wall that blocked his further progress. This street, whose name I have forgotten, is no thoroughfare.

He was not the first who had wandered there that morning; for as he raised his eyes with an agreeable deliberation, they alighted on the figure of a girl, in whom he was struck to recognise the third of the incongruous fugitives. She had run there, seemingly, blindfold; the wall had checked her career, and being entirely wearied, she had sunk upon the ground beside the garden railings, soiling her dress among the summer dust. Each saw the other in the same instant of time; and she, with one wild look, sprang to her feet and began to hurry from the scene.

Challoner was doubly startled to meet once more the heroine of his adventure and to observe the fear with which she shunned him. Pity and alarm, in nearly equal forces, contested the possession of his mind, and yet, in spite of both, he saw himself condemned to follow in the lady's wake. He did so gingerly, as fearing to increase her terrors; but tread as lightly as he might, his footfalls eloquently echoed in the empty street. Their sound appeared

to strike in her some strong emotion, for scarce had
he begun to follow ere she paused. A second time
she addressed herself to flight, and a second time
she paused. Then she turned about, and with
doubtful steps and the most attractive appearance
of timidity, drew near to the young man. He on
his side continued to advance with similar signals
of distress and bashfulness. At length, when they
were but some steps apart, he saw her eyes brim
over, and she reached out both her hands in eloquent appeal.

"Are you an English gentleman?" she cried.

The unhappy Challoner regarded her with consternation. He was the spirit of fine courtesy, and
would have blushed to fail in his devoirs to any
lady; but, in the other scale, he was a man averse
from amorous adventures. He looked east and
west, but the houses that looked down upon this
interview remained inexorably shut, and he saw
himself, though in the full glare of the day's eye,
cut off from any human intervention. His looks
returned at last upon the suppliant. He remarked
with irritation that she was charming both in face
and figure, elegantly dressed and gloved: a lady
undeniable; the picture of distress and innocence;
weeping and lost in the city of diurnal sleep.

"Madam," he said, "I protest you have no
cause to fear intrusion, and if I have appeared to
follow you, the fault is in this street, which has
deceived us both."

An unmistakable relief appeared upon the lady's
face. "I might have guessed it!" she exclaimed.

" Thank you a thousand times! But at this hour, in this appalling silence, and among all these staring windows, I am lost in terrors — oh, lost in them!" she cried, her face blanching at the words. " I beg you to lend me your arm," she added with the loveliest, suppliant inflection. " I dare not go alone; my nerve is gone — I had a shock, oh, what a shock! I beg of you to be my escort."

" My dear madam," responded Challoner, heavily, " my arm is at your service."

She took it and clung to it for a moment, struggling with her sobs, and the next, with feverish hurry, began to lead him in the direction of the city. One thing was plain, among so much that was obscure: it was plain her fears were genuine. Still, as she went, she spied around as if for dangers, and now she would shiver like a person in a chill and now clutch his arm in hers. To Challoner her terror was at once repugnant and infectious; it gained and mastered, while it still offended him, and he wailed in spirit and longed for release.

" Madam," he said at last, " I am, of course, charmed to be of use to any lady, but I confess I was bound in a direction opposite to that you follow, and a word of explanation —— "

" Hush!" she sobbed, " not here — not here."

The blood of Challoner ran cold. He might have thought the lady mad, but his memory was charged with more perilous stuff, and in view of the detonation, the smoke and the flight of the ill-assorted trio, his mind was lost among mysteries.

2

So they continued to thread the maze of streets in silence with the speed of a guilty flight, and both thrilling with incommunicable terrors. In time, however, and above all by their quick pace of walking, the pair began to rise to firmer spirits; the lady ceased to peer about the corners; and Challoner, emboldened by the resonant tread and distant figure of a constable, returned to the charge with more of spirit and directness.

"I thought," said he, in the tone of conversation, "that I had indistinctly perceived you leaving a villa in the company of two gentlemen."

"Oh!" she said, "you need not fear to wound me by the truth. You saw me flee from a common lodging-house, and my companions were not gentlemen. In such a case, the best of compliments is to be frank."

"I thought," resumed Challoner, encouraged as much as he was surprised by the spirit of her reply, "to have perceived, besides, a certain odour. A noise, too — I do not know to what I should compare it —— "

"Silence!" she cried. "You do not know the danger you invoke. Wait, only wait; and as soon as we have left those streets and got beyond the reach of listeners, all shall be explained. Meanwhile, avoid the topic. What a sight is this sleeping city!" she exclaimed; and then, with a most thrilling voice, "'Dear God,'" she quoted, "'the very houses seem asleep. And all that mighty heart is lying still.'"

"I perceive, madam," said he, "you are a reader."

"I am more than that," she answered, with a sigh. "I am a girl condemned to thoughts beyond her age; and so untoward is my fate, that this walk upon the arm of a stranger is like an interlude of peace."

They had come by this time to the neighbourhood of the Victoria Station; and here, at a street corner, the young lady paused, withdrew her arm from Challoner's, and looked up and down as though in pain or indecision. Then, with a lovely change of countenance, and laying her gloved hand upon his arm:

"What you already think of me," she said, "I tremble to conceive; yet I must here condemn myself still further. Here I must leave you, and here I beseech you to wait for my return. Do not attempt to follow me or spy upon my actions. Suspend yet awhile your judgment of a girl as innocent as your own sister; and do not, above all, desert me. Stranger as you are, I have none else to look to. You see me in sorrow and great fear; you are a gentleman, courteous and kind; and when I beg for a few minutes' patience, I make sure beforehand you will not deny me."

Challoner grudgingly promised; and the young lady, with a grateful eye-shot, vanished round the corner. But the force of her appeal had been a little blunted; for the young man was not only destitute of sisters, but of any female relative nearer than a great-aunt in Wales. Now he was alone; besides, the spell that he had hitherto obeyed began to weaken; he considered his be-

haviour with a sneer; and plucking up the spirit
of revolt, he started in pursuit. The reader, if
he has ever plied the fascinating trade of the noc-
tambulist, will not be unaware that, in the neighbourhood of the great railway centres, certain early
taverns inaugurate the business of the day. It was
into one of these that Challoner, coming round the
corner of the block, beheld his charming companion disappear. To say he was surprised were
inexact, for he had long since left that sentiment
behind him. Acute disgust and disappointment
seized upon his soul; and with silent oaths he
damned this commonplace enchantress. She had
scarce been gone a second, ere the swing-doors
reopened, and she appeared again in company with
a young man of mean and slouching attire. For
some five or six exchanges they conversed together
with an animated air: then the fellow shouldered
again into the tap; and the young lady, with something swifter than a walk, retraced her steps
toward Challoner. He saw her coming, a miracle
of grace; her ankle, as she hurried, flashing from
her dress; her movements eloquent of speed and
youth; and though he still entertained some
thoughts of flight, they grew miserably fainter as
the distance lessened. Against mere beauty he was
proof: it was her unmistakable gentility that now
robbed him of the courage of his cowardice. With
a proved adventuress he had acted strictly on his
right; with one whom, in spite of all, he could not
quite deny to be a lady, he found himself disarmed.
At the very corner from whence he had spied upon

her interview, she came upon him, still transfixed, and — "Ah!" she cried, with a bright flush of colour. "Ah! Ungenerous!"

The sharpness of the attack somewhat restored the Squire of Dames to the possession of himself.

"Madam," he returned, with a fair show of stoutness, "I do not think that hitherto you can complain of any lack of generosity; I have suffered myself to be led over a considerable portion of the metropolis; and if I now request you to discharge me of my office of protector, you have friends at hand who will be glad of the succession."

She stood a moment dumb.

"It is well," she said. "Go! go, and may God help me! You have seen me — me, an innocent girl! fleeing from a dire catastrophe and haunted by sinister men; and neither pity, curiosity, nor honour move you to await my explanation or to help me in my distress. Go!" she repeated. "I am lost indeed." And with a passionate gesture she turned and fled along the street.

Challoner observed her retreat and disappear, an almost intolerable sense of guilt contending with the profound sense that he was being gulled. She was no sooner gone than the first of these feelings took the upper hand; he felt, if he had done her less than justice, that his conduct was a perfect model of the ungracious; the cultured tone of her voice, her choice of language, and the elegant decorum of her movements cried out aloud against a harsh construction; and between penitence and curiosity he began slowly to follow in her wake. At the corner he had her once more full in view. Her speed was failing like a stricken bird's. Even as he looked, she threw her arm out gropingly, and fell and leaned against the wall. At the spectacle, Challoner's fortitude gave way. In a few strides he overtook her and, for the first time removing his hat, assured her in the most moving terms of his entire respect and firm desire to help her. He spoke at first unheeded; but gradually it appeared that she began to comprehend his words; she moved a little, and drew herself upright; and finally, as with a sudden movement of forgiveness, turned on the young man a countenance in which reproach and gratitude were mingled. " Ah, madam," he cried, " use me as you will! " And once more, but now with a great air of deference, he offered her the conduct of his arm. She took it with a sigh that struck him to the heart; and they began once more to trace the deserted streets. But now her steps, as though exhausted by emotion, began to linger on the way; she leaned the more heavily upon his arm; and he, like the parent bird, stooped fondly above his drooping convoy. Her physical distress was not accompanied by any failing of her spirits; and hearing her strike so soon into a playful and charming vein of talk, Challoner could not sufficiently admire the elasticity of his companion's nature. " Let me forget," she had said, " for one half-hour, let me forget "; and sure enough, with the very word, her sorrows appeared to be forgotten. Before every house she paused, invented a name for the proprietor, and sketched his character: here lived the old general whom she was to marry on the fifth of the next month, there was the mansion of the rich widow who had set her heart on Challoner; and though she still hung wearily on the young man's arm, her laughter sounded low and pleasant in his ears. "Ah," she sighed, by way of commentary, "in such a life as mine I must seize tight hold of any happiness that I can find."

When they arrived, in this leisurely manner, at the head of Grosvenor Place, the gates of the park were opening and the bedraggled company of night-walkers were being at last admitted into that paradise of lawns. Challoner and his companion followed the movement, and walked for awhile in silence in that tatterdemalion crowd; but as one after another, weary with the night's patrolling of the city pavement, sank upon the benches or wandered into separate paths, the vast extent of the park had soon utterly swallowed up the last of these intruders; and the pair proceeded on their way alone in the grateful quiet of the morning.

Presently they came in sight of a bench, standing very open on a mound of turf. The young lady looked about her with relief.

"Here," she said, "here at last we are secure from listeners. Here, then, you shall learn and judge my history. I could not bear that we should part, and that you should still suppose your kindness squandered upon one who was unworthy."

Thereupon she sat down upon the bench, and motioning Challoner to take a place immediately beside her, began in the following words, and with the greatest appearance of enjoyment, to narrate the story of her life.

STORY OF THE DESTROYING ANGEL

MY father was a native of England, son of a cadet of a great, ancient, but untitled family; and by some event, fault, or misfortune he was driven to flee from the land of his birth and to lay aside the name of his ancestors. He sought the States; and instead of lingering in effeminate cities, pushed at once into the far west with an exploring party of frontiersmen. He was no ordinary traveller; for he was not only brave and impetuous by character, but learned in many sciences, and above all in botany, which he particularly loved. Thus it fell that, before many months, Fremont himself, the nominal leader of the troop, courted and bowed to his opinion.

They had pushed, as I have said, into the still unknown regions of the west. For some time they followed the track of Mormon caravans, guiding themselves in that vast and melancholy desert by the skeletons of men and animals. Then they inclined their route a little to the north and, losing even these dire memorials, came into a country of forbidding stillness. I have often heard my father dwell upon the features of that ride: rock, cliff, and barren moor alternated; the streams were very far between; and neither beast nor bird disturbed the solitude. On the fortieth day they had already run so short of food that it was judged advisable to call a halt and scatter upon all sides to hunt. A great fire was built, that its smoke might serve to rally them; and each man of the party mounted and struck off at a venture into the surrounding desert.

My father rode for many hours with a steep range of cliffs upon the one hand, very black and horrible; and upon the other an unwatered vale dotted with boulders like the site of some subverted city. At length he found the slot of a great animal, and from the claw-marks and the hair among the brush, judged that he was on the track of a cinnamon bear of most unusual size. He quickened the pace of his steed, and still following the quarry, came at last to the division of two watersheds. On the far side the country was exceedingly intricate and difficult, heaped with boulders, and dotted here and there with a few pines, which seemed to indicate the neighbourhood of water. Here, then, he picketed his horse, and relying on his trusty rifle, advanced alone into that wilderness.

Presently, in the great silence that reigned, he was aware of the sound of running water to his right; and leaning in that direction, was rewarded by a scene of natural wonder and human pathos strangely intermixed. The stream ran at the bottom of a narrow and winding passage, whose wall-like sides of rock were sometimes for miles

together unscalable by man. The water, when the
stream was swelled with rains, must have filled
it from side to side; the sun's rays only plumbed
it in the hour of noon; the wind, in that narrow
and damp funnel, blew tempestuously. And yet,
in the bottom of this den, immediately below my
father's eyes as he leaned over the margin of the
cliff, a party of some half a hundred men, women,
and children lay scattered uneasily among the
rocks. They lay some upon their backs, some
prone, and not one stirring; their upturned faces
seemed all of an extraordinary paleness and ema-
ciation; and from time to time, above the wash-
ing of the stream, a faint sound of moaning
mounted to my father's ears.

While he thus looked, an old man got staggering
to his feet, unwound his blanket, and laid it, with
great gentleness, on a young girl who sat hard by
propped against a rock. The girl did not seem to
be conscious of the act; and the old man, after
having looked upon her with the most engaging
pity, returned to his former bed and lay down
again uncovered on the turf. But the scene had
not passed without observation even in that starving camp. From the very outskirts of the party,
a man with a white beard and seemingly of vener-
able years, rose upon his knees and came crawling
stealthily among the sleepers toward the girl; and
judge of my father's indignation, when he beheld
this cowardly miscreant strip from her both the
coverings and return with them to his original
position. Here he lay down for awhile below his

spoils, and, as my father imagined, feigned to be asleep; but presently he had raised himself again upon one elbow, looked with sharp scrutiny at his companions, and then swiftly carried his hand into his bosom and thence to his mouth. By the movement of his jaws he must be eating; in that camp of famine he had reserved a store of nourishment; and while his companions lay in the stupor of approaching death, secretly restored his powers.

My father was so incensed at what he saw that he raised his rifle; and but for an accident, he has often declared, he would have shot the fellow dead upon the spot. How different would then have been my history! But it was not to be: even as he raised the barrel, his eye lighted on the bear, as it crawled along a ledge some way below him; and ceding to the hunter's instinct, it was at the brute, not at the man, that he discharged his piece. The bear leaped and fell into a pool of the river; the cañon re-echoed the report; and in a moment the camp was afoot. With cries that were scarce human, stumbling, falling, and throwing each other down, these starving people rushed upon the quarry; and before my father, climbing down by the ledge, had time to reach the level of the stream, many were already satisfying their hunger on the raw flesh, and a fire was being built by the more dainty.

His arrival was for some time unremarked. He stood in the midst of these tottering and clay-faced marionettes; he was surrounded by their cries; but their whole soul was fixed on the dead carcase;

even those who were too weak to move, lay, half turned over, with their eyes riveted upon the bear; and my father, seeing himself stand as though invisible in the thick of this dreary hubbub, was seized with a desire to weep. A touch upon the arm restrained him. Turning about he found himself face to face with the old man he had so nearly killed; and yet, at the second glance, recognised him for no old man at all, but one in the full strength of his years, and of a strong, speaking, and intellectual countenance, stigmatised by weariness and famine. He beckoned my father near the cliff, and there, in the most private whisper, begged for brandy. My father looked at him with scorn: "You remind me," he said, "of a neglected duty. Here is my flask; it contains enough, I trust, to revive the women of your party; and I will begin with her whom I saw you robbing of her blankets." And with that, not heeding his appeals, my father turned his back upon the egoist.

The girl still lay reclined against the rock; she lay too far sunk in the first stage of death to have observed the bustle round her couch; but when my father had raised her head, put the flask to her lips, and forced or aided her to swallow some drops of the restorative, she opened her languid eyes and smiled upon him faintly. Never was there a smile of more touching sweetness; never were eyes more deeply violet, more honestly eloquent of the soul! I speak with knowledge, for these were the same eyes that smiled upon me in the cradle. From her who was to be his wife, my father, still jealously watched and followed by the man with the grey beard, carried his attentions to all the women of the party, and gave the last drainings of his flask to those among the men who seemed in the most need.

" Is there none left? not a drop for me? " said the man with the beard.

" Not one drop," replied my father; " and if you find yourself in want, let me counsel you to put your hand into the pocket of your coat."

" Ah! " cried the other, " you misjudge me. You think me one who clings to life for selfish and commonplace considerations. But let me tell you, that were all this caravan to perish, the world would but be lightened of a weight. These are but human insects, pullulating, thick as may-flies, in the slums of European cities, whom I myself have plucked from degradation and misery, from the dung-heap and gin-palace door. And you compare their lives with mine! "

" You are then a Mormon missionary? " asked my father.

" Oh! " cried the man, with a strange smile, " a Mormon missionary if you will! I value not the title. Were I no more than that, I could have died without a murmur. But with my life as a physician is bound up the knowledge of great secrets and the future of man. This it was, when we missed the caravan, tried for a short cut and wandered to this desolate ravine, that ate into my soul and, in five days, has changed my beard from ebony to silver."

" And you are a physician," mused my father, looking on his face, " bound by oath to succour man in his distresses."

" Sir," returned the Mormon, " my name is Grierson: you will hear that name again; and you will then understand that my duty was not to this caravan of paupers, but to mankind at large."

My father turned to the remainder of the party, who were now sufficiently revived to hear; told them that he would set off at once to bring help from his own party; " and," he added, " if you be again reduced to such extremities, look round you, and you will see the earth strewn with assistance. Here, for instance, growing on the under-side of fissures in this cliff, you will perceive a yellow moss. Trust me, it is both edible and excellent."

" Ha!" said Dr. Grierson, " you know botany!"

" Not I alone," returned my father, lowering his voice; " for see where these have been scraped away. Am I right? Was that your secret store?"

My father's comrades, he found, when he returned to the signal-fire, had made a good day's hunting. They were thus the more easily persuaded to extend assistance to the Mormon caravan; and the next day beheld both parties on the march for the frontiers of Utah. The distance to be traversed was not great; but the nature of the country and the difficulty of procuring food, extended the time to nearly three weeks; and my father had thus ample leisure to know and appreciate the girl whom he had succoured. I will call my mother Lucy. Her family name I am not at

liberty to mention; it is one you would know well.
By what series of undeserved calamities this innocent flower of maidenhood, lovely, refined by education, ennobled by the finest taste, was thus cast
among the horrors of a Mormon caravan, I must
not stay to tell you. Let it suffice, that even in
these untoward circumstances, she found a heart
worthy of her own. The ardour of attachment
which united my father and mother was perhaps
partly due to the strange manner of their meeting;
it knew, at least, no bounds either divine or human;
my father, for her sake, determined to renounce
his ambitions and abjure his faith; and a week
had not yet passed upon the march before he had
resigned from his party, accepted the Mormon
doctrine, and received the promise of my mother's
hand on the arrival of the party at Salt Lake.

The marriage took place, and I was its only offspring. My father prospered exceedingly in his
affairs, remained faithful to my mother; and
though you may wonder to hear it, I believe there
were few happier homes in any country than that
in which I saw the light and grew to girlhood.
We were, indeed, and in spite of all our wealth,
avoided as heretics and half-believers by the more
precise and pious of the faithful: Young himself,
that formidable tyrant, was known to look askance
upon my father's riches; but of this I had no
guess. I dwelt, indeed, under the Mormon system,
with perfect innocence and faith. Some of our
friends had many wives; but such was the custom; and why should it surprise me more than

marriage itself? From time to time one of our
rich acquaintances would disappear, his family be
broken up, his wives and houses shared among the
elders of the church, and his memory only recalled
with bated breath and dreadful headshakings.
When I had been very still and my presence perhaps was forgotten, some such topic would arise
among my elders by the evening fire; I would see
them draw the closer together and look behind
them with scared eyes; and I might gather from
their whisperings how some one, rich, honoured,
healthy, and in the prime of his days, some one,
perhaps, who had taken me on his knees a week
before, had in one hour been spirited from home
and family, and vanished like an image from a
mirror, leaving not a print behind. It was terrible,
indeed; but so was death, the universal law. And
even if the talk should wax still bolder, full of
ominous silences and nods, and I should hear named
in a whisper the Destroying Angels, how was a
child to understand these mysteries? I heard of
a Destroying Angel as some more happy child
might hear in England of a bishop or a rural dean,
with vague respect and without the wish for further information. Life anywhere, in society as
in nature, rests upon dread foundations; I beheld
safe roads, a garden blooming in the desert, pious
people crowding to worship; I was aware of my
parents' tenderness and all the harmless luxuries
of my existence; and why should I pry beneath
this honest seeming surface for the mysteries on
which it stood?

3

We dwelt originally in the city; but at an early date we moved to a beautiful house in a green dingle, musical with splashing water, and surrounded on almost every side by twenty miles of poisonous and rocky desert. The city was thirty miles away; there was but one road, which went no further than my father's door; the rest were bridle-tracks impassable in winter; and we thus dwelt in a solitude inconceivable to the European. Our only neighbour was Dr. Grierson. To my young eyes, after the hair-oiled, chin-bearded elders of the city, and the ill-favoured and mentally stunted women of their harems, there was something agreeable in the correct manner, the fine bearing, the thin white hair and beard, and the piercing looks of the old doctor. Yet, though he was almost our only visitor, I never wholly overcame a sense of fear in his presence; and this disquietude was rather fed by the awful solitude in which he lived and the obscurity that hung about his occupations. His house was but a mile or two from ours, but very differently placed. It stood overlooking the road on the summit of a steep slope, and planted close against a range of overhanging bluffs. Nature, you would say, had here desired to imitate the works of man; for the slope was even like the glacis of a fort, and the cliffs of a constant height, like the ramparts of a city. Not even spring could change one feature of that desolate scene; and the windows looked down across a plain, snowy with alkali, to ranges of cold stone sierras on the north. Twice or thrice I remember passing within view of this forbidding residence; and seeing it always shuttered, smokeless, and deserted, I remarked to my parents that some day it would certainly be robbed.

"Ah, no," said my father, "never robbed"; and I observed a strange conviction in his tone.

At last, and not long before the blow fell on my unhappy family, I chanced to see the doctor's house in a new light. My father was ill; my mother confined to his bedside; and I was suffered to go, under the charge of our driver, to the lonely house some twenty miles away, where our packages were left for us. The horse cast a shoe; night overtook us half-way home; and it was well on for three in the morning when the driver and I, alone in a light wagon, came to that part of the road which ran below the doctor's house. The moon swam clear; the cliffs and mountains in this strong light lay utterly deserted; but the house, from its station on the top of the long slope and close under the bluff, not only shone abroad from every window like a place of festival, but from the great chimney at the west end poured forth a coil of smoke so thick and so voluminous, that it hung for miles along the windless night air, and its shadow lay far abroad in the moonlight upon the glittering alkali. As we continued to draw near, besides, a regular and panting throb began to divide the silence. First it seemed to me like the beating of a heart; and next it put into my mind the thought of some giant smothered under mountains and still, with incalculable effort, fetching

breath. I had heard of the railway, though I had
not seen it, and I turned to ask the driver if this
resembled it. But some look in his eye, some
pallor, whether of fear or moonlight on his face,
caused the words to die upon my lips. We continued, therefore, to advance in silence, till we
were close below the lighted house; when suddenly, without one premonitory rustle, there burst
forth a report of such a bigness that it shook the
earth and set the echoes of the mountains thunder-
ing from cliff to cliff. A pillar of amber flame
leaped from the chimney-top and fell in multitudes
of sparks; and at the same time the lights in the
windows turned for one instant ruby red and then
expired. The driver had checked his horse in-
stinctively, and the echoes were still rumbling further off among the mountains, when there broke
from the now darkened interior a series of yells —
whether of man or woman it was impossible to
guess — the door flew open, and there ran forth
into the moonlight, at the top of the long slope, a
figure clad in white, which began to dance and leap
and throw itself down, and roll as if in agony, before the house. I could no more restrain my cries;
the driver laid his lash about the horse's flank,
and we fled up the rough track at the peril of our
lives; and did not draw rein till, turning the corner
of the mountain, we beheld my father's ranch and
deep, green groves and gardens, sleeping in the
tranquil light.

This was the one adventure of my life, until my
father had climbed to the very topmost point of

material prosperity, and I myself had reached the age of seventeen. I was still innocent and merry like a child; tended my garden or ran upon the hills in glad simplicity; gave not a thought to coquetry or to material cares; and if my eye rested on my own image in a mirror or some sylvan spring, it was to seek and recognise the features of my parents. But the fears which had long pressed on others were now to be laid on my youth. I had thrown myself, one sultry, cloudy afternoon, on a divan; the windows stood open on the veranda, where my mother sat with her embroidery; and when my father joined her from the garden, their conversation, clearly audible to me, was of so startling a nature that it held me enthralled where I lay.

"The blow has come," my father said, after a long pause.

I could hear my mother start and turn, but in words she made no reply.

"Yes," continued my father, "I have received to-day a list of all that I possess; of all, I say; of what I have lent privately to men whose lips are sealed with terror; of what I have buried with my own hand on the bare mountain, when there was not a bird in heaven. Does the air, then, carry secrets? Are the hills of glass? Do the stones we tread upon preserve the footprint to betray us? Oh, Lucy, Lucy, that we should have come to such a country!"

"But this," returned my mother, "is no very new or very threatening event. You are accused

of some concealment. You will pay more taxes in
the future, and be mulcted in a fine. It is disquieting, indeed, to find our acts so spied upon, and
the most private known. But is this new? Have
we not long feared and suspected every blade of
grass?"

"Ay, and our shadows!" cried my father.
"But all this is nothing. Here is the letter that
accompanied the list."

I heard my mother turn the pages; and she was
some time silent.

"I see," she said at last; and then with the
tone of one reading: "'From a believer so largely
blessed by Providence with this world's goods,'"
she continued, "'the Church awaits in confidence
some signal mark of piety.' There lies the sting.
Am I not right? These are the words you fear?"

"These are the words," replied my father.
"Lucy, you remember Priestley? Two days before he disappeared, he carried me to the summit
of an isolated butte; we could see around us for
ten miles; sure, if in any quarter of this land a
man were safe from spies, it were in such a
station; but it was in the very ague-fit of terror
that he told me, and that I heard, his story. He
had received a letter such as this; and he submitted to my approval an answer in which he
offered to resign a third of his possessions. I con-
jured him, as he valued his life, to raise his offer-
ing; and, before we parted, he had doubled the
amount. Well, two days later he was gone — gone
from the chief street of the city in the hour of noon

— and gone for ever. O God!" cried my father, "by what art do they thus spirit out of life the solid body? What death do they command that leaves no traces? that this material structure, these strong arms, this skeleton that can resist the grave for centuries, should be thus reft in a moment from the world of sense? A horror dwells in that thought more awful than mere death."

"Is there no hope in Grierson?" asked my mother.

"Dismiss the thought," replied my father. "He now knows all that I can teach, and will do naught to save me. His power, besides, is small, his own danger not improbably more imminent than mine; for he, too, lives apart; he leaves his wives neglected and unwatched; he is openly cited for an unbeliever; and unless he buys security at a more awful price — but no; I will not believe it; I have no love for him, but I will not believe it."

"Believe what?" asks my mother; and then, with a change of note, "But oh, what matters it?" she cried. "Abimelech, there is but one way open: we must fly!"

"It is in vain," returned my father. "I should but involve you in my fate. To leave this land is hopeless: we are closed in it as men are closed in life; and there is no issue but the grave."

"We can but die then," replied my mother. "Let us at least die together. Let not Asenath [1] and myself survive you. Think to what a faith we should be doomed!"

[1] In this name the accent falls upon the *e;* the *s* is sibilant.

My father was unable to resist her tender violence; and though I could see he nourished not one spark of hope, he consented to desert his whole estate, beyond some hundreds of dollars that he had by him at the moment, and to flee that night, which promised to be dark and cloudy. As soon as the servants were asleep, he was to load two mules with provisions; two others were to carry my mother and myself; and, striking through the mountains by an unfrequented trail, we were to make a fair stroke for liberty and life. As soon as they had thus decided, I showed myself at the window, and, owning that I had heard all, assured them that they could rely on my prudence and devotion. I had no fear, indeed, but to show myself unworthy of my birth; I held my life in my hand without alarm; and when my father, weeping upon my neck, had blessed Heaven for the courage of his child, it was with a sentiment of pride and some of the joy that warriors take in war, that I began to look forward to the perils of our flight.

Before midnight, under an obscure and starless heaven, we had left far behind us the plantations of the valley, and were mounting a certain cañon in the hills, narrow, encumbered with great rocks, and echoing with the roar of a tumultuous torrent. Cascade after cascade thundered and hung up its flag of whiteness in the night, or fanned our faces with the wet wind of its descent. The trail was breakneck, and led to famine-guarded deserts; it had been long since deserted for more practicable

routes; and it was now a part of the world untrod
from year to year by human footing. Judge of our
dismay, when turning suddenly an angle of the
cliffs, we found a bright bonfire blazing by itself
under an impending rock; and on the face of the
rock, drawn very rudely with charred wood, the
great Open Eye which is the emblem of the Mormon faith. We looked upon each other in the firelight; my mother broke into a passion of tears;
but not a word was said. The mules were turned
about; and leaving that great eye to guard the
lonely cañon, we retraced our steps in silence.
Day had not yet broken ere we were once more
at home, condemned beyond reprieve.

What answer my father sent I was not told; but
two days later, a little before sundown, I saw a
plain, honest-looking man ride slowly up the road
in a great pother of dust. He was clad in home-
spun, with a broad straw hat; wore a patriarchal
beard; and had an air of a simple rustic farmer,
that was, in my eyes, very reassuring. He was,
indeed, a very honest man and pious Mormon;
with no liking for his errand, though neither he
nor any one in Utah dared to disobey; and it
was with every mark of diffidence that he had himself announced as Mr. Aspinwall, and entered the
room where our unhappy family was gathered.
My mother and me he awkwardly enough dismissed; and as soon as he was alone with my
father laid before him a blank signature of President Young's, and offered him a choice of services:
either to set out as a missionary to the tribes about

the White Sea, or to join the next day, with a
party of Destroying Angels, in the massacre of
sixty German immigrants. The last, of course,
my father could not entertain, and the first he
regarded as a pretext: even if he could consent to
leave his wife defenceless, and to collect fresh
victims for the tyranny under which he was himself
oppressed, he felt sure he would never be suffered
to return. He refused both; and Aspinwall, he
said, betrayed sincere emotion, part religious, at
the spectacle of such disobedience, but part human,
in pity for my father and his family. He besought
him to reconsider his decision; and at length, finding he could not prevail, gave him till the moon
rose to settle his affairs, and say farewell to wife
and daughter. " For," said he, " then, at the latest,
you must ride with me."

I dare not dwell upon the hours that followed:
they fled all too fast; and presently the moon out-
topped the eastern range, and my father and Mr.
Aspinwall set forth, side by side, on their nocturnal
journey. My mother, though still bearing a heroic
countenance, had hastened to shut herself in her
apartment, thenceforward solitary; and I, alone
in the dark house, and consumed by grief and apprehension, made haste to saddle my Indian pony,
to ride up to the corner of the mountain, and to
enjoy one farewell sight of my departing father.
The two men had set forth at a deliberate pace;
nor was I long behind them, when I reached the
point of view. I was the more amazed to see no
moving creature in the landscape. The moon, as

the saying is, shone bright as day; and nowhere, under the whole arch of night, was there a growing tree, a bush, a farm, a patch of tillage, or any evidence of man, but one. From the corner where I stood, a rugged bastion of the line of bluffs concealed the doctor's house; and across the top of that projection the soft night wind carried and unwound about the hills a coil of sable smoke. What fuel could produce a vapour so sluggish to dissipate in that dry air, or what furnace pour it forth so copiously, I was unable to conceive; but I knew well enough that it came from the doctor's chimney; I saw well enough that my father had already disappeared; and in despite of reason, I connected in my mind the loss of that dear protector with the ribbon of foul smoke that trailed along the mountains.

Days passed, and still my mother and I waited in vain for news; a week went by, a second followed, but we heard no word of the father and husband. As smoke dissipates, as the image glides from the mirror, so in the ten or twenty minutes that I had spent in getting my horse and following upon his trail, had that strong and brave man vanished out of life. Hope, if any hope we had, fled with every hour; the worst was now certain for my father, the worst was to be dreaded for his defenceless family. Without weakness, with a desperate calm at which I marvel when I look back upon it, the widow and the orphan awaited the event. On the last day of the third week we rose in the morning to find ourselves alone in the

house, alone, so far as we searched, on the estate;
all our attendants, with one accord, had fled; and
as we knew them to be gratefully devoted, we drew
the darkest intimations from their flight. The day
passed, indeed, without event; but in the fall of
the evening we were called at last into the veranda
by the approaching clink of horse's hoofs.

The doctor, mounted on an Indian pony, rode
into the garden, dismounted, and saluted us. He
seemed much more bent, and his hair more silvery
than ever; but his demeanour was composed, serious, and not unkind.

" Madam," said he, " I am come upon a weighty
errand; and I would have you recognise it as an
effect of kindness in the President, that he should
send as his ambassador your only neighbour and
your husband's oldest friend in Utah."

" Sir," said my mother, " I have but one concern, one thought. You know well what it is.
Speak: my husband?"

" Madam," returned the doctor, taking a chair
on the veranda, " if you were a silly child, my
position would now be painfully embarrassing.
You are, on the other hand, a woman of great
intelligence and fortitude; you have, by my
forethought, been allowed three weeks to draw
your own conclusions and to accept the inev-
itable. Further words from me are, I conceive,
superfluous."

My mother was as pale as death, and trembled
like a reed; I gave her my hand, and she kept it in
the folds of her dress and wrung it till I could have

cried aloud. " Then, sir," said she at last, " you speak to deaf ears. If this be indeed so, what have I to do with errands? what do I ask of Heaven but to die?"

" Come," said the doctor, " command yourself. I bid you dismiss all thoughts of your late husband, and bring a clear mind to bear upon your own future and the fate of that young girl."

" You bid me dismiss —— " began my mother. " Then you know!" she cried.

" I know," replied the doctor.

" You know?" broke out the poor woman. " Then it was you who did the deed! I tear off the mask, and with dread and loathing see you as you are — you, whom the poor fugitive beholds in nightmares, and awakes raving — you, the Destroying Angel!"

" Well, madam, and what then?" returned the doctor. " Have not my fate and yours been similar? Are we not both immured in this strong prison of Utah? Have you not tried to flee, and did not the Open Eye confront you in the cañon? Who can escape the watch of that unsleeping eye of Utah? Not I, at least. Horrible tasks have, indeed, been laid upon me; and the most ungrateful was the last; but had I refused my offices, would that have spared your husband? You know well it would not. I, too, had perished along with him; nor would I have been able to alleviate his last moments, nor could I to-day have stood between his family and the hand of Brigham Young."

"Ah!" cried I, "and could you purchase life by such concessions?"

"Young lady," answered the doctor, "I both could and did; and you will live to thank me for that baseness. You had a spirit, Asenath, that it pleases me to recognise. But we waste time. Mr. Fonblanque's estate reverts, as you doubtless imagine, to the church; but some part of it has been reserved for him who is to marry the family; and that person, I should perhaps tell you without delay, is no other than myself."

At this odious proposal my mother and I cried out aloud, and clung together like lost souls.

"It is as I supposed," resumed the doctor, with the same measured utterance. "You recoil from this arrangement. Do you expect me to convince you? You know very well that I have never held the Mormon view of women. Absorbed in the most arduous studies, I have left the slatterns whom they call my wives to scratch and quarrel among themselves; of me, they have had nothing but my purse; such was not the union I desired, even if I had the leisure to pursue it. No: you need not, madam, and my old friend — " and here the doctor rose and bowed with something of gallantry — "you need not apprehend my importunities. On the contrary, I am rejoiced to read in you a Roman spirit; and if I am obliged to bid you follow me at once, and that in the name, not of my wish, but of my orders, I hope it will be found that we are of a common mind."

So, bidding us dress for the road, he took a

lamp (for the night had now fallen) and set off to the stable to prepare our horses.

" What does it mean? — what will become of us?" I cried.

" Not that, at least," replied my mother, shuddering. " So far we can trust him. I seem to read among his words a certain tragic promise. Asenath, if I leave you, if I die, you will not forget your miserable parents?"

Thereupon we fell to cross-purposes: I beseeching her to explain her words; she putting me by, and continuing to recommend the doctor for a friend. " The doctor!" I cried at last; " the man who killed my father?"

" Nay," said she, " let us be just. I do believe, before Heaven, he played the friendliest part. And he alone, Asenath, can protect you in this land of death."

At this the doctor returned, leading our two horses; and when we were all in the saddle, he bade me ride on before, as he had matter to discuss with Mrs. Fonblanque. They came at a foot's pace, eagerly conversing in a whisper; and presently after the moon rose and showed them looking eagerly into each other's faces as they went, my mother laying her hand upon the doctor's arm, and the doctor himself, against his usual custom, making vigorous gestures of protest or asseveration.

At the foot of the track which ascended the talus of the mountain to his door, the doctor overtook me at a trot.

" Here," he said, " we shall dismount; and as your mother prefers to be alone, you and I shall walk together to my house."

" Shall I see her again? " I asked.

" I give you my word," he said, and helped me to alight. " We leave the horses here," he added. " There are no thieves in this stone wilderness."

The track mounted gradually, keeping the house in view. The windows were once more bright; the chimney once more vomited smoke; but the most absolute silence reigned, and, but for the figure of my mother very slowly following in our wake, I felt convinced that there was no human soul within a range of miles. At the thought, I looked upon the doctor, gravely walking by my side, with bowed shoulders, and then once more at his house, lit up and pouring smoke like some industrious factory. And then my curiosity broke forth. " In Heaven's name," I cried, " what do you make in this inhuman desert? "

He looked at me with a peculiar smile, and answered with an evasion:

" This is not the first time," said he, " that you have seen my furnaces alight. One morning, in the small hours, I saw you driving past; a delicate experiment miscarried; and I cannot acquit myself of having startled either your driver or the horse that drew you."

" What! " cried I, beholding again in fancy the antics of the figure, " could that be you? "

" It was I," he replied; " but do not fancy that

I was mad. I was in agony. I had been scalded cruelly."

We were now near the house, which, unlike the ordinary houses of the country, was built of hewn stone and very solid. Stone, too, was its foundation, stone its background. Not a blade of grass sprouted among the broken mineral about the walls, not a flower adorned the windows. Over the door, by way of sole adornment, the Mormon Eye was rudely sculptured; I had been brought up to view that emblem from my childhood; but since the night of our escape, it had acquired a new significance, and set me shrinking. The smoke rolled voluminously from the chimney-top, its edges ruddy with the fire; and from the far corner of the building, near the ground, angry puffs of steam shone snow-white in the moon and vanished.

The doctor opened the door and paused upon the threshold. "You ask me what I make here," he observed: "Two things: Life and Death." And he motioned me to enter.

"I shall await my mother," said I.

"Child," he replied, "look at me: am I not old and broken? Of us two, which is the stronger, the young maiden or the withered man?"

I bowed, and passing by him, entered a vestibule or kitchen, lighted by a good fire and a shaded reading-lamp. It was furnished only with a dresser, a rude table, and some wooden benches; and on one of these the doctor motioned me to take a seat; and passing by another door into the interior of

4

the house, he left me to myself. Presently I heard
the jar of iron from the far end of the building;
and this was followed by the same throbbing noise
that had startled me in the valley, but now so near
at hand as to be menacing by loudness, and even
to shake the house with every recurrence of the
stroke. I had scarce time to master my alarm
when the doctor returned, and almost in the same
moment my mother appeared upon the threshold.
But how am I to describe to you the peace and
ravishment of that face? Years seemed to have
passed over her head during that brief ride, and
left her younger and fairer; her eyes shone, her
smile went to my heart; she seemed no more a
woman, but the angel of ecstatic tenderness. I ran
to her in a kind of terror; but she shrank a little
back and laid her finger on her lips, with something arch and yet unearthly. To the doctor, on
the contrary, she reached out her hand as to a
friend and helper; and so strange was the scene
that I forgot to be offended.

"Lucy," said the doctor, "all is prepared. Will
you go alone, or shall your daughter follow us?"

"Let Asenath come," she answered, "dear
Asenath! At this hour, when I am purified of fear
and sorrow, and already survive myself and my
affections, it is for your sake, and not for mine.
that I desire her presence. Were she shut out,
dear friend, it is to be feared she might misjudge
your kindness."

"Mother," I cried wildly, "mother, what is
this?"

But my mother, with her radiant smile, said only " Hush ! " as though I were a child again, and tossing in some fever-fit; and the doctor bade me be silent and trouble her no more. " You have made a choice," he continued, addressing my mother, " that has often strangely tempted me. The two extremes: all, or else nothing; never, or this very hour upon the clock — these have been my incongruous desires. But to accept the middle term, to be content with a half-gift, to flicker awhile and to burn out — never for an hour, never since I was born, has satisfied the appetite of my ambition." He looked upon my mother fixedly, much of admiration and some touch of envy in his eyes; then, with a profound sigh, he led the way into the inner room.

It was very long. From end to end it was lit up by many lamps, which by the changeful colour of their light, and by the incessant snapping sounds with which they burned, I have since divined to be electric. At the extreme end an open door gave us a glimpse into what must have been a lean-to shed beside the chimney: and this, in strong contrast to the room, was painted with a red reverberation, as from furnace-doors. The walls were lined with books and glazed cases, the tables crowded with the implements of chemical research; great glass accumulators glittered in the light; and through a hole in the gable near the shed door, a heavy driving belt entered the apartment and ran overhead upon steel pulleys, with clumsy activity and many ghostly and fluttering sounds. In one corner I perceived a chair resting upon crystal feet, and curiously wreathed with wire. To this my mother advanced with a decisive swiftness.

" Is this it? " she asked.

The doctor bowed in silence.

" Asenath," said my mother, " in this sad end of my life I have found one helper. Look upon him: it is Dr. Grierson. Be not, O my daughter, be not ungrateful to that friend!"

She sat upon the chair, and took in her hands the globes that terminated the arms.

" Am I right? " she asked, and looked upon the doctor with such a radiancy of face that I trembled for her reason. Once more the doctor bowed, but this time leaning hard against the wall. He must have touched a spring. The least shock agitated my mother where she sat; the least passing jar appeared to cross her features; and she sank back in the chair like one resigned to weariness. I was at her knees that moment; but her hands fell loosely in my grasp; her face, still beatified with the same touching smile, sank forward on her bosom; her spirit had for ever fled.

I do not know how long may have elapsed before, raising for a moment my tearful face, I met the doctor's eyes. They rested upon mine with such a depth of scrutiny, pity, and interest, that even from the freshness of my sorrow, I was startled into attention.

" Enough," he said, " to lamentation. Your mother went to death as to a bridal, dying where her husband died. It is time, Asenath, to think of the survivors. Follow me to the next room."

I followed him, like a person in a dream; he made me sit by the fire, he gave me wine to drink; and then, pacing the stone floor, he thus began to address me:

"You are now, my child, alone in the world, and under the immediate watch of Brigham Young. It would be your lot, in ordinary circumstances, to become the fiftieth bride of some ignoble elder, or by particular fortune, as fortune is counted in this land, to find favour in the eyes of the president himself. Such a fate for a girl like you were worse than death; better to die as your mother died than to sink daily deeper in the mire of this pit of woman's degradation. But is escape conceivable? Your father tried; and you beheld yourself with what security his jailers acted, and how a dumb drawing on a rock was counted a sufficient sentry over the avenues of freedom. Where your father failed, will you be wiser or more fortunate? or are you, too, helpless in the toils?"

I had followed his words with changing emotion, but now I believed I understood.

"I see," I cried; "you judge me rightly. I must follow where my parents led; and oh! I am not only willing, I am eager!"

"No," replied the doctor, "not death for you. The flawed vessel we may break, but not the perfect. No, your mother cherished a different hope, and so do I. I see," he cried, "the girl develop to the completed woman, the plan reach fulfilment,

the promise — ay, outdone! I could not bear to
arrest so lively, so comely a process. It was your
mother's thought," he added, with a change of
tone, "that I should marry you myself." I fear
I must have shown a perfect horror of aversion
from this fate, for he made haste to quiet me.

"Reassure yourself, Asenath," he resumed.
"Old as I am, I have not forgotten the tumultuous
fancies of youth. I have passed my days, indeed,
in laboratories; but in all my vigils I have not
forgotten the tune of a young pulse. Age asks
with timidity to be spared intolerable pain; youth,
taking fortune by the beard, demands joy like a
right. These things I have not forgotten; none,
rather, has more keenly felt, none more jealously
considered them; I have but postponed them to
their day. See, then; you stand without support;
the only friend left to you, this old investigator,
old in cunning, young in sympathy. Answer me
but one question. Are you free from the entanglement of what the world calls love? Do you still
command your heart and purposes? or are you
fallen in some bond-slavery of the eye and ear?"

I answered him in broken words; my heart, I
think I must have told him, lay with my dead
parents.

"It is enough," he said. "It has been my fate
to be called on often, too often, for those services
of which we spoke to-night; none in Utah could
carry them so well to a conclusion; hence there has
fallen into my hands a certain share of influence
which I now lay at your service, partly for the sake

of my dead friends, your parents; partly for the interest I bear you in your own right. I shall send you to England, to the great city of London, there to await the bridegroom I have selected. He shall be a son of mine, a young man suitable in age and not grossly deficient in that quality of beauty that your years demand. Since your heart is free, you may well pledge me the sole promise that I ask in return for much expense and still more danger; to await the arrival of that bridegroom with the delicacy of a wife."

I sat awhile stunned. The doctor's marriages, I remembered to have heard, had been unfruitful; and this added perplexity to my distress. But I was alone, as he had said, alone in that dark land; the thought of escape, of any equal marriage, was already enough to revive in me some dawn of hope; and in what words I know not, I accepted the proposal.

He seemed more moved by my consent than I could reasonably have looked for. " You shall see," he cried; " you shall judge for yourself." And hurrying to the next room he returned with a small portrait somewhat coarsely done in oils. It showed a man in the dress of nearly forty years before, young indeed, but still recognisable to be the doctor. " Do you like it?" he asked. " That is myself when I was young. My — my boy will be like that, like but nobler; with such health as angels might condescend to envy; and a man of mind, Asenath, of commanding mind. That should be a man, I think, that should be one among ten thousand. A man like that — one to combine the passions of youth with the restraint, the force, the dignity of age — one to fill all the parts and faculties, one to be man's epitome — say, will that not satisfy the needs of an ambitious girl? Say, is not that enough?" And as he held the picture close before my eyes, his hands shook.

I told him briefly I would ask no better, for I was transpierced with this display of fatherly emotion; but even as I said the words, the most insolent revolt surged through my arteries. I held him in horror, him, his portrait, and his son; and had there been any choice but death or a Mormon marriage, I declare before heaven I had embraced it.

"It is well," he replied, "and I had rightly counted on your spirit. Eat, then, for you have far to go." So saying, he set meat before me; and while I was endeavouring to obey, he left the room and returned with an armful of coarse raiment. "There," said he, "is your disguise. I leave you to your toilette."

The clothes had probably belonged to a somewhat lubberly boy of fifteen; and they hung about me like a sack, and cruelly hampered my movements. But what filled me with uncontrollable shudderings, was the problem of their origin and the fate of the lad to whom they had belonged. I had scarcely effected the exchange when the doctor returned, opened a back window, helped me out into the narrow space between the house and the overhanging bluffs, and showed me a ladder of

iron footholds mortised in the rock. "Mount,"
he said, swiftly. "When you are at the summit,
walk so far as you are able, in the shadow of the
smoke. The smoke will bring you, sooner or later,
to a cañon; follow that down, and you will find
a man with two horses. Him you will implicitly
obey. And remember, silence! That machinery
which I now put in motion for your service, may
by one word be turned against you. Go; heaven
prosper you!"

The ascent was easy. Arrived at the top of the
cliff, I saw before me on the other side a vast and
gradual declivity of stone, lying bare to the moon
and the surrounding mountains. Nowhere was
any vantage or concealment; and knowing how
these deserts were beset with spies, I made haste
to veil my movements under the blowing trail of
smoke. Sometimes it swam high, rising on the
night wind, and I had no more substantial curtain
than its moon-thrown shadow; sometimes again it
crawled upon the earth, and I would walk in it,
no higher than to my shoulders, like some mountain fog. But one way or another, the smoke of
that ill-omened furnace protected the first step of
my escape, and led me unobserved to the cañon.

There, sure enough, I found a taciturn and
sombre man beside a pair of saddle-horses; and
thenceforward, all night long, we wandered in
silence by the most occult and dangerous paths
among the mountains. A little before the day-
spring we took refuge in a wet and gusty cavern at
the bottom of a gorge; lay there all day concealed;

and the next night, before the glow had faded out
of the west, resumed our wanderings. About noon
we stopped again, in a lawn upon a little river,
where was a screen of bushes; and here my guide,
handing me a bundle from his pack, bade me
change my dress once more. The bundle contained
clothing of my own, taken from our house, with
such necessaries as a comb and soap. I made my
toilette by the mirror of a quiet pool; and as I
was so doing and smiling with some complacency
to see myself restored to my own image, the mountains rang with a scream of far more than human
piercingness; and while I still stood astonished,
there sprang up and swiftly increased a storm of
the most awful and earth-rending sounds. Shall
I own to you that I fell upon my face and shrieked?
And yet this was but the overland train winding
among the near mountains: the very means of my
salvation: the strong wings that were to carry me
from Utah!

When I was dressed, the guide gave me a bag,
which contained, he said, both money and papers;
and telling me that I was already over the borders
in the territory of Wyoming, bade me follow the
stream until I reached the railway station, half
a mile below. "Here," he added, "is your ticket
as far as Council Bluffs. The East express will
pass in a few hours." With that, he took both
horses and, without further words or any saluta-
tion, rode off by the way that we had come.

Three hours afterwards I was seated on the
end platform of the train as it swept eastward

through the gorges and thundered in tunnels of the mountain. The change of scene, the sense of escape, the still throbbing terror of pursuit — above all, the astounding magic of my new conveyance, kept me from any logical or melancholy thought. I had gone to the doctor's house two nights before prepared to die, prepared for worse than death; what had passed, terrible although it was, looked almost bright compared to my anticipations; and it was not till I had slept a full night in the flying palace car, that I awoke to the sense of my irreparable loss and to some reasonable alarm about the future. In this mood, I examined the contents of the bag. It was well supplied with gold; it contained tickets and complete directions for my journey as far as Liverpool, and a long letter from the doctor, supplying me with a fictitious name and story, recommending the most guarded silence, and bidding me to await faithfully the coming of his son. All then had been arranged beforehand: he had counted upon my consent, and what was tenfold worse, upon my mother's voluntary death. My horror of my only friend, my aversion for this son who was to marry me, my revolt against the whole current and conditions of my life, were now complete. I was sitting stupefied by my distress and helplessness, when to my joy, a very pleasant lady offered me her conversation. I clutched at the relief; and I was soon glibly telling her the story in the doctor's letter: how I was a Miss Gould, of Nevada City, going to England to an uncle, what money I had, what family, my age, and so

forth, until I had exhausted my instructions, and
as the lady still continued to ply me with questions,
began to embroider on my own account. This
soon carried one of my inexperience beyond her
depth; and I had already remarked a shadow on
the lady's face, when a gentleman drew near and
very civilly addressed me:

"Miss Gould, I believe?" said he; and then,
excusing himself to the lady by the authority of
my guardian, drew me to the fore platform of the
Pullman car. "Miss Gould," he said in my ear,
"is it possible that you suppose yourself in safety?
Let me completely undeceive you. One more such
indiscretion and you return to Utah. And, in the
meanwhile, if this woman should again address
you, you are to reply with these words: 'Madam,
I do not like you, and I will be obliged if you will
suffer me to choose my own associates.'"

Alas, I had to do as I was bid; this lady, to
whom I already felt myself drawn with the strong-
est cords of sympathy, I dismissed with insult; and
thenceforward, through all that day I sat in silence,
gazing on the bare plains and swallowing my tears.
Let that suffice: it was the pattern of my journey.
Whether on the train, at the hotels, or on board the
ocean steamer, I never exchanged a friendly word
with any fellow-traveller but I was certain to be
interrupted. In every place, on every side, the
most unlikely persons, man or woman, rich or poor,
became protectors to forward me upon my journey
or spies to observe and regulate my conduct. Thus
I crossed the States, thus passed the ocean, the

Mormon Eye still following my movements; and
when at length a cab had set me down before that
London lodging-house from which you saw me
fleeing this morning, I had already ceased to
struggle and ceased to hope.

The landlady, like every one else through all that
journey, was expecting my arrival. A fire was
lighted in my room, which looked upon the garden;
there were books on the table, clothes in the
drawers; and there (I had almost said with con-
tentment, and certainly with resignation) I saw
month follow month over my head. At times my
landlady took me for a walk or an excursion, but
she would never suffer me to leave the house alone;
and I, seeing that she also lived under the shadow
of that widespread Mormon terror, felt too much
pity to resist. To the child born on Mormon soil,
as to the man who accepts the engagements of a
secret order, no escape is possible; so I had clearly
read, and I was thankful even for this respite.
Meanwhile, I tried honestly to prepare my mind
for my approaching nuptials. The day drew near
when my bridegroom was to visit me, and gratitude and fear alike obliged me to consent. A son
of Dr. Grierson's, be he what he pleased, must still
be young, and it was even probable he should be
handsome; on more than that, I felt I dared not
reckon; and in moulding my mind toward consent I dwelt the more carefully on these physical
attractions which I felt I might expect, and averted
my eyes from moral or intellectual considerations.
We have a great power upon our spirits; and as

time passed I worked myself into a frame of acquiescence, nay, and I began to grow impatient for the hour. At night sleep forsook me; I sat all day by the fire, absorbed in dreams, conjuring up the features of my husband, and anticipating in fancy the touch of his hand and the sound of his voice. In the dead level and solitude of my existence, this was the one eastern window and the one door of hope. At last, I had so cultivated and prepared my will, that I began to be besieged with fears upon the other side. How if it was I that did not please? How if this unseen lover should turn from me with disaffection? And now I spent hours before the glass, studying and judging my attractions, and was never weary of changing my dress or ordering my hair.

When the day came I was long about my toilette; but at last, with a sort of hopeful desperation, I had to own that I could do no more, and must now stand or fall by nature. My occupation ended, I fell a prey to the most sickening impatience, mingled with alarms; giving ear to the swelling rumour of the streets, and at each change of sound or silence, starting, shrinking, and colouring to the brow. Love is not to be prepared, I know, without some knowledge of the object; and yet, when the cab at last rattled to the door and I heard my visitor mount the stairs, such was the tumult of hopes in my poor bosom that love itself might have been proud to own their parentage. The door opened, and it was Dr. Grierson that appeared. I believe I must have screamed aloud,

and I know, at least, that I fell fainting to the
floor.

When I came to myself he was standing over
me, counting my pulse. " I have startled you," he
said. " A difficulty unforeseen — the impossi-
bility of obtaining a certain drug in its full purity
— has forced me to resort to London unprepared.
I regret that I should have shown myself once more
without those poor attractions which are much,
perhaps, to you, but to me are no more considerable
than rain that falls into the sea. Youth is but a
state, as passing as that syncope from which you
are but just awakened, and, if there be truth in
science, as easy to recall; for I find, Asenath, that
I must now take you for my confidant. Since my
first years, I have devoted every hour and act of
life to one ambitious task; and the time of my
success is at hand. In these new countries, where
I was so long content to stay, I collected indis-
pensable ingredients; I have fortified myself on
every side from the possibility of error; what was
a dream now takes the substance of reality; and
when I offered you a son of mine I did so in a
figure. That son — that husband, Asenath, is myself — not as you now behold me, but restored to
the first energy of youth. You think me mad? It
is the customary attitude of ignorance. I will not
argue; I will leave facts to speak. When you
behold me purified, invigorated, renewed, re-
stamped in the original image — when you recognise in me (what I shall be) the first perfect
expression of the powers of mankind — I shall be

able to laugh with a better grace at your passing
and natural incredulity. To what can you aspire
— fame, riches, power, the charm of youth, the
dear-bought wisdom of age — that I shall not be
able to afford you in perfection? Do not deceive
yourself. I already excel you in every human gift
but one: when that gift also has been restored to
me you will recognise your master."

Hereupon, consulting his watch, he told me he
must now leave me to myself; and bidding me
consult reason, and not girlish fancies, he withdrew. I had not the courage to move; the night
fell and found me still where he had laid me during my faint, my face buried in my hands, my
soul drowned in the darkest apprehensions. Late
in the evening he returned, carrying a candle, and,
with a certain irritable tremor, bade me rise and
sup. " Is it possible," he added, " that I have been
deceived in your courage? A cowardly girl is no
fit mate for me."

I flung myself before him on my knees, and with
floods of tears besought him to release me from
this engagement, assuring him that my cowardice
was abject, and that in every point of intellect and
character I was his hopeless and derisible inferior.

" Why, certainly," he replied. " I know you
better than yourself; and I am well enough acquainted with human nature to understand this
scene. It is addressed to me," he added with a
smile, " in my character of the still untransformed.
But do not alarm yourself about the future. Let
me but attain my end, and not you only, Asenath,

but every woman on the face of the earth becomes my willing slave."

Thereupon he obliged me to rise and eat; sat down with me to table; helped and entertained me with the attentions of a fashionable host; and it was not till a late hour, that, bidding me courteously good-night, he once more left me alone to my misery.

In all this talk of an elixir and the restoration of his youth, I scarce knew from which hypothesis I should the more eagerly recoil. If his hopes reposed on any base of fact, if indeed, by some abhorrent miracle, he should discard his age, death were my only refuge from that most unnatural, that most ungodly union. If, on the other hand, these dreams were merely lunatic, the madness of a life waxed suddenly acute, my pity would become a load almost as heavy to bear as my revolt against the marriage. So passed the night, in alternations of rebellion and despair, of hate and pity; and with the next morning I was only to comprehend more fully my enslaved position. For though he appeared with a very tranquil countenance, he had no sooner observed the marks of grief upon my brow than an answering darkness gathered on his own. "Asenath," he said, "you owe me much already; with one finger I still hold you suspended over death; my life is full of labour and anxiety; and I choose," said he, with a remarkable accent of command, "that you shall greet me with a pleasant face." He never needed to repeat the recommendation; from that day forward I was always ready to receive him with apparent cheerfulness; and he rewarded me with a good deal of his company, and almost more than I could bear of his confidence. He had set up a laboratory in the back part of the house, where he toiled day and night at his elixir, and he would come thence to visit me in my parlour; now with passing humours of discouragement; now, and far more often, radiant with hope. It was impossible to see so much of him, and not to recognise that the sands of his life were running low; and yet all the time he would be laying out vast fields of future, and planning, with all the confidence of youth, the most unbounded schemes of pleasure and ambition. How I replied I know not; but I found a voice and words to answer, even while I wept and raged to hear him.

A week ago the doctor entered my room with the marks of great exhilaration contending with pitiful bodily weakness. " Asenath," said he, " I have now obtained the last ingredient. In one week from now the perilous moment of the last projection will draw nigh. You have once before assisted, although unconsciously, at the failure of a similar experiment. It was the elixir which so terribly exploded one night when you were passing my house; and it is idle to deny that the conduct of so delicate a process, among the million jars and trepidations of so great a city, presents a certain element of danger. From this point of view, I cannot but regret the perfect stillness of my house among the deserts; but on the other hand, I have

succeeded in proving that the singularly unstable
equilibrium of the elixir, at the moment of projection, is due rather to the impurity than to the
nature of the ingredients; and as all are now of
an equal and exquisite nicety, I have little fear for
the result. In a week then from to-day, my dear
Asenath, this period of trial will be ended." And
he smiled upon me in a manner unusually paternal.

I smiled back with my lips, but at my heart
there raged the blackest and most unbridled terror.
What if he failed? And oh, tenfold worse! what
if he succeeded? What detested and unnatural
changeling would appear to claim my hand? And
could there, I asked myself with a dreadful sinking,
be any truth in his boasts of an assured victory
over my reluctance? I knew him, indeed, to be
masterful, to lead my life at a sign. Suppose, then,
this experiment to succeed; suppose him to return
to me, hideously restored, like a vampire in a
legend; and suppose that, by some devilish fascina-
tion . . . My head turned; all former fears deserted me; and I felt I could embrace the worst
in preference to this.

My mind was instantly made up. The doctor's
presence in London was justified by the affairs of
the Mormon polity. Often in our conversation,
he would gloat over the details of that great or-
ganisation, which he feared even while yet he
wielded it; and would remind me, that even in the
humming labyrinth of London, we were still visible
to that unsleeping eye in Utah. His visitors, indeed, who were of every sort, from the missionary

to the Destroying Angel, and seemed to belong to every rank of life, had, up to that moment, filled me with unmixed repulsion and alarm. I knew that if my secret were to reach the ear of any leader my fate were sealed beyond redemption; and yet in my present pass of horror and despair, it was to these very men that I turned for help. I waylaid upon the stair one of the Mormon missionaries, a man of a low class, but not inaccessible to pity; told him I scarce remember what elaborate fable to explain my application; and by his interme-diacy entered into correspondence with my father's family. They recognised my claim for help, and on this very day I was to begin my escape.

Last night I sat up fully dressed, awaiting the result of the doctor's labours, and prepared against the worst. The nights at this season and in this northern latitude are short; and I had soon the company of the returning daylight. The silence in and around the house was only broken by the movements of the doctor in the laboratory; to these I listened, watch in hand, awaiting the hour of my escape, and yet consumed by anxiety about the strange experiment that was going forward overhead. Indeed, now that I was conscious of some protection for myself, my sympathies had turned more directly to the doctor's side; I caught myself even praying for his success; and when some hours ago a low, peculiar cry reached my ears from the laboratory, I could no longer control my impatience, but mounted the stairs and opened the door.

The doctor was standing in the middle of the room; in his hand a large, round-bellied, crystal flask, some three parts full of a bright amber-coloured liquid; on his face a rapture of gratitude and joy unspeakable. As he saw me he raised the flask at arm's length. "Victory!" he cried. "Victory, Asenath!" And then — whether the flask escaped his trembling fingers, or whether the explosion was spontaneous, I cannot tell — enough that we were thrown, I against the door-post, the doctor into the corner of the room; enough that we were shaken to the soul by the same explosion that must have startled you upon the street; and that, in the brief space of an indistinguishable instant, there remained nothing of the labours of the doctor's lifetime but a few shards of broken crystal and those voluminous and ill-smelling vapours that pursued me in my flight.

THE SQUIRE OF DAMES

(concluded)

WHAT with the lady's animated manner and dramatic conduct of her voice, Challoner had thrilled to every incident with genuine emotion. His fancy, which was not perhaps of a very lively character, applauded both the matter and the style; but the more judicial functions of his mind refused assent. It was an excellent story; and it might be true, but he believed it was not. Miss Fonblanque was a lady, and it was doubtless possible for a lady to wander from the truth; but how was a gentleman to tell her so? His spirits for some time had been sinking, but they now fell to zero; and long after her voice had died away he still sat with a troubled and averted countenance, and could find no form of words to thank her for her narrative. His mind, indeed, was empty of everything beyond a dull longing for escape. From this pause, which grew more embarrassing with every second, he was roused by the sudden laughter of the lady. His vanity was alarmed; he turned and faced her; their eyes met; and he caught from hers a spark of such frank merriment as put him instantly at ease.

" You certainly," he said, " appear to bear your calamities with excellent spirit."

" Do I not? " she cried, and fell once more into delicious laughter. But from this access she more speedily recovered. " This is all very well," said she, nodding at him gravely, " but I am still in a most distressing situation, from which, if you deny me your help, I shall find it difficult indeed to free myself."

At this mention of help Challoner fell back to his original gloom.

" My sympathies are much engaged with you," he said, " and I should be delighted, I am sure. But our position is most unusual; and circumstances over which I have, I can assure you, no control, deprive me of the power — the pleasure — unless, indeed," he added, somewhat brightening at the thought, " I were to recommend you to the care of the police? "

She laid her hand upon his arm and looked hard into his eyes; and he saw with wonder that, for the first time since the moment of their meeting, every trace of colour had faded from her cheek.

" Do so," she said, " and — weigh my words well — you kill me as certainly as with a knife."

" God bless me! " exclaimed Challoner.

" Oh," she cried, " I can see you disbelieve my story and make light of the perils that surround me; but who are you to judge? My family share my apprehensions; they help me in secret; and you saw yourself by what an emissary, and in what a place, they have chosen to supply me with the funds for my escape. I admit that you are brave and clever and have impressed me most favourably; but how are you to prefer your opinion before that of my uncle, an ex-minister of state, a man with the ear of the Queen, and of a long political experience? If I am mad, is he? And you must allow me, besides, a special claim upon your help. Strange as you may think my story, you know that much of it is true; and if you who heard the explosion and saw the Mormon at Victoria, refuse to credit and assist me, to whom am I to turn?"

"He gave you money then?" asked Challoner, who had been dwelling singly on that fact.

"I begin to interest you," she cried. "But, frankly, you are condemned to help me. If the service I had to ask of you were serious, were suspicious, were even unusual, I should say no more. But what is it? To take a pleasure trip (for which, if you will suffer me, I propose to pay) and to carry from one lady to another a sum of money! What can be more simple?"

"Is the sum," asked Challoner, "considerable?"

She produced a packet from her bosom; and observing that she had not yet found time to make the count, tore open the cover and spread upon her knees a considerable number of Bank of England notes. It took some time to make the reckoning, for the notes were of every degree of value; but at last, and counting a few loose sovereigns, she made out the sum to be a little under 710*l.* sterling.

The sight of so much money worked an immediate revolution in the mind of Challoner.

"And you propose, madam," he cried, "to intrust that money to a perfect stranger?"

"Ah!" said she with a charming smile, "but I no longer regard you as a stranger."

"Madam," said Challoner, "I perceive I must make you a confession. Although of a very good family — through my mother, indeed, a lineal descendant of the patriot Bruce — I dare not conceal from you that my affairs are deeply, very deeply involved. I am in debt, my pockets are practically empty; and, in short, I am fallen to that state when a considerable sum of money would prove to many men an irresistible temptation."

"Do you not see," returned the young lady, "that by these words you have removed my last hesitation? Take them." And she thrust the notes into the young man's hand.

He sat so long, holding them, like a baby at the font, that Miss Fonblanque once more bubbled into laughter.

"Pray," she said, "hesitate no further; put them in your pocket; and to relieve our position of a shadow of embarrassment, tell me by what name I am to address my knight-errant, for I find myself reduced to the awkwardness of the pronoun."

Had borrowing been in question, the wisdom of our ancestors had come lightly to the young man's aid; but upon what pretext could he refuse so generous a trust? Upon none, he saw, that was

not unpardonably wounding; and the bright eyes
and the high spirits of his companion had already
made a breach in the rampart of Challoner's
caution. The whole thing, he reasoned, might be
a mere mystification, which it were the height of
solemn folly to resent. On the other hand the
explosion, the interview at the public-house, and
the very money in his hands, seemed to prove
beyond denial the existence of some serious danger;
and if that were so, could he desert her? There
was a choice of risks: the risk of behaving with
extraordinary incivility and unhandsomeness to a
lady, and the risk of going on a fool's errand. The
story seemed false; but then the money was undeniable. The whole circumstances were questionable and obscure; but the lady was charming,
and had the speech and manners of society. While
he still hung in the wind, a recollection returned
upon his mind with some of the dignity of proph-
ecy. Had he not promised Somerset to break with
the traditions of the commonplace, and to accept
the first adventure offered? Well, here was the
adventure.

He thrust the money into his pocket.

"My name is Challoner," said he.

"Mr. Challoner," she replied, "you have come
very generously to my aid when all was against
me. Though I am myself a very humble person,
my family commands great interest; and I do not
think you will repent this handsome action."

Challoner flushed with pleasure.

"I imagine that, perhaps, a consulship," she

added, her eyes dwelling on him with a judicial admiration, "a consulship in some great town or capital — or else —— But we waste time; let us set about the work of my delivery."

She took his arm with a frank confidence that went to his heart; and once more laying by all serious thoughts, she entertained him, as they crossed the park, with her agreeable gaiety of mind. Near the Marble Arch they found a hansom, which rapidly conveyed them to the terminus at Euston Square; and here, in the hotel, they sat down to an excellent breakfast. The young lady's first step was to call for writing materials and write, upon one corner of the table, a hasty note; still, as she did so, glancing with smiles at her companion. "Here," said she, "here is the letter which will introduce you to my cousin." She began to fold the paper. "My cousin, although I have never seen her, has the character of a very charming woman and a recognised beauty; of that I know nothing, but at least she has been very kind to me; so has my lord her father; so have you — kinder than all — kinder than I can bear to think of." She said this with unusual emotion; and, at the same time, sealed the envelope. "Ah!" she cried, "I have shut my letter! It is not quite courteous: and yet, as between friends, it is perhaps better so. I introduce you, after all, into a family secret; and though you and I are already old comrades, you are still unknown to my uncle. You go, then, to this address, Richard Street, Glasgow; go, please, as soon as you arrive; and give this letter with your own hands into those of Miss Fonblanque, for that is the name by which she is to pass. When we next meet, you will tell me what you think of her," she added, with a touch of the provocative.

"Ah," said Challoner, almost tenderly, "she can be nothing to me."

"You do not know," replied the young lady with a sigh. "By the bye, I had forgotten — it is very childish, and I am almost ashamed to mention it — but when you see Miss Fonblanque, you will have to make yourself a little ridiculous; and I am sure the part in no way suits you. We had agreed upon a watchword. You will have to address an earl's daughter in these words: '*Nigger, nigger, never die*'; but reassure yourself," she added, laughing, "for the fair patrician will at once finish the quotation. Come now, say your lesson."

"'Nigger, nigger, never die,'" repeated Challoner, with undisguised reluctance.

Miss Fonblanque went into fits of laughter. "Excellent," said she, "it will be the most humourous scene." And she laughed again.

"And what will be the counterword?" asked Challoner, stiffly.

"I will not tell you till the last moment," said she; "for I perceive you are growing too imperious."

Breakfast over, she accompanied the young man to the platform, bought him the "Graphic," the "Athenæum," and a paper-cutter, and stood on the step conversing till the whistle sounded. Then she put her head into the carriage. '*Black face and shining eye!*' she whispered, and instantly leaped down upon the platform, with a trill of gay and musical laughter. As the train steamed out of the great arch of glass, the sound of that laughter still rang in the young man's ears.

Challoner's position was too unusual to be long welcome to his mind. He found himself projected the whole length of England, on a mission beset with obscure and ridiculous circumstances, and yet, by the trust he had accepted, irrevocably bound to persevere. How easy it appeared, in the retrospect, to have refused the whole proposal, returned the money, and gone forth again upon his own affairs, a free and happy man! And it was now impossible: the enchantress who had held him with her eye had now disappeared, taking his honour in pledge; and as she had failed to leave him an address, he was denied even the inglorious safety of retreat. To use the paper-knife, or even to read the periodicals with which she had presented him, was to renew the bitterness of his remorse; and as he was alone in the compartment, he passed the day staring at the landscape in impotent repentance, and long before he was landed on the platform of St. Enoch's, had fallen to the lowest and coldest zones of self-contempt.

As he was hungry, and elegant in his habits, he would have preferred to dine and to remove the stains of travel; but the words of the young lady, and his own impatient eagerness, would suffer no delay. In the late, luminous, and lamp-starred dusk of the summer evening, he accordingly set forward with brisk steps.

The street to which he was directed had first seen the day in the character of a row of small suburban villas on a hillside; but the extension of the city had, long since and on every hand, surrounded it with miles of streets. From the top of the hill a range of very tall buildings, densely inhabited by the very poorest classes of the population and variegated by drying-poles from every second window, overplumbed the villas and their little gardens like a seaboard cliff. But still, under the grime of years of city smoke, these antiquated cottages, with their venetian blinds and rural porticos, retained a somewhat melancholy savour of the past.

The street, when Challoner entered it, was perfectly deserted. From hard by, indeed, the sound of a thousand footfalls filled the ear; but in Richard Street itself there was neither light nor sound of human habitation. The appearance of the neighbourhood weighed heavily on the mind of the young man; once more, as in the streets of London, he was impressed with the sense of city deserts; and as he approached the number indicated, and somewhat falteringly rang the bell, his heart sank within him.

The bell was ancient, like the house; it had a thin and garrulous note; and it was some time before it ceased to sound from the rear quarters of the building. Following upon this an inner door was stealthily opened, and careful and catlike steps drew near along the hall. Challoner, supposing he was to be instantly admitted, produced his letter and, as well as he was able, prepared a smiling face. To his indescribable surprise, however, the footsteps ceased, and then, after a pause and with the like stealthiness, withdrew once more, and died away in the interior of the house. A second time the young man rang violently at the bell; a second time, to his keen hearkening, a certain bustle of discreet footing moved upon the hollow boards of the old villa; and again the faint-hearted garrison only drew near to retreat. The cup of the visitor's endurance was now full to overflowing; and, committing the whole family of Fonblanque to every mood and shade of condemnation, he turned upon his heel and redescended the steps. Perhaps the mover in the house was watching from a window, and plucked up courage at the sight of this desistance; or perhaps, where he lurked trembling in the back part of the villa, reason in its own right had conquered his alarms. Challoner, at least, had scarce set foot upon the pavement when he was arrested by the sound of the withdrawal of an inner bolt; one followed another rattling in their sockets; the key turned harshly in the lock; the door opened; and there appeared upon the threshold a man of a very stalwart figure in his shirt sleeves. He was a person neither of great manly beauty nor of a refined exterior; he was not the man, in ordinary moods, to attract the eyes of the observer; but as he now stood in the doorway, he was marked so legibly with the **extreme** passion of **terror** that Challoner stood wonder-struck. For a fraction of a minute they gazed upon each other in silence; and then, the man of the house, with ashen lips and gasping voice, inquired the business of his visitor. Challoner replied, in tones from which he strove to banish his surprise, that he was the bearer of a letter to a certain Miss Fonblanque. At this name, as at a talisman, the man fell back and impatiently invited him to enter; and no sooner had the adventurer crossed the threshold, than the door was closed behind him and his retreat cut off.

It was already long past eight at night; and though the late twilight of the north still lingered in the streets, in the passage it was already groping dark. The man led Challoner directly to a parlour looking on the garden to the back. Here he had apparently been supping; for by the light of a tallow dip, the table was seen to be covered with a napkin, and set out with a quart of bottled ale and the heel of a Gouda cheese. The room, on the other hand, was furnished with faded solidity, and the walls were lined with scholarly and costly volumes in glazed cases. The house must have been taken furnished; for it had no congruity with this man of the shirt sleeves and the mean supper. As for the earl's daughter, the earl and the visionary consulships in foreign cities, they had long ago begun to fade in Challoner's imagination. Like Dr. Grierson and the Mormon angels, they were plainly woven of the stuff of dreams. Not an illusion remained to the knight-errant; not a hope was left him, but to be speedily relieved from this disreputable business.

The man had continued to regard his visitor with undisguised anxiety, and began once more to press him for his errand.

"I am here," said Challoner, "simply to do a service between two ladies; and I must ask you, without further delay, to summon Miss Fonblanque, into whose hands alone I am authorised to deliver the letter that I bear."

A growing wonder began to mingle on the man's face with the lines of solicitude. "I am Miss Fonblanque," he said; and then, perceiving the effect of this communication, "Good God!" he cried, "what are you staring at? I tell you, I am Miss Fonblanque."

Seeing the speaker wore a chin-beard of considerable length, and the remainder of his face was blue with shaving, Challoner could only suppose himself the subject of a jest. He was no longer under the spell of the young lady's presence; and with men, and above all with his inferiors, he was capable of some display of spirit.

"Sir," said he, pretty roundly, "I have put myself to great inconvenience for persons of whom I know too little, and I begin to be weary of the business. Either you shall immediately summon Miss Fonblanque, or I leave this house and put myself under the direction of the police."

"This is horrible!" exclaimed the man. "I declare before Heaven I am the person meant, but how shall I convince you? It must have been

6

Clara, I perceive, that sent you on this errand — a
mad woman, who jests with the most deadly interests; and here we are incapable, perhaps, of an
agreement, and Heaven knows what may depend
on our delay!"

He spoke with a really startling earnestness;
and at the same time there flashed upon the mind
of Challoner the ridiculous jingle which was to
serve as a password. "This may, perhaps, assist
you," he said; and then, with some embarrassment:
"'Nigger, nigger, never die.'"

A light of relief broke upon the troubled countenance of the man with the chin-beard. "'Black
face and shining eye' — give me the letter," he
panted in one gasp.

"Well," said Challoner, though still with some
reluctance, "I suppose I must regard you as the
proper recipient; and though I may justly complain of the spirit in which I have been treated, I
am only too glad to be done with all responsibility.
Here it is"; and he produced the envelope.

The man leaped upon it like a beast, and with
hands that trembled in a manner painful to behold,
tore it open and unfolded the letter. As he read,
terror seemed to mount upon him to the pitch of
nightmare. He struck one hand upon his brow,
while with the other, as if unconsciously, he
crumpled the paper to a ball. "My gracious
powers!" he cried; and then, dashing to the window, which stood open on the garden, he clapped
forth his head and shoulders, and whistled long
and shrill. Challoner fell back into a corner, and

resolutely grasping his staff, prepared for the most desperate events; but the thoughts of the man with the chin-beard were far removed from violence. Turning again into the room, and once more beholding his visitor, whom he appeared to have forgotten, he fairly danced with trepidation. " Impossible! " he cried. " Oh, quite impossible! O Lord, I have lost my head." And then, once more striking his hand upon his brow, " The money! " he exclaimed. " Give me the money."

" My good friend," replied Challoner, " this is a very painful exhibition; and until I see you reasonably master of yourself, I decline to proceed with any business."

" You are quite right," said the man. " I am of a very nervous habit; a long course of the dumb ague has undermined my constitution. But I know you have money; it may be still the saving of me; and oh, dear young gentleman, in pity's name be expeditious! "

Challoner, sincerely uneasy as he was, could scarce refrain from laughter; but he was himself in a hurry to be gone, and without more delay produced the money. " You will find the sum, I trust, correct," he observed; " and let me ask you to give me a receipt."

But the man heeded him not. He seized the money, and disregarding the sovereigns that rolled loose upon the floor, thrust the bundle of notes into his pocket.

" A receipt," repeated Challoner with some asperity, " I insist on a receipt."

" Receipt? " repeated the man a little wildly.
" A receipt? Immediately! Await me here."

Challoner, in reply, begged the gentleman to
lose no unnecessary time, as he was himself desirous of catching a particular train.

" Ah, by God, and so am I! " exclaimed the man
with the chin-beard; and with that he was gone
out of the room, and had rattled up-stairs, four at
a time, to the upper storey of the villa.

" This is certainly a most amazing business,"
thought Challoner, " certainly a most disquieting
affair; and I cannot conceal from myself that I
have become mixed up with either lunatics or malefactors. I may truly thank my stars that I am so
nearly and so creditably done with it." Thus
thinking and perhaps remembering the episode of
the whistle, he turned to the open window. The
garden was still faintly clear; he could distinguish
the stairs and terraces with which the small domain
had been adorned by former owners, and the blackened bushes and dead trees that had once afforded
shelter to the country birds; beyond these he saw
the strong retaining wall, some thirty feet in
height, which inclosed the garden to the back; and
again above that, the pile of dingy buildings rear-
ing its frontage high into the night. A peculiar
object lying stretched upon the lawn for some time
baffled his eyesight; but at length he made it out
to be a long ladder, or series of ladders bound into
one; he was still wondering of what service so
great an instrument could be in such a scant inclosure, when he was recalled to himself by the

noise of some one running violently down the
stairs. This was followed by the sudden, clamor-
ous banging of the house door; and that again,
by rapid and retreating footsteps in the street.

Challoner sprang into the passage. He ran
from room to room, up-stairs and down-stairs; and
in that old dingy and worm-eaten house, he found
himself alone. Only in one apartment looking to
the front, were there any traces of the late inhab-
itant: a bed that had been recently slept in and not
made, a chest of drawers disordered by a hasty
search, and on the floor a roll of crumpled paper.
This he picked up. The light in this upper story
looking to the front was considerably brighter
than in the parlour; and he was able to make out
that the paper bore the mark of the hotel at Euston,
and even, by peering closely, to decipher the following lines in a very elegant and careful female
hand:

"DEAR M'GUIRE, — It is certain your retreat is known.
We have just had another failure, clockwork thirty hours too
soon, with the usual humiliating result. Zero is quite dis-
heartened. We are all scattered, and I could find no one
but the *solemn ass* who brings you this and the money. I
would love to see your meeting. — Ever yours,
                                        "SHINING EYE."

Challoner was stricken to the heart. He perceived by what facility, by what unmanly fear of
ridicule, he had been brought down to be the gull
of this intriguer; and his wrath flowed forth in
almost equal measure against himself, against the
woman, and against Somerset, whose idle counsels

had impelled him to embark on that adventure.
At the same time a great and troubled curiosity,
and a certain chill of fear, possessed his spirit.
The conduct of the man with the chin-beard, the
terms of the letter, and the explosion of the early
morning, fitted together like parts in some obscure and mischievous imbroglio. Evil was certainly afoot; evil, secrecy, terror, and falsehood
were the conditions and the passions of the people
among whom he had begun to move, like a blind
puppet; and he who began as a puppet, his experience told him, was often doomed to perish as a
victim.

From the stupor of deep thought into which he
had glided with the letter in his hand, he was
awakened by the clatter of the bell. He glanced
from the window; and, conceive his horror and
surprise when he beheld, clustered on the steps, in
the front garden and on the pavement of the street,
a formidable posse of police! He started to the
full possession of his powers and courage. Escape,
and escape at any cost, was the one idea that possessed him. Swiftly and silently he redescended
the creaking stairs; he was already in the passage
when a second and more imperious summons from
the door awoke the echoes of the empty house; nor
had the bell ceased to jangle before he had be-
stridden the window-sill of the parlour and was
lowering himself into the garden. His coat was
hooked upon the iron flower basket; for a moment
he hung dependent heels and head below; and then,
with the noise of rending cloth and followed by

several pots, he dropped upon the sod. Once more
the bell was rung, and now with furious and repeated peals. The desperate Challoner turned his
eyes on every side. They fell upon the ladder, and
he ran to it, and with strenuous but unavailing
effort sought to raise it from the ground. Suddenly the weight, which was thus resisting his
whole strength, began to lighten in his hands; the
ladder, like a thing of life, reared its bulk from
off the sod; and Challoner, leaping back with a cry
of almost superstitious terror, beheld the whole
structure mount, foot by foot, against the face of
the retaining wall. At the same time, two heads
were dimly visible above the parapet, and he was
hailed by a guarded whistle. Something in its
modulation recalled, like an echo, the whistle of the
man with the chin-beard.

Had he chanced upon a means of escape prepared beforehand by those very miscreants whose
messenger and gull he had become? Was this,
indeed, a means of safety, or but the starting-point
of further complication and disaster? He paused
not to reflect. Scarce was the ladder reared to its
full length than he had sprung already on the
rounds; hand over hand, swift as an ape, he scaled
the tottering stairway. Strong arms received, embraced, and helped him; he was lifted and set once
more upon the earth; and with the spasm of his
alarm yet unsubsided, found himself, in the company of two rough-looking men, in the paved back-
yard of one of the tall houses that crowned the
summit of the hill. Meanwhile, from below, the

note of the bell had been succeeded by the sound
of vigorous and redoubling blows.

"Are you all out?" asked one of his companions; and as soon as he had babbled an answer in
the affirmative, the rope was cut from the top
round, and the ladder thrust roughly back into the
garden, where it fell and broke with clattering
reverberations.   Its fall was hailed with many
broken cries; for the whole of Richard Street was
now in high emotion, the people crowding to the
windows or clambering on the garden walls.   The
same man who had already addressed Challoner
seized him by the arm; whisked him through the
basement of the house and across the street upon
the other side; and before the unfortunate adventurer had time to realise his situation, a door was
opened and he was thrust into a low and dark
compartment.

"Bedad," observed his guide, "there was no
time to lose.   Is M'Guire gone, or was it you that
whistled?"

"M'Guire is gone," said Challoner.

The guide now struck a light.   "Ah," said he,
"this will never do.   You dare not go upon the
streets in such a figure.   Wait quietly here and I
will bring you something decent."

With that the man was gone, and Challoner, his
attention thus rudely awakened, began ruefully to
consider the havoc that had been worked in his
attire.   His hat was gone; his trousers were
cruelly ripped; and the best part of one tail of his
very elegant frock-coat had been left hanging from

the iron crockets of the window. He had scarce
had time to measure these disasters when his host
re-entered the apartment and proceeded, without
a word, to envelop the refined and urbane Challoner in a long ulster of the cheapest material and
of a pattern so gross and vulgar that his spirit
sickened at the sight. This calumnious disguise
was crowned and completed by a soft felt hat of
the Tyrolese design and several sizes too small.
At another moment Challoner would simply have
refused to issue forth upon the world thus trav-
estied; but the desire to escape from Glasgow was
now too strongly and too exclusively impressed
upon his mind. With one haggard glance at the
spotted tails of his new coat, he inquired what
was to pay for this accoutrement. The man assured him that the whole expense was easily met
from funds in his possession, and begged him,
instead of wasting time, to make his best speed
out of the neighbourhood.

The young man was not loath to take the hint.
True to his usual courtesy, he thanked the speaker
and complimented him upon his taste in great-
coats; and leaving the man somewhat abashed
by these remarks and the manner of their delivery,
he hurried forth into the lamp-lighted city. The
last train was gone ere, after many deviations, he
had reached the terminus. Attired as he was he
dared not present himself at any reputable inn;
and he felt keenly that the unassuming dignity of
his demeanour would serve to attract attention,
perhaps mirth, and possibly suspicion, in any

humbler hostelry. He was thus condemned to pass the solemn and uneventful hours of a whole night in pacing the streets of Glasgow; supperless; a figure of fun for all beholders; waiting the dawn, with hope indeed, but with unconquerable shrinkings; and above all things, filled with a profound sense of the folly and weakness of his conduct. It may be conceived with what curses he assailed the memory of the fair narrator of Hyde Park; her parting laughter rang in his ears all night with damning mockery and iteration; and when he could spare a thought from this chief artificer of his confusion, it was to expend his wrath on Somerset and the career of the amateur detective. With the coming of day, he found in a shy milk-shop the means to appease his hunger. There were still many hours to wait before the departure of the south express; these he passed wandering with indescribable fatigue in the obscurer by-streets of the city; and at length slipped quietly into the station and took his place in the darkest corner of a third-class carriage. Here, all day long, he jolted on the bare boards, distressed by heat and continually re-awakened from uneasy slumbers. By the half return ticket in his purse, he was entitled to make the journey on the easy cushions and with the ample space of the first-class; but alas! in his absurd attire he durst not for decency comingle with his equals; and this small annoyance, coming last in such a series of disasters, cut him to the heart.

That night, when, in his Putney lodging, he reviewed the expense, anxiety, and weariness of his adventure; when he beheld the ruins of his last good trousers and his last presentable coat; and above all, when his eye by any chance alighted on the Tyrolese hat or the degrading ulster, his heart would overflow with bitterness, and it was only by a serious call on his philosophy that he maintained the dignity of his demeanour.

SOMERSET'S ADVENTURE: THE SUPERFLUOUS MANSION

MR. PAUL SOMERSET was a young gentleman of a lively and fiery imagination, with very small capacity for action. He was one who lived exclusively in dreams and in the future: the creature of his own theories, and an actor in his own romances. From the cigar divan he proceeded to parade the streets, still heated with the fire of his eloquence, and scouting upon every side for the offer of some fortunate adventure. In the continual stream of passers-by, on the sealed fronts of houses, on the posters that covered the hoardings, and in every lineament and throb of the great city he saw a mysterious and hopeful hieroglyph. But although the elements of adventure were streaming by him as thick as drops of water in the Thames, it was in vain that, now with a beseeching, now with something of a braggadocio air, he courted and provoked the notice of the passengers; in vain that, putting fortune to the touch, he even thrust himself into the way and came into direct collision with those of the more promising demeanour. Persons brimful of secrets, persons pining for affection, persons perishing for lack of help or counsel, he was sure he could perceive on every side; but by some contrariety of fortune, each passed upon his way without remarking the young gentleman, and went further (surely to fare worse!) in quest of the confidant, the friend, or the adviser. To thousands he must have turned an appealing countenance, and yet not one regarded him.

A light dinner, eaten to the accompaniment of his impetuous aspirations, broke in upon the series of his attempts on fortune; and when he returned to the task, the lamps were already lighted, and the nocturnal crowd was dense upon the pavement. Before a certain restaurant, whose name will readily occur to any student of our Babylon, people were already packed so closely that passage had grown difficult; and Somerset, standing in the kennel, watched, with a hope that was beginning to grow somewhat weary, the faces and the manners of the crowd. Suddenly he was startled by a gentle touch upon the shoulder, and facing about, he was aware of a very plain and elegant brougham, drawn by a pair of powerful horses, and driven by a man in sober livery. There were no arms upon the panel; the window was open, but the interior was obscure; the driver yawned behind his palm; and the young man was already beginning to suppose himself the dupe of his own fancy, when a hand, no larger than a child's and smoothly gloved in white, appeared in a corner of the window and privily beckoned him to approach. He did so, and looked in. The carriage was occupied by a single small and dainty figure, swathed head and shoulders in impenetrable folds of white lace; and a voice, speaking low and silvery, addressed him in these words:

"Open the door and get in."

"It must be," thought the young man with an almost unbearable thrill, "it must be that duchess at last!" Yet, although the moment was one to which he had long looked forward, it was with a certain share of alarm that he opened the door, and, mounting into the brougham, took his seat beside the lady of the lace. Whether or no she had touched a spring, or given some other signal, the young man had hardly closed the door before the carriage, with considerable swiftness, and with a very luxurious and easy movement on its springs, turned and began to drive toward the west.

Somerset, as I have written, was not unprepared; it had long been his particular pleasure to rehearse his conduct in the most unlikely situations; and this, among others, of the patrician ravisher, was one he had familiarly studied. Strange as it may seem, however, he could find no apposite remark; and as the lady, on her side, vouchsafed no further sign, they continued to drive in silence through the streets. Except for alternate flashes from the passing lamps, the carriage was plunged in obscurity; and beyond the fact that the fittings were luxurious, and that the lady was singularly small and slender in person, and, all but one gloved hand, still swathed in her costly veil, the young man could decipher no detail of an inspiring nature. The suspense began to grow unbearable. Twice he cleared his throat, and twice the whole resources of the language failed him. In similar scenes, when he had forecast them on the theatre of fancy, his presence of mind had always been complete, his eloquence remarkable; and at this disparity between the rehearsal and the performance, he began to be seized with a panic of apprehension. Here, on the very threshold of adventure, suppose him ignominiously to fail; suppose that after ten, twenty, or sixty seconds of still uninterrupted silence, the lady should touch the check-string and re-deposit him, weighed and found wanting, on the common street! Thousands of persons of no mind at all, he reasoned, would be found more equal to the part; could, that very instant, by some decisive step, prove the lady's choice to have been well inspired, and put a stop to this intolerable silence.

His eye, at this point, lighted on the hand. It was better to fall by desperate councils than to continue as he was; and with one tremulous swoop he pounced on the gloved fingers and drew them to himself. One overt step, it had appeared to him, would dissolve the spell of his embarrassment; in act, he found it otherwise: he found himself no less incapable of speech or further progress; and with the lady's hand in his, sat helpless. But worse was in store. A peculiar quivering began to agitate the form of his companion; the hand that lay unresistingly in Somerset's trembled as with ague; and presently there broke forth, in the shadow of the carriage, the bubbling and musical sound of laughter, resisted but triumphant. The young man dropped his prize; had it been possible, he would have bounded from the carriage. The lady, meanwhile, lying back upon the cushions, passed on from trill to trill of the most heartfelt, high-pitched, clear, and fairy-sounding merriment.

"You must not be offended," she said at last, catching an opportunity between two paroxysms. "If you have been mistaken in the warmth of your attentions, the fault is solely mine; it does not flow from your presumption, but from my eccentric manner of recruiting friends; and, believe me, I am the last person in the world to think the worse of a young man for showing spirit. As for to-night, it is my intention to entertain you to a little supper; and if I shall continue to be as much pleased with your manners as I was taken with your face, I may perhaps end by making you an advantageous offer."

Somerset sought in vain to find some form of answer, but his discomfiture had been too recent and complete.

"Come," returned the lady, "we must have no display of temper; that is for me the one disqualifying fault; and as I perceive we are drawing near our destination, I shall ask you to descend and offer me your arm."

Indeed, at that very moment the carriage drew up before a stately and severe mansion in a spacious square; and Somerset, who was possessed of an excellent temper, with the best grace in the

world assisted the lady to alight. The door was
opened by an old woman of a grim appearance,
who ushered the pair into a dining-room somewhat
dimly lighted, but already laid for supper, and
occupied by a prodigious company of large and
valuable cats. Here, as soon as they were alone,
the lady divested herself of the lace in which she
was infolded; and Somerset was relieved to find,
that although still bearing the traces of great
beauty, and still distinguished by the fire and colour
of her eye, her hair was of a silvery whiteness and
her faced lined with years.

"And now, *mon preux*," said the old lady, nodding at him with a quaint gaiety, "you perceive
that I am no longer in my first youth. You will
soon find that I am all the better company for
that."

As she spoke, the maid re-entered the apartment
with a light but tasteful supper. They sat down,
accordingly, to table, the cats with savage pantomime surrounding the old lady's chair, and what
with the excellence of the meal and the gaiety of
his entertainer, Somerset was soon completely at
his ease. When they had well eaten and drunk, the
old lady leaned back in her chair, and taking a cat
upon her lap, subjected her guest to a prolonged
but evidently mirthful scrutiny.

"I fear, madam," said Somerset, "that my manners have not risen to the height of your precon-
ceived opinion."

"My dear young man," she replied, "you were
never more mistaken in your life. I find you

charming, and you may very well have lighted on a fairy godmother. I am not one of those who are given to change their opinions, and short of substantial demerit, those who have once gained my favour continue to enjoy it; but I have a singular swiftness of decision, read my fellow men and women with a glance, and have acted throughout life on first impressions. Yours, as I tell you, has been favourable: and if, as I suppose, you are a young fellow of somewhat idle habits, I think it not improbable that we may strike a bargain."

"Ah, madam," returned Somerset, "you have divined my situation. I am a man of birth, parts and breeding; excellent company, or at least so I find myself; but by a peculiar iniquity of fate, destitute alike of trade or money. I was, indeed, this evening upon the quest of an adventure, resolved to close with any offer of interest, emolument or pleasure; and your summons, which I profess I am still at some loss to understand, jumped naturally with the inclination of my mind. Call it, if you will, impudence; I am here, at least, prepared for any proposition you can find it in your heart to make, and resolutely determined to accept."

"You express yourself very well," replied the old lady, "and are certainly a droll and curious young man. I should not care to affirm that you were sane, for I have never found any one entirely so besides myself; but at least the nature of your madness entertains me, and I will reward you with some description of my character and life."

Thereupon the old lady, still fondling the cat upon her lap, proceeded to narrate the following particulars.

NARRATIVE OF THE SPIRITED
OLD LADY

I WAS the eldest daughter of the Reverend Bernard Fanshawe, who held a valuable living in the diocese of Bath and Wells. Our family, a very large one, was noted for a sprightly and incisive wit, and came of a good old stock where beauty was an heirloom. In Christian grace of character we were unhappily deficient. From my earliest years I saw and deplored the defects of those relatives whose age and position should have enabled them to conquer my esteem; and while I was yet a child, my father married a second wife, in whom (strange to say) the Fanshawe failings were exaggerated to a monstrous and almost laughable degree. Whatever may be said against me, it cannot be denied I was a pattern daughter; but it was in vain that, with the most touching patience, I submitted to my stepmother's demands; and from the hour she entered my father's house, I may say that I met with nothing but injustice and ingratitude.

I stood not alone, however, in the sweetness of my disposition; for one other of the family besides myself was free from any violence of character. Before I had reached the age of sixteen, this cousin,

John by name, had conceived for me a sincere but silent passion; and although the poor lad was too timid to hint at the nature of his feelings, I had soon divined and begun to share them. For some days I pondered on the odd situation created for me by the bashfulness of my admirer: and at length, perceiving that he began, in his distress, rather to avoid than seek my company, I determined to take the matter into my own hands. Finding him alone in a retired part of the rectory garden, I told him that I had divined his amiable secret; that I knew with what disfavour our union was sure to be regarded; and that, under the circumstances, I was prepared to flee with him at once. Poor John was literally paralysed with joy; such was the force of his emotions, that he could find no words in which to thank me; and that I, seeing him thus helpless, was obliged to arrange, myself, the details of our flight, and of the stolen marriage which was immediately to crown it. John had been at that time projecting a visit to the metropolis. In this I bade him persevere, and promised on the following day to join him at the Tavistock Hotel.

True, on my side, to every detail of our arrangement, I arose, on the day in question, before the servants, packed a few necessaries in a bag, took with me the little money I possessed, and bade farewell for ever to the rectory. I walked with good spirits to a town some thirty miles from home, and was set down the next morning in this great city of London. As I walked from the

coach-office to the hotel, I could not help exulting
in the pleasant change that had befallen me; beholding, meanwhile, with innocent delight, the
traffic of the streets, and depicting, in all the colours of fancy, the reception that awaited me from
John. But alas! when I inquired for Mr. Fanshawe, the porter assured me there was no such
gentleman among the guests. By what channel
our secret had leaked out, or what pressure had
been brought to bear on the too facile John, I
could never fathom. Enough that my family had
triumphed; that I found myself alone in London,
tender in years, smarting under the most sensible
mortification, and by every sentiment of pride and
self-respect debarred for ever from my father's
house.

I rose under the blow, and found lodgings in the
neighbourhood of Euston Road, where, for the first
time in my life, I tasted the joys of independence.
Three days afterwards, an advertisement in *The
Times* directed me to the office of a solicitor whom
I knew to be in my father's confidence. There
I was given the promise of a very moderate
allowance, and a distinct intimation that I must
never look to be received at home. I could not but
resent so cruel a desertion, and I told the lawyer it
was a meeting I desired as little as themselves.
He smiled at my courageous spirit, paid me the
first quarter of my income, and gave me the remainder of my personal effects, which had been
sent to me under his care, in a couple of rather
ponderous boxes. With these I returned in triumph

to my lodgings, more content with my position than I should have thought possible a week before and fully determined to make the best of the future.

All went well for several months; and, indeed, it was my own fault alone that ended this pleasant and secluded episode of life. I have, I must confess, the fatal trick of spoiling my inferiors. My landlady, to whom I had as usual been overkind, impertinently called me in fault for some particular too small to mention; and I, annoyed that I had allowed her the freedom upon which she thus presumed, ordered her to leave my presence. She stood a moment dumb, and then, recalling her self-possession, " Your bill," said she, " shall be ready this evening, and to-morrow, madam, you shall leave my house. See," she added, " that you are able to pay what you owe me; for if I do not receive the uttermost farthing, no box of yours shall pass my threshold."

I was confounded at her audacity, but as a whole quarter's income was due to me, not otherwise affected by the threat. That afternoon, as I left the solicitor's door, carrying in one hand, and done up in a paper parcel, the whole amount of my fortune, there befell me one of those decisive incidents that sometimes shape a life. The lawyer's office was situate in a street that opened at the upper end upon the Strand and was closed at the lower, at the time of which I speak, by a row of iron railings looking on the Thames. Down this street, then, I beheld my stepmother advancing to meet me, and doubtless bound to the very house I had just left. She was attended by a maid whose face was new to me; but her own was too clearly printed on my memory; and the sight of it, even from a distance, filled me with generous indignation. Flight was impossible. There was nothing left but to retreat against the railing, and with my back turned to the street, pretend to be admiring the barges on the river or the chimneys of transpontine London.

I was still standing, and had not yet fully mastered the turbulence of my emotions, when a voice at my elbow addressed me with a trivial question. It was the maid whom my stepmother, with characteristic hardness, had left to await her on the street, while she transacted her business with the family solicitor. The girl did not know who I was; the opportunity too golden to be lost; and I was soon hearing the latest news of my father's rectory and parish. It did not surprise me to find that she detested her employers; and yet the terms in which she spoke of them were hard to bear, hard to let pass unchallenged. I heard them, however, without dissent, for my self-command is wonderful; and we might have parted as we met had she not proceeded, in an evil hour, to criticise the rector's missing daughter, and with the most shocking perversions, to narrate the story of her flight. My nature is so essentially generous that I can never pause to reason. I flung up my hand sharply, by way, as well as I remember, of indignant protest; and, in the act, the packet slipped from my fingers, glanced between the railings, and fell and sunk in the river. I stood for a moment petrified, and then, struck by the drollery of the incident, gave way to peals of laughter. I was still laughing when my stepmother reappeared, and the maid, who doubtless considered me insane, ran off to join her; nor had I yet recovered my gravity when I presented myself before the lawyer to solicit a fresh advance. His answer made me serious enough, for it was a flat refusal; and it was not until I had besought him even with tears, that he consented to lend me ten pounds from his own pocket. " I am a poor man," said he, " and you must look for nothing further at my hands."

The landlady met me at the door. " Here, madam," said she, with a curtsey insolently low, " here is my bill. Would it inconvenience you to settle it at once?"

" You shall be paid, madam," said I, " in the morning, in the proper course." And I took the paper with a very high air, but inwardly quaking.

I had no sooner looked at it than I perceived myself to be lost. I had been short of money and had allowed my debt to mount; and it had now reached the sum, which I shall never forget, of twelve pounds thirteen shillings and fourpence halfpenny. All evening I sat by the fire considering my situation. I could not pay the bill; my landlady would not suffer me to remove my boxes; and without either baggage or money, how was I to find another lodging? For three months, unless I could invent some remedy, I was condemned to be without a roof and without a penny. It can surprise no one that I decided on immediate flight; but even here I was confronted by a difficulty, for I had no sooner packed my boxes than I found I was not strong enough to move, far less to carry them.

In this strait I did not hesitate a moment, but throwing on a shawl and bonnet, and covering my face with a thick veil, I betook myself to that great bazar of dangerous and smiling chances, the pavement of the city. It was already late at night, and the weather being wet and windy, there were few abroad besides policemen. These, on my present mission, I had wit enough to know for enemies; and wherever I perceived their moving lanterns, I made haste to turn aside and choose another thoroughfare. A few miserable women still walked the pavement; here and there were young fellows returning drunk, or ruffians of the lowest class lurking in the mouths of alleys; but of any one to whom I might appeal in my distress, I began almost to despair.

At last, at the corner of a street, I ran into the arms of one who was evidently a gentleman, and who, in all his appointments, from his furred greatcoat to the fine cigar which he was smoking, comfortably breathed of wealth. Much as my face has changed from its original beauty, I still retain (or so I tell myself) some traces of the youthful lightness of my figure. Even veiled as I then was, I could perceive the gentleman was struck by my appearance; and this emboldened me for my adventure.

" Sir," said I with a quickly beating heart, " are you one in whom a lady can confide?"

" Why, my dear," said he, removing his cigar, " that depends on circumstances. If you will raise your veil —— "

" Sir," I interrupted, " let there be no mistake. I ask you, as a gentleman, to serve me, but I offer no reward."

" That is frank," said he, " but hardly tempting. And what, may I inquire, is the nature of the service?"

But I knew well enough it was not my interest to tell him on so short an interview. " If you will accompany me," said I, " to a house not far from here, you can see for yourself."

He looked at me awhile with hesitating eyes; and then, tossing away his cigar, which was not yet a quarter smoked, " Here goes!" said he, and with perfect politeness offered me his arm. I was wise enough to take it; to prolong our walk as far as possible, by more than one excursion from the shortest line; and to beguile the way with that sort of conversation which should prove to him indubitably from what station in society I sprang. By the time we reached the door of my lodging I felt sure I had confirmed his interest, and might venture, before I turned the pass-key, to beseech him to moderate his voice and to tread softly. He promised to obey me; and I admitted him into the passage and thence into my sitting-room, which was fortunately next the door.

"And now," said he, when with trembling fingers I had lighted a candle, "what is the meaning of all this?"

"I wish you," said I, speaking with great difficulty, "to help me out with these boxes — and I wish nobody to know."

He took up the candle. "And I wish to see your face," he said.

I turned back my veil without a word, and looked at him with every appearance of resolve that I could summon up. For some time he gazed into my face, still holding up the candle. "Well," said he at last, "and where do you wish them taken?"

I knew that I had gained my point; and it was with a tremor in my voice that I replied, "I had thought we might carry them between us to the corner of Euston Road," said I, "where, even at this late hour, we may still find a cab."

"Very good," was his reply; and he immediately hoisted the heavier of my trunks upon his shoulder, and taking one handle of the second, signed to me to help him at the other end. In this order we made good our retreat from the house, and without the least adventure, drew pretty near to the corner of Euston Road. Before a house, where there was a light still burning, my companion paused. "Let us here," said he, "set down our boxes, while we go forward to the end of the street in quest of a cab. By doing so, we can still keep an eye upon their safety; and we avoid the very extraordinary figure we should otherwise present — a young man, a young lady, and a mass of baggage, standing castaway at midnight on the streets of London." So it was done, and the event proved him to be wise; for long before there was any word of a cab, a policeman appeared upon the scene, turned upon us the full glare of his lantern, and hung suspiciously behind us in a doorway.

"There seem to be no cabs about, policeman," said my champion, with affected cheerfulness. But the constable's answer was ungracious; and as for the offer of a cigar, with which this rebuff was most unwisely followed up, he refused it point-blank, and without the least civility. The young gentleman looked at me with a warning grimace, and there we continued to stand, on the edge of the pavement, in the beating rain, and with the policeman still silently watching our movements from the doorway.

At last, and after a delay that seemed interminable, a four-wheeler appeared lumbering along in the mud, and was instantly hailed by my companion. "Just pull up here, will you?" he cried. "We have some baggage up the street."

And now came the hitch of our adventure; for when the policeman, still closely following us, beheld my two boxes lying in the rain, he arose from mere suspicion to a kind of certitude of something evil. The light in the house had been extinguished; the whole frontage of the street was dark; there was nothing to explain the presence of these unguarded trunks; and no two innocent people were ever, I believe, detected in such questionable circumstances.

"Where have these things come from?" asked the policeman, flashing his light full into my companion's face.

"Why, from that house, of course," replied the young gentleman, hastily shouldering a trunk.

The policeman whistled and turned to look at the dark windows; he then took a step toward the door, as though to knock, a course which had infallibly proved our ruin; but seeing us already hurrying down the street under our double burden, thought better or worse of it, and followed in our wake.

"For God's sake," whispered my companion, "tell me where to drive to."

"Anywhere," I replied, with anguish. "I have no idea. Anywhere you like."

Thus it befell that, when the boxes had been stowed and I had already entered the cab, my deliverer called out in clear tones the address of the house in which we are now seated. The policeman, I could see, was staggered. This neighbourhood, so retired, so aristocratic, was far from what he had expected. For all that, he took the number, and spoke for a few seconds and with a decided manner, in the cabman's ear.

"What can he have said?" I gasped, as soon as the cab had rolled away.

"I can very well imagine," replied my champion; "and I can assure you that you are now condemned to go where I have said; for, should we attempt to change our destination by the way, the jarvey will drive us straight to a police office. Let me compliment you on your nerves," he added. " I have had, I believe, the most horrible fright of my existence."

But my nerves, which he so much misjudged, were in so strange a disarray that speech was now become impossible; and we made the drive thenceforward in unbroken silence. When we arrived before the door of our destination, the young gentleman alighted, opened it with a pass-key like one who was at home, bade the driver carry the trunks into the hall, and dismissed him with a handsome fee. He then led me into this diningroom, looking nearly as you behold it, but with certain marks of bachelor occupancy, and hastened to pour out a glass of wine, which he insisted on my drinking. As soon as I could find my voice, " In God's name," I cried, " where am I ? "

He then told me I was in his house, where I was very welcome, and had no more urgent business than to rest myself and recover my spirits. As he spoke he offered me another glass of wine, of which, indeed, I stood in great want, for I was faint, and inclined to be hysterical. Then he sat down beside the fire, lighted another cigar, and for some time observed me curiously and in silence.

" And now," said he, " that you have somewhat restored yourself, will you be kind enough to tell me in what sort of crime I have become a partner? Are you murderess, smuggler, thief, or only the harmless and domestic moonlight flitter? "

I had been already shocked by his lighting a cigar without permission, for I had not forgotten the one he threw away on our first meeting; and now, at these explicit insults, I resolved at once to reconquer his esteem. The judgment of the world I have consistently despised, but I had already begun to set a certain value on the good opinion of my entertainer. Beginning with a note of pathos, but soon brightening into my habitual vivacity and humour, I rapidly narrated the circumstances of my birth, my flight, and subsequent misfortunes. He heard me to an end in silence, gravely smoking. "Miss Fanshawe," said he, when I had done, "you are a very comical and most enchanting creature; and I see nothing for it but that I should return to-morrow morning and satisfy your landlady's demands."

"You strangely misinterpret my confidence," was my reply; "and if you had at all appreciated my character, you would understand that I can take no money at your hands."

"Your landlady will doubtless not be so particular," he returned; "neither do I at all despair of persuading even your unconquerable self. I desire you to examine me with critical indulgence. My name is Henry Luxmore, Lord Southwark's second son. I possess nine thousand a year, the house in which we are now sitting, and seven others in the best neighbourhoods in town. I do not believe I am repulsive to the eye, and as for my character, you have seen me under trial. I think you simply the most original of created beings; I need not tell you what you know very well, that you are ravishingly pretty; and I have nothing more to add, except that, foolish as it may appear, I am already head over heels in love with you."

" Sir," said I, " I am prepared to be misjudged; but while I continue to accept your hospitality that fact alone should be enough to protect me from insult."

" Pardon me," said he; " I offer you marriage." And leaning back in his chair he replaced his cigar between his lips.

I own I was confounded by an offer, not only so unprepared, but couched in terms so singular. But he knew very well how to obtain his purposes, for he was not only handsome in person, but his very coolness had a charm; and to make a long story short, a fortnight later I became the wife of the Honourable Henry Luxmore.

For nearly twenty years I now led a life of almost perfect quiet. My Henry had his weaknesses; I was twice driven to flee from his roof, but not for long; for though he was easily over-excited, his nature was placable below the surface, and with all his faults, I loved him tenderly. At last he was taken from me; and such is the power of self-deception, and so strange are the whims of the dying, he actually assured me, with his latest breath, that he forgave the violence of my temper!

There was but one pledge of the marriage, my daughter Clara. She had, indeed, inherited a

shadow of her father's failing; but in all things
else, unless my partial eyes deceived me, she de-
rived her qualities from me, and might be called
my moral image. On my side, whatever else I
may have done amiss, as a mother I was above
reproach. Here, then, was surely every promise
for the future; here, at last, was a relation in
which I might hope to taste repose. But it was
not to be. You will hardly credit me when I inform you that she ran away from home; yet such
was the case. Some whim about oppressed na-
tionalities — Ireland, Poland, and the like — has
turned her brain; and if you should anywhere
encounter a young lady (I must say, of remarkable attractions) answering to the name of Luxmore, Lake, or Fonblanque (for I am told she
uses these indifferently, as well as many others),
tell her for me, that I forgive her cruelty, and
though I will never more behold her face, I
am at any time prepared to make her a liberal
allowance.

On the death of Mr. Luxmore, I sought oblivion
in the details of business. I believe I have mentioned that seven mansions, besides this, formed
part of Mr. Luxmore's property: I have found
them seven white elephants. The greed of tenants,
the dishonesty of solicitors, and the incapacity that
sits upon the bench, have combined together to
make these houses the burthen of my life. I had
no sooner, indeed, begun to look into these matters for myself, than I discovered so many injus-
tices and met with so much studied incivility, that

I was plunged into a long series of law suits, some of which are pending to this day. You must have heard my name already; I am the Mrs. Luxmore of the Law Reports: a strange destiny, indeed, for one born with an almost cowardly desire for peace! But I am of the stamp of those who, when they have once begun a task, will rather die than leave their duty unfulfilled. I have met with every obstacle: insolence and ingratitude from my own lawyers; in my adversaries, that fault of obstinacy which is to me perhaps the most distasteful in the calendar; from the bench, civility indeed — always, I must allow, civility — but never a spark of independence, never that knowledge of the law and love of justice which we have a right to look for in a judge, the most august of human officers. And still, against all these odds, I have undissuadably persevered.

It was after the loss of one of my innumerable cases (a subject on which I will not dwell) that it occurred to me to make a melancholy pilgrimage to my various houses. Four were at that time tenantless and closed, like pillars of salt, commemorating the corruption of the age and the decline of private virtue. Three were occupied by persons who had wearied me by every conceivable unjust demand and legal subterfuge — persons whom, at that very hour, I was moving heaven and earth to turn into the street. This was perhaps the sadder spectacle of the two; and my heart grew hot within me to behold them occupying, in my very teeth, and with an insolent ostentation, these handsome structures which were as much mine as the flesh upon my body.

One more house remained for me to visit, that in which we now are. I had let it (for at that period I lodged in a hotel, the life that I have always preferred) to a Colonel Geraldine, a gentleman attached to Prince Florizel of Bohemia, whom you must certainly have heard of; and I had supposed, from the character and position of my tenant, that here, at least, I was safe against annoyance. What was my surprise to find this house also shuttered and apparently deserted! I will not deny that I was offended; I conceived that a house, like a yacht, was better to be kept in commission; and I promised myself to bring the matter before my solicitor the following morning. Meanwhile the sight recalled my fancy naturally to the past; and yielding to the tender influence of sentiment, I sat down opposite the door upon the garden parapet. It was August, and a sultry afternoon, but that spot is sheltered, as you may observe by daylight, under the branches of a spreading chestnut; the square, too, was deserted; there was a sound of distant music in the air; and all combined to plunge me into that most agreeable of states, which is neither happiness nor sorrow, but shares the poignancy of both.

From this I was recalled by the arrival of a large van, very handsomely appointed, drawn by valuable horses, mounted by several men of an appearance more than decent, and bearing on its panels, instead of a trader's name, a coat-of-arms too modest to be deciphered from where I sat. It drew up before my house, the door of which was immediately opened by one of the men. His companions — I counted seven of them in all — proceeded, with disciplined activity, to take from the van and carry into the house a variety of hampers, bottle-baskets, and boxes, such as are designed for plate and napery. The windows of the dining-room were thrown widely open, as though to air it; and I saw some of those within laying the table for a meal. Plainly, I concluded, my tenant was about to return; and while still determined to submit to no aggression on my rights, I was gratified by the number and discipline of his attendants, and the quiet profusion that appeared to reign in his establishment. I was still so thinking when, to my extreme surprise, the windows and shutters of the dining-room were once more closed; the men began to reappear from the interior and resume their stations on the van; the last closed the door behind his exit; the van drove away; and the house was once more left to itself, looking blindly on the square with shuttered windows, as though the whole affair had been a vision.

It was no vision, however; for, as I rose to my feet and thus brought my eyes a little nearer to the level of the fanlight over the door, I saw that, though the day had still some hours to run, the hall lamps had been lighted and left burning. Plainly, then, guests were expected, and not expected before night. For whom, I asked myself with indignation, were such secret preparations likely to be made? Although no prude, I am a woman of decided views upon morality; if my house, to which my husband had brought me, was to serve in the character of a *petite maison*, I saw myself forced, however unwillingly, into a new course of litigation; and, determined to return and know the worst, I hastened to my hotel for dinner.

I was at my post by ten. The night was clear and quiet; the moon rode very high and put the lamps to shame; and the shadow below the chestnut was black as ink. Here, then, I ensconced myself on the low parapet, with my back against the railings, face to face with the moonlit front of my old home, and ruminating gently on the past. Time fled; eleven struck on all the city clocks; and presently after I was aware of the approach of a gentleman of stately and agreeable demeanour. He was smoking as he walked; his light paletôt, which was open, did not conceal his evening clothes; and he bore himself with a serious grace that immediately awakened my attention. Before the door of this house he took a pass-key from his pocket, quietly admitted himself, and disappeared into the lamplighted hall.

He was scarcely gone when I observed another and a much younger man approaching hastily from the opposite side of the square. Considering the season of the year and the genial mildness of the night, he was somewhat closely muffled up; and as he came, for all his hurry, he kept looking nervously behind him. Arrived before my door, he halted and set one foot upon the step, as though about to enter; then, with a sudden change, he turned and began to hurry away; halted a second time, as if in painful indecision; and lastly, with a violent gesture, wheeled about, returned straight to the door, and rapped upon the knocker. He was almost immediately admitted by the first arrival.

My curiosity was now broad awake. I made myself as small as I could in the very densest of the shadow, and waited for the sequel. Nor had I long to wait. From the same side of the square a second young man made his appearance, walking slowly and softly, and like the first, muffled to the nose. Before the house he paused; looked all about him with a swift and comprehensive glance; and seeing the square lie empty in the moon and lamplight, leaned far across the area railings and appeared to listen to what was passing in the house. From the dining-room there came the report of a champagne cork, and following upon that, the sound of rich and manly laughter. The listener took heart of grace, produced a key, unlocked the area gate, shut it noiselessly behind him, and descended the stair. Just when his head had reached the level of the pavement, he turned half round and once more raked the square with a suspicious eyeshot. The mufflings had fallen lower round his neck; the moon shone full upon him; and I was startled to observe the pallor and passionate agitation of his face.

I could remain no longer passive. Persuaded that something deadly was afoot, I crossed the roadway and drew near the area railings. There was no one below; the man must therefore have entered the house, with what purpose I dreaded to imagine. I have at no part of my career lacked courage; and now, finding the area gate was merely laid to, I pushed it gently open and descended the stairs. The kitchen door of the house, like the area gate, was closed but not fastened. It flashed upon me that the criminal was thus preparing his escape; and the thought, as it confirmed the worst of my suspicions, lent me new resolve. I entered the house; and being now quite reckless of my life, I shut and locked the door.

From the dining-room above I could hear the pleasant tones of a voice in easy conversation. On the ground floor all was not only profoundly silent, but the darkness seemed to weigh upon my eyes. Here, then, I stood for some time, having thrust myself uncalled into the utmost peril, and being destitute of any power to help or interfere. Nor will I deny that fear had begun already to assail me, when I became aware, all at once and as though by some immediate but silent incandescence, of a certain glimmering of light upon the passage floor. Toward this I groped my way with infinite precaution; and having come at length as far as the angle of the corridor, beheld the door of the butler's pantry standing just ajar and a narrow thread of brightness falling from

the chink. Creeping still closer, I put my eyes
to the aperture. The man sat within upon a
chair, listening, I could see, with the most rapt
attention. On a table before him he had laid a
watch, a pair of steel revolvers, and a bull's-eye
lantern. For one second many contradictory theories and projects whirled together in my head;
the next, I had slammed the door and turned the
key upon the malefactor. Surprised at my own
decision, I stood and panted, leaning on the wall.
From within the pantry not a sound was to be
heard; the man, whatever he was, had accepted
his fate without a struggle, and now, as I hugged
myself to fancy, sat frozen with terror and looking for the worst to follow. I promised myself
that he should not be disappointed; and the better
to complete my task, I turned to ascend the stairs.

The situation, as I groped my way to the first
floor, appealed to me suddenly by my strong sense
of humour. Here was I, the owner of the house,
burglariously present in its walls; and there, in
the dining-room, were two gentlemen, unknown
to me, seated complacently at supper, and only
saved by my promptitude from some surprising
or deadly interruption. It were strange if I could
not manage to extract the matter of amusement
from so unusual a situation.

Behind this dining-room, there is a small apartment intended for a library. It was to this that
I cautiously groped my way; and you will see
how fortune had exactly served me. The weather,
I have said, was sultry: in order to ventilate the

dining-room and yet preserve the uninhabited appearance of the mansion to the front, the window of the library had been widely opened and the door of communication between the two apartments left ajar. To this interval I now applied my eye.

Wax tapers, set in silver candlesticks, shed their chastened brightness on the damask of the table-cloth and the remains of a cold collation of the rarest delicacy. The two gentlemen had finished supper, and were now trifling with cigars and maraschino; while in a silver spirit lamp, coffee of the most captivating fragrance was preparing in the fashion of the East. The elder of the two, he who had first arrived, was placed directly facing me; the other was set on his left hand. Both, like the man in the butler's pantry, seemed to be intently listening; and on the face of the second I thought I could perceive the marks of fear. Oddly enough, however, when they came to speak, the parts were found to be reversed.

" I assure you," said the elder gentleman, " I not only heard the slamming of a door, but the sound of very guarded footsteps."

" Your Highness was certainly deceived," replied the other. " I am endowed with the acutest hearing, and I can swear that not a mouse has rustled." Yet the pallor and contraction of his features were in total discord with the tenor of his words.

His Highness (whom, of course, I readily divined to be Prince Florizel) looked at his companion for the least fraction of a second; and though nothing shook the easy quiet of his attitude, I could see that he was far from being duped. "It is well," said he; "let us dismiss the topic. And now, sir, that I have very freely explained the sentiments by which I am directed, let me ask you, according to your promise, to imitate my frankness."

"I have heard you," replied the other, "with great interest."

"With singular patience," said the Prince politely.

"Ay, your Highness, and with unlooked-for sympathy," returned the young man. "I know not how to tell the change that has befallen me. You have, I must suppose, a charm, to which even your enemies are subject." He looked at the clock on the mantel-piece and visibly blanched. "So late!" he cried. "Your Highness — God knows I am speaking from the heart — before it be too late, leave this house!"

The Prince glanced once more at his companion, and then very deliberately shook the ash from his cigar. "That is a strange remark," said he; "and *à propos de bottes,* I never continue a cigar when once the ash is fallen; the spell breaks, the soul of the flavour flies away, and there remains but the dead body of tobacco; and I make it a rule to throw away that husk and choose another." He suited the action to the words.

"Do not trifle with my appeal," resumed the young man in tones that trembled with emotion. "It is made at the price of my honour and to the peril of my life. Go — go now! lose not a moment; and if you have any kindness for a young man, miserably deceived indeed, but not devoid of better sentiments, look not behind you as you leave."

"Sir," said the Prince, "I am here upon your honour; I assure you upon mine that I shall continue to rely upon that safeguard. The coffee is ready; I must again trouble you, I fear." And with a courteous movement of the hand, he seemed to invite his companion to pour out the coffee.

The unhappy young man rose from his seat. "I appeal to you," he cried, "by every holy sentiment, in mercy to me, if not in pity to yourself, begone before it is too late."

"Sir," replied the Prince, "I am not readily accessible to fear; and if there is one defect to which I must plead guilty, it is that of a curious disposition. You go the wrong way about to make me leave this house, in which I play the part of your entertainer; and, suffer me to add, young man, if any peril threaten us, it was of your contriving, not of mine."

"Alas, you do not know to what you condemn me," cried the other. "But I at least will have no hand in it." With these words he carried his hand to his pocket, hastily swallowed the contents of a phial, and, with the very act, reeled back and fell across his chair upon the floor. The Prince left his place and came and stood above him, where he lay convulsed upon the carpet. "Poor moth!" I heard his Highness murmur. "Alas, poor moth!

must we again inquire which is the more fatal — weakness or wickedness? And can a sympathy with ideas, surely not ignoble in themselves, conduct a man to this dishonourable death?"

By this time I had pushed the door open and walked into the room. "Your Highness," said I, "this is no time for moralising; with a little promptness we may save this creature's life; and as for the other, he need cause you no concern, for I have him safely under lock and key."

The Prince had turned about upon my entrance, and regarded me certainly with no alarm, but with a profundity of wonder which almost robbed me of my self-possession. "My dear madam," he cried at last, "and who the devil are you?"

I was already on the floor beside the dying man. I had, of course, no idea with what drug he had attempted his life, and I was forced to try him with a variety of antidotes. Here were both oil and vinegar, for the Prince had done the young man the honour of compounding for him one of his celebrated salads; and of each of these I administered from a quarter to half a pint, with no apparent efficacy. I next plied him with the hot coffee, of which there may have been near upon a quart.

"Have you no milk?" I inquired.

"I fear, madam, that milk has been omitted," returned the Prince.

"Salt, then," said I; "salt is a revulsive. Pass the salt."

"And possibly the mustard?" asked his High-

ness, as he offered me the contents of the various
salt-cellars poured together on a plate.

" Ah! " cried I, " the thought is excellent!   Mix
me about half a pint of mustard, drinkably dilute."

Whether it was the salt or the mustard, or the
mere combination of so many subversive agents,
as soon as the last had been poured over his throat,
the young sufferer obtained relief.

" There! " I exclaimed, with natural triumph,
" I have saved a life! "

" And yet, madam," returned the Prince, " your
mercy may be cruelty disguised.   Where the honour
is lost, it is, at least, superfluous to prolong the
life."

" If you had led a life as changeable as mine,
your Highness," I replied, " you would hold a very
different opinion.   For my part, and after whatever extremity of misfortune or disgrace, I should
still count to-morrow worth a trial."

" You speak as a lady, madam," said the Prince;
" and for such you speak the truth.   But to men
there is permitted such a field of license, and the
good behaviour asked of them is at once so easy
and so little, that to fail in that is to fall beyond
the reach of pardon.   But will you suffer me to
repeat a question, put to you at first, I am afraid,
with some defect of courtesy; and to ask you once
more, who you are and how I have the honour
of your company? "

" I am the proprietor of the house in which we
stand," said I.

" And still I am at fault," returned the Prince.

But at that moment the timepiece on the mantel-shelf began to strike the hour of twelve; and the young man, raising himself upon one elbow, with an expression of despair and horror that I have never seen excelled, cried lamentably: " Midnight? O just God." We stood frozen to our places, while the tingling hammer of the timepiece measured the remaining strokes; nor had we yet stirred, so tragic had been the tones of the young man, when the various bells of London began in turn to declare the hour. The timepiece was inaudible beyond the walls of the chamber where we stood; but the second pulsation of Big Ben had scarcely throbbed into the night, before a sharp detonation rang about the house. The Prince sprang for the door by which I had entered; but quick as he was, I yet contrived to intercept him.

" Are you armed? " I cried.

" No, madam," replied he. " You remind me appositely; I will take the poker."

" The man below," said I, " has two revolvers. Would you confront him at such odds? "

He paused, as though staggered in his purpose. " And yet, madam," said he, " we cannot continue to remain in ignorance of what has passed."

" No! " cried I. " And who proposes it? I am as curious as yourself, but let us rather send for the police; or, if your Highness dreads a scandal, for some of your own servants."

" Nay, madam," he replied, smiling, " for so brave a lady, you surprise me. Would you have me, then, send others where I fear to go myself? "

" You are perfectly right," said I, " and I was entirely wrong. Go, in God's name, and I will hold the candle!"

Together, therefore, we descended to the lower story, he carrying the poker, I the light; and together we approached and opened the door of the butler's pantry. In some sort, I believe, I was prepared for the spectacle that met our eyes; I was prepared, that is, to find the villain dead, but the rude details of such a violent suicide I was unable to endure. The Prince, unshaken by horror as he had remained unshaken by alarm, assisted me with the most respectful gallantry to regain the dining-room.

There we found our patient, still, indeed, deadly pale, but vastly recovered and already seated on a chair. He held out both his hands with a most pitiful gesture of interrogation.

" He is dead," said the Prince.

" Alas!" cried the young man, " and it should be I! What do I do, thus lingering on the stage I have disgraced, while he, my sure comrade, blameworthy indeed for much, but yet the soul of fidelity, has judged and slain himself for an involuntary fault? Ah, sir," said he, " and you too, madam, without whose cruel help I should be now beyond the reach of my accusing conscience, you behold in me the victim equally of my own faults and virtues. I was born a hater of injustice; from my most tender years my blood boiled against heaven when I beheld the sick, and against men when I witnessed the sorrows of the poor; the pauper's crust stuck in my throat when I sat down to eat my dainties, and the crippled child has set me weeping. What was there in that, but what was noble? and yet observe to what a fall these thoughts have led me! Year after year this passion for the lost besieged me closer. What hope was there in kings? what hope in these well-feathered classes that now roll in money? I had observed the course of history; I knew the burgess, our ruler of to-day, to be base, cowardly and dull; I saw him, in every age, combine to pull down that which was immediately above and to prey upon those that were below; his dulness, I knew, would ultimately bring about his ruin; I knew his days were numbered, and yet how was I to wait? how was I to let the poor child shiver in the rain? The better days, indeed, were coming, but the child would die before that. Alas, your Highness, in surely no ungenerous impatience I enrolled myself among the enemies of this unjust and doomed society; in surely no unnatural desire to keep the fires of my philanthropy alight, I bound myself by an irrevocable oath.

" That oath is all my history. To give freedom to posterity, I have forsworn my own. I must attend upon every signal; and soon my father complained of my irregular hours and turned me from his house. I was engaged in betrothal to an honest girl; from her also I had to part, for she was too shrewd to credit my inventions and too innocent to be intrusted with the truth. Behold me, then, alone with conspirators! Alas! as

9

the years went on, my illusions left me. Surrounded as I was by the fervent disciples and
apologists of revolution, I beheld them daily advance in confidence and desperation; I beheld myself, upon the other hand, and with an almost
equal regularity, decline in faith. I had sacrificed
all to further that cause in which I still believed;
and daily I began to grow in doubts if we were
advancing it indeed. Horrible was the society with
which we warred, but our own means were not
less horrible.

"I will not dwell upon my sufferings; I will
not pause to tell you how, when I beheld young
men still free and happy, married, fathers of children, cheerfully toiling at their work, my heart
reproached me with the greatness and vanity of
my unhappy sacrifice. I will not describe to you
how, worn by poverty, poor lodging, scanty food,
and an unquiet conscience, my health began to fail,
and in the long nights, as I wandered bedless in
the rainy streets, the most cruel sufferings of the
body were added to the tortures of the mind.
These things are not personal to me; they are
common to all unfortunates in my position. An
oath, so light a thing to swear, so grave a thing
to break: an oath, taken in the heat of youth,
repented with what sobbings of the heart, but yet
in vain repented, as the years go on: an oath,
that was once the very utterance of the truth of
God, but that falls to be the symbol of a meaningless and empty slavery; such is the yoke that
many young men joyfully assume, and under

whose dead weight they live to suffer worse than death.

"It is not that I was patient. I have begged to be released; but I knew too much, and was still refused. I have fled; ay, and for the time successfully. I reached Paris. I found a lodging in the Rue St. Jacques, almost opposite the Val de Grâce. My room was mean and bare, but the sun looked into it toward evening: it commanded a peep of a green garden; a bird hung by a neighbour's window and made the morning beautiful; and I, who was sick, might lie in bed and rest myself: I who was in full revolt against the principles that I had served, and was no longer at the beck of the council, and was no longer charged with shameful and revolting tasks. Oh! what an interval of peace was that! I still dream at times that I can hear the note of my neighbour's bird.

"My money was running out, and it became necessary that I should find employment. Scarcely had I been three days upon the search, ere I thought that I was being followed. I made certain of the features of the man, which were quite strange to me, and turned into a small café, where I whiled away an hour, pretending to read the papers, but inwardly convulsed with terror. When I came forth into the street, it was quite empty, and I breathed again; but alas, I had not turned three corners, when I once more observed the human hound pursuing me. Not an hour was to be lost; timely submission might yet preserve a life which otherwise was forfeited and dishonoured; and I fled with what speed you may conceive, to the Paris agency of the society I served.

"My submission was accepted. I took up once more the hated burthen of that life; once more I was at the call of men whom I despised and hated, while yet I envied and admired them. They were whole-hearted in the things they proposed; but I, who had once been such as they, had fallen from the brightness of my faith, and now laboured, like a hireling, for the wages of a loathed existence. Ay, sir, to that I was condemned; I obeyed to continue to live, and lived but to obey.

"The last charge that was laid upon me was the one which has to-night so tragically ended. Boldly telling who I was, I was to request from your Highness, on behalf of my society, a private audience, where it was designed to murder you. If one thing remained to me of my old convictions, it was the hate of kings; and when this task was offered me, I took it gladly. Alas, sir, you triumphed. As we supped, you gained upon my heart. Your character, your talents, your designs for our unhappy country, all had been misrepresented. I began to forget you were a prince; I began, all too feelingly, to remember that you were a man. As I saw the hour approach, I suffered agonies untold; and when, at last, we heard the slamming of the door which announced in my unwilling ears the arrival of the partner of my crime, you will bear me out with what instancy

I besought you to depart. You would not, alas! and what could I? Kill you, I could not; my heart revolted, my hand turned back from such a deed. Yet it was impossible that I should suffer you to stay; for when the hour struck and my companion came, true to appointment, and he, at least, true to design, I could neither suffer you to be killed nor yet him to be arrested. From such a tragic passage, death, and death alone, could save me; and it is no fault of mine if I continue to exist.

"But you, madam," continued the young man, addressing himself more directly to myself, "were doubtless born to save the Prince and to confound our purposes. My life you have prolonged; and by turning the key on my companion, you have made me the author of his death. He heard the hour strike; he was impotent to help; and thinking himself forfeit to honour, thinking that I should fall alone upon his Highness and perish for lack of his support, he has turned his pistol on himself."

"You are right," said Prince Florizel: "it was in no ungenerous spirit that you brought these burthens on yourself; and when I see you so nobly to blame, so tragically punished, I stand like one reproved. For is it not strange, madam, that you and I, by practising accepted and inconsiderable virtues, and commonplace but still unpardonable faults, should stand here, in the sight of God, with what we call clean hands and quiet consciences; while this poor youth, for an error that I could almost envy him, should be sunk beyond the reach of hope?"

"Sir," resumed the Prince, turning to the young man, "I cannot help you; my help would but unchain the thunderbolt that overhangs you; and I can but leave you free."

"And, sir," said I, "as this house belongs to me, I will ask you to have the kindness to remove the body. You and your conspirators, it appears to me, can hardly in civility do less."

"It shall be done," said the young man, with a dismal accent.

"And you, dear madam," said the Prince, "you, to whom I owe my life, how can I serve you?"

"Your Highness," I said, "to be very plain, this is my favourite house, being not only a valuable property, but endeared to me by various associations. I have endless troubles with tenants of the ordinary class; and at first applauded my good fortune when I found one of the station of your Master of the Horse. I now begin to think otherwise: dangers set a siege about great personages; and I do not wish my tenement to share these risks. Procure me the resiliation of the lease, and I shall feel myself your debtor."

"I must tell you, madam," replied his Highness, "that Colonel Geraldine is but a cloak for myself; and I should be sorry indeed to think myself so unacceptable a tenant."

"Your Highness," said I, "I have conceived a sincere admiration for your character; but on the subject of house property, I cannot allow the interference of my feelings. I will, however, to prove to you that there is nothing personal in my request, here solemnly engage my word that I will never put another tenant in this house."

"Madam," said Florizel, "you plead your cause too charmingly to be refused."

Thereupon we all three withdrew. The young man, still reeling in his walk, departed by himself to seek the assistance of his fellow conspirators; and the Prince, with the most attentive gallantry, lent me his escort to the door of my hotel. The next day, the lease was cancelled; nor from that hour to this, though sometimes regretting my engagement, have I suffered a tenant in this house.

THE SUPERFLUOUS MANSION

(*continued*)

A S soon as the old lady had finished her relation, Somerset made haste to offer her his compliments.

"Madam," said he, "your story is not only entertaining but instructive; and you have told it with infinite vivacity. I was much affected toward the end, as I held at one time very liberal opinions, and should certainly have joined a secret society if I had been able to find one. But the whole tale came home to me; and I was the better able to feel for you in your various perplexities, as I am myself of somewhat hasty temper."

"I do not understand you," said Mrs. Luxmore, in a very high key. "You must have strangely misinterpreted what I have told you. You must be a singularly dense young man."

Somerset, seeing no probable termination to the lady's anger, hurried to recant.

"Dear Mrs. Luxmore," said he, "you certainly misconstrue my remark. As a man of somewhat fiery humour, my conscience repeatedly pricked me when I heard what you had suffered at the hands of persons similarly constituted."

"Oh, very well indeed," replied the old lady; "and a very proper spirit. I regret that I have met with it so rarely."

"But in all this," resumed the young man, "I perceive nothing that concerns myself."

"I am about to come to that," she returned. "And you have already before you, in the pledge I gave Prince Florizel, one of the elements of the affair. I am a woman of the nomadic sort, and when I have no case before the courts I make it a habit to visit the continental spas: not that I have ever been ill, but then I am no longer young, and I am always happy in a crowd. Well, to come more shortly to the point, I am now on the wing for Evian; this incubus of a house, which I must leave behind and dare not let, hangs heavily upon my hands; and I propose to rid myself of that concern, and do you a very good turn into the bargain, by lending you the mansion, with all its fittings, as it stands. The idea was sudden; it appealed to me as humourous; and I am sure it will cause my relatives, if they should ever hear of it, the keenest possible chagrin. Here, then, is the key, and when you return at two to-morrow afternoon, you will find neither me nor my cats to disturb you in your new possession."

So saying, the old lady arose, as if to dismiss her visitor, but Somerset, looking somewhat blankly on the key, began to protest.

"Dear Mrs. Luxmore," said he, "this is a most unusual proposal. You know nothing of me, beyond the fact that I displayed both impudence and

timidity. I may be the worst kind of scoundrel;
I may sell your furniture —— "

" You may blow up the house with gunpowder
for what I care! " cried Mrs. Luxmore. " It is
in vain to reason. Such is the force of my character that, when I have one idea clearly in my
head, I do not care two straws for any side consideration. It amuses me to do it, and let that
suffice. On your side, you may do what you please
— let apartments, or keep a private hotel; on my
part, I promise you a full month's warning before
I return, and I never fail religiously to keep my
promises."

The young man was about to renew his protest,
when he observed a sudden and significant change
in the old lady's countenance.

" If I thought you capable of disrespect! " she
cried.

" Madam," said Somerset, with the extreme fervour of asseveration, " madam, I accept. I beg
you to understand that I accept with joy and
gratitude."

" Ah, well," returned Mrs. Luxmore, " if I am
mistaken, let it pass. And now, since all is comfortably settled, I wish you a good-night."

Thereupon, as if to leave him no room for repentance, she hurried Somerset out of the front
door, and left him standing, key in hand, upon
the pavement.

The next day, about the hour appointed, the
young man found his way to the Square, which
I will here call Golden Square, though that was

not its name. What to expect, he knew not;
for a man may live in dreams, and yet be unprepared for their realisation. It was already with
a certain pang of surprise that he beheld the mansion, standing in the eye of day, a solid among
solids. The key, upon trial, readily opened the
front door; he entered that great house, a privi-
leged burglar; and escorted by the echoes of desertion, rapidly reviewed the empty chambers.
Cats, servant, old lady, the very marks of habitation, like writing on a slate, had been in these
few hours obliterated. He wandered from floor
to floor, and found the house of great extent; the
kitchen offices commodious and well-appointed; the
rooms many and large; and the drawing-room, in
particular, an apartment of princely size and tasteful decoration. Although the day without was
warm, genial, and sunny, with a ruffling wind from
the quarter of Torquay, a chill, as it were, of suspended animation inhabited the house. Dust and
shadows met the eye; and but for the ominous
procession of the echoes, and the rumour of the
wind among the garden trees, the ear of the young
man was stretched in vain.

Behind the dining-room, that pleasant library,
referred to by the old lady in her tale, looked
upon the flat roofs and netted cupolas of the
kitchen quarters, and on a second visit this room
appeared to greet him with a smiling countenance.
He might as well, he thought, avoid the expense
of lodging: the library, fitted with an iron bed-
stead which he had remarked in one of the upper

chambers, would serve his purpose for the night; while in the dining-room, which was large, airy, and lightsome, looking on the square and garden, he might very agreeably pass his days, cook his meals, and study to bring himself to some proficiency in that art of painting which he had recently determined to adopt. It did not take him long to make the change; he had soon returned to the mansion with his modest kit, and the cabman who brought him was readily induced, by the young man's pleasant manner and a small gratuity, to assist him in the installation of the iron bed. By six in the evening, when Somerset went forth to dine, he was able to look back upon the mansion with a sense of pride and property. Four-square it stood, of an imposing frontage, and flanked on either side by family hatchments. His eye, from where he stood whistling in the key, with his back to the garden railings, reposed on every feature of reality, and yet his own possession seemed as flimsy as a dream.

In the course of a few days the genteel inhabitants of the square began to remark the customs of their neighbour. The sight of a young gentleman discussing a clay pipe about four o'clock in the afternoon in the drawing-room balcony of so discreet a mansion, and perhaps still more, his periodical excursion to a decent tavern in the neighbourhood, and his unabashed return, nursing the full tankard, had presently raised to a high pitch the interest and indignation of the liveried servants of the square. The disfavour of some of these gentlemen at first proceeded to the length of insult; but Somerset knew how to be affable with any class of men; and a few rude words merrily accepted and a few glasses amicably shared, gained for him the right of toleration.

The young man had embraced the art of Raphael, partly from a notion of its ease, partly from an inborn distrust of offices. He scorned to bear the yoke of any regular schooling, and proceeded to turn one half of the dining-room into a studio for the reproduction of still life. There he amassed a variety of objects, indiscriminately chosen from the kitchen, the drawing-room, and the back garden, and there spent his days in smiling assiduity. Meantime, the great bulk of empty building overhead lay like a load upon his imagination. To hold so great a stake and to do nothing, argued some defect of energy, and he at length determined to act upon the hint given by Mrs. Luxmore herself, and to stick with wafers in the window of the dining-room a small hand-bill announcing furnished lodgings. At half-past six of a fine July morning he affixed the bill and went forth into the square to study the result. It seemed, to his eye, promising and unpretentious, and he returned to the drawing-room balcony to consider over a studious pipe the knotty problem of how much he was to charge.

Thereupon he somewhat relaxed in his devotion to the art of painting. Indeed, from that time forth, he would spend the best part of the day in the front balcony, like the attentive angler poring on his float; and the better to support the tedium, he would frequently console himself with his clay pipe. On several occasions passers-by appeared to be arrested by the ticket, and on several others ladies and gentlemen drove to the very doorstep by the carriageful; but it appeared there was something repulsive in the appearance of the house, for with one accord, they would cast but one look upward and hastily resume their onward progress or direct the driver to proceed. Somerset had thus the mortification of actually meeting the eye of a large number of lodging-seekers; and though he hastened to withdraw his pipe and to compose his features to an air of invitation, he was never rewarded by so much as an inquiry. " Can there," he thought, " be anything repellent in myself?" But a candid examination in one of the pier-glasses of the drawing-room led him to dismiss the fear.

Something, however, was amiss. His vast and accurate calculations on the fly-leaves of books, or on the backs of playbills, appeared to have been an idle sacrifice of time. By these, he had variously computed the weekly takings of the house, from sums as modest as five-and-twenty shillings, up to the more majestic figure of a hundred pounds; and yet, in despite of the very elements of arithmetic, here he was making literally nothing.

This incongruity impressed him deeply and occupied his thoughtful leisure on the balcony; and at last it seemed to him that he had detected the error of his method. " This," he reflected, " is an age of generous display: the age of the sandwich-man, of Griffiths, of Pears' legendary soap, and of Eno's fruit salt, which, by sheer brass and notoriety, and the most disgusting pictures I ever remember to have seen, has overlaid that comforter of my childhood, Lamplough's pyretic saline. Lamplough was genteel, Eno was omnipresent; Lamplough was trite, Eno original and abominably vulgar; and here have I, a man of some pretensions to knowledge of the world, contented myself with half a sheet of note-paper, a few cold words which do not directly address the imagination, and the adornment (if adornment it may be called) of four red wafers! Am I, then, to sink with Lamplough, or to soar with Eno? Am I to adopt that modesty which is doubtless becoming in a duke? or to take hold of the red facts of life with the emphasis of the tradesman and the poet?"

Pursuant upon these meditations, he procured several sheets of the very largest size of drawing-paper; and laying forth his paints, proceeded to compose an ensign that might attract the eye and at the same time, in his own phrase, directly address the imagination of the passenger. Something taking in the way of colour, a good, savoury choice of words, and a realistic design setting forth the life a lodger might expect to lead within the walls of that palace of delight: these, he perceived, must be the elements of his advertisement. It was possible, upon the one hand, to depict the sober pleasures of domestic life, the evening fire, blond-headed urchins and the hissing urn; but on the other, it was possible (and he almost felt as if it were more suited to his muse) to set forth the charms of an existence somewhat wider in its range, or, boldly say, the paradise of the Mohammedan. So long did the artist waver between these two views, that, before he arrived at a conclusion, he had finally conceived and completed both designs. With the proverbially tender heart of the parent, he found himself unable to sacrifice either of these offspring of his art; and decided to expose them on alternate days. "In this way," he thought, "I shall address myself indifferently to all classes of the world."

The tossing of a penny decided the only remaining point; and the more imaginative canvas received the suffrages of fortune and appeared first in the window of the mansion. It was of a high fancy, the legend eloquently writ, the scheme of colour taking and bold; and but for the imperfection of the artist's drawing, it might have been taken for a model of its kind. As it was, however, when viewed from his favourite point against the garden railings, and with some touch of distance, it caused a pleasurable rising of the artist's heart. "I have thrown away," he ejaculated, "an invaluable motive; and this shall be the subject of my first academy picture."

The fate of neither of these works was equal to its merit. A crowd would certainly, from time to time, collect before the area-railings; but they came to jeer and not to speculate; and those who pushed their inquiries further, were too plainly animated by the spirit of derision. The racier of the two cartoons displayed, indeed, no symptom of attractive merit; and though it had a certain share of that success called scandalous, failed utterly of its effect. On the day, however, of the second appearance of the companion work, a real inquirer did actually present himself before the eyes of Somerset.

This was a gentlemanly man, with some marks of recent merriment, and his voice under inadequate control.

"I beg your pardon," said he, "but what is the meaning of your extraordinary bill?"

"I beg yours," returned Somerset hotly. "Its meaning is sufficiently explicit." And being now, from dire experience, fearful of ridicule, he was preparing to close the door, when the gentleman thrust his cane into the aperture.

"Not so fast, I beg of you," said he. "If you really let apartments, here is a possible tenant at your door; and nothing would give me greater pleasure than to see the accommodation and to learn your terms."

His heart joyously beating, Somerset admitted the visitor, showed him over the various apartments, and with some return of his persuasive eloquence, expounded their attractions. The gentleman was particularly pleased by the elegant proportions of the drawing-room.

"This," he said, "would suit me very well,

What, may I ask, would be your terms a week for this floor and the one above it?"

" I was thinking," returned Somerset, " of a hundred pounds."

" Surely not," exclaimed the gentleman.

" Well, then," returned Somerset, " fifty."

The gentleman regarded him with an air of some amazement. " You seem to be strangely elastic in your demands," said he. " What if I were to proceed on your own principle of division, and offer you twenty-five?"

" Done!" cried Somerset; and then, overcome by a sudden embarrassment, " You see," he added, apologetically, " it is all found money for me."

" Really?" said the stranger, looking at him all the while with growing wonder. " Without extras, then?"

" I — I suppose so," stammered the keeper of the lodging-house.

" Service included?" pursued the gentleman.

" Service?" cried Somerset. " Do you mean that you expect me to empty your slops?"

The gentleman regarded him with a very friendly interest. " My dear fellow," said he, " if you take my advice, you will give up this business." And thereupon he resumed his hat and took himself away.

This smarting disappointment produced a strong effect on the artist of the cartoons; and he began with shame to eat up his rosier illusions. First one and then the other of his great works was condemned, withdrawn from exhibition, and relegated, as a mere wall-picture, to the decoration of the dining-room. Their place was taken by a replica of the original wafered announcement, to which, in particularly large letters, he had added the pithy rubric: "*No service.*" Meanwhile he had fallen into something as nearly bordering on low spirits as was consistent with his disposition; depressed, at once by the failure of his scheme, the laughable turn of his late interview, and the judicial blindness of the public to the merit of the twin cartoons.

Perhaps a week had passed before he was again startled by the note of the knocker. A gentleman of a somewhat foreign and somewhat military air, yet closely shaven and wearing a soft hat, desired in the politest terms to visit the apartments. He had (he explained) a friend, a gentleman in tender health, desirous of a sedate and solitary life, apart from interruption and the noises of the common lodging-house. "The unusual clause," he continued, "in your announcement, particularly struck me. 'This,' I said, 'is the place for Mr. Jones.' You are yourself, sir, a professional gentleman?" concluded the visitor, looking keenly in Somerset's face.

"I am an artist," replied the young man lightly.

"And these," observed the other, taking a side glance through the open door of the dining-room, which they were then passing, "these are some of your works. Very remarkable." And he again and still more sharply peered into the countenance of the young man.

Somerset, unable to suppress a blush, made the more haste to lead his visitor up-stairs and to display the apartments.

"Excellent," observed the stranger, as he looked from one of the back windows. "Is that a mews behind, sir? Very good. Well, sir, see here. My friend will take your drawing-room floor; he will sleep in the back drawing-room; his nurse, an excellent Irish widow, will attend on all his wants and occupy a garret; he will pay you the round sum of ten dollars a week; and you, on your part, will engage to receive no other lodger? I think that fair."

Somerset had scarcely words in which to clothe his gratitude and joy.

"Agreed," said the other; "and to spare you trouble, my friend will bring some men with him to make the changes. You will find him a retiring inmate, sir; receives but few, and rarely leaves the house except at night."

"Since I have been in this house," returned Somerset, "I have myself, unless it were to fetch beer, rarely gone abroad except in the evening. But a man," he added, "must have some amusement."

An hour was then agreed on; the gentleman departed; and Somerset sat down to compute in English money the value of the figure named. The result of this investigation filled him with amazement and disgust; but it was now too late; nothing remained but to endure; and he awaited the arrival of his tenant, still trying, by various arithmetical expedients, to obtain a more favour-

able quotation for the dollar. With the approach
of dusk, however, his impatience drove him once
more to the front balcony. The night fell, mild
and airless; the lamps shone around the central
darkness of the garden; and through the tall
grove of trees that intervened, many warmly illuminated windows on the further side of the square
told their tale of white napery, choice wine, and
genial hospitality. The stars were already thicken-
ing overhead, when the young man's eyes alighted
on a procession of three four-wheelers, coasting
round the garden railing and bound for the Superfluous Mansion. They were laden with formidable
boxes; moving in a military order, one following
another; and, by the extreme slowness of their
advance, inspired Somerset with the most serious
ideas of his tenant's malady.

By the time he had the door open, the cabs
had drawn up beside the pavement; and from the
two first, there had alighted the military gentleman of the morning and two very stalwart por-
ters. These proceeded instantly to take possession
of the house; with their own hands, and firmly
rejecting Somerset's assistance, they carried in the
various crates and boxes; with their own hands
dismounted and transferred to the back drawing-
room the bed in which the tenant was to sleep;
and it was not until the bustle of arrival had sub-
sided, and the arrangements were complete, that
there descended, from the third of the three vehi-
cles, a gentleman of great stature and broad shoulders, leaning on the shoulder of a woman in a

widow's dress, and himself covered by a long cloak and muffled in a coloured comforter.

Somerset had but a glimpse of him in passing; he was soon shut into the back drawing-room; the other men departed; silence redescended on the house; and had not the nurse appeared a little before half-past ten, and, with a strong brogue, asked if there were a decent public-house in the neighbourhood, Somerset might have still supposed himself to be alone in the Superfluous Mansion.

Day followed day: and still the young man had never come by speech or sight of his mysterious lodger. The doors of the drawing-room flat were never open; and although Somerset could hear him moving to and fro, the tall man never quitted the privacy of his apartments. Visitors, indeed, arrived; sometimes in the dusk, sometimes at intempestuous hours of night or morning; men, for the most part; some meanly attired, some decently; some loud, some cringing; and yet all, in the eyes of Somerset, displeasing. A certain air of fear and secrecy was common to them all; they were all voluble, he thought, and ill at ease; even the military gentleman proved, on a closer inspection, to be no gentleman at all; and as for the doctor who attended the sick man, his manners were not suggestive of a university career. The nurse, again, was scarcely a desirable house-fellow. Since her arrival, the fall of whisky in the young man's private bottle was much accelerated; and though never communicative, she was at times unpleasantly familiar. When asked about the patient's health, she would dolorously shake her head, and declare that the poor gentleman was in a pitiful condition.

Yet somehow Somerset had early begun to entertain the notion that his complaint was other than bodily. The ill-looking birds that gathered to the house, the strange noises that sounded from the drawing-room in the dead hours of night, the careless attendance and intemperate habits of the nurse, the entire absence of correspondence, the entire seclusion of Mr. Jones himself, whose face, up to that hour, he could not have sworn to in a court of justice — all weighed unpleasantly upon the young man's mind. A sense of something evil, irregular, and underhand, haunted and depressed him; and this uneasy sentiment was the more firmly rooted in his mind, when, in the fulness of time, he had an opportunity of observing the features of his tenant. It fell in this way. The young landlord was awakened about four in the morning by a noise in the hall. Leaping to his feet, and opening the door of the library, he saw the tall man, candle in hand, in earnest conversation with the gentleman who had taken the rooms. The faces of both were strongly illuminated; and in that of his tenant Somerset could perceive none of the marks of disease, but every sign of health, energy, and resolution. While he was still looking, the visitor took his departure; and the invalid, having carefully fastened the front door, sprang up-stairs without a trace of lassitude.

That night upon his pillow, Somerset began to kindle once more into the hot fit of the detective fever; and the next morning resumed the practice of his art with careless hand and an abstracted mind. The day was destined to be fertile in surprises; nor had he long been seated at the easel ere the first of these occurred. A cab laden with baggage drew up before the door; and Mrs. Luxmore in person rapidly mounted the steps and began to pound upon the knocker. Somerset hastened to attend the summons.

"My dear fellow," she said, with the utmost gaiety, "here I come dropping from the moon. I am delighted to find you faithful; and I have no doubt you will be equally pleased to be restored to liberty."

Somerset could find no words, whether of protest or welcome; and the spirited old lady pushed briskly by him and paused on the threshold of the dining-room. The sight that met her eyes was one well calculated to inspire astonishment. The mantel-piece was arrayed with saucepans and empty bottles; on the fire some chops were frying; the floor was littered from end to end with books, clothes, walking-canes, and the materials of the painter's craft; but what far outstripped the other wonders of the place was the corner which had been arranged for the study of still life. This formed a sort of rockery; conspicuous upon which, according to the principles of the art of composition, a cabbage was relieved against a copper kettle,

and both contrasted with the mail of a boiled
lobster.

"My gracious goodness!" cried the lady of the
house; and then, turning in wrath on the young
man, "From what rank in life are you sprung?"
she demanded. "You have the exterior of a gentleman; but from the astonishing evidences before
me, I should say you can only be a green-grocer's
man. Pray, gather up your vegetables, and let me
see no more of you."

"Madam," babbled Somerset, "you promised
me a month's warning."

"That was under a misapprehension," returned
the old lady. "I now give you warning to leave
at once."

"Madam," said the young man, "I wish I
could; and indeed, as far as I am concerned, it
might be done. But then, my lodger!"

"Your lodger?" echoed Mrs. Luxmore.

"My lodger; why should I deny it?" returned
Somerset. "He is only here by the week."

The old lady sat down upon a chair. "You
have a lodger? — you?" she cried. "And pray,
how did you get him?"

"By advertisement," replied the young man.
"O madam, I have not lived unobservantly. I
adopted" — his eyes involuntarily shifted to the
cartoons — "I adopted every method."

Her eyes had followed his; for the first
time in Somerset's experience, she produced a
double eyeglass; and as soon as the full merit
of the works flashed upon her, she gave way

to peal after peal of her thrilling and soprano laughter.

"Oh, I think you are perfectly delicious!" she cried. "I do hope you had them in the window. M'Pherson," she continued, crying to her maid, who had been all this time grimly waiting in the hall, "I lunch with Mr. Somerset. Take the cellar key and bring some wine."

In this gay humour, she continued throughout the luncheon; presented Somerset with a couple of dozen of wine, which she made M'Pherson bring up from the cellar — "as a present, my dear," she said, with another burst of tearful merriment, "for your charming pictures, which you must be sure to leave me when you go"; and finally, protesting that she dared not spoil the absurdest houseful of madmen in the whole of London, departed (as she vaguely phrased it) for the continent of Europe.

She was no sooner gone, than Somerset encountered in the corridor the Irish nurse; sober, to all appearance, and yet a prey to singularly strong emotion. It was made to appear, from her account, that Mr. Jones had already suffered acutely in his health from Mrs. Luxmore's visit, and that nothing short of a full explanation could allay the invalid's uneasiness. Somerset, somewhat staring, told what he thought fit of the affair.

"Is that all?" cried the woman. "As God sees you, is that all?"

"My good woman," said the young man, "I

have no idea what you can be driving at. Suppose the lady were my friend's wife, suppose she
were my fairy godmother, suppose she were the
Queen of Portugal; and how should that affect
yourself or Mr. Jones?"

"Blessed Mary!" cried the nurse, "it's he
that will be glad to hear it!"

And immediately she fled up-stairs.

Somerset, on his part, returned to the dining-
room, and with a very thoughtful brow and ruminating many theories, disposed of the remainder
of the bottle. It was port; and port is a wine,
sole among its equals and superiors, that can in
some degree support the competition of tobacco.
Sipping, smoking, and theorising, Somerset moved
on from suspicion to suspicion, from resolve to
resolve, still growing braver and rosier as the
bottle ebbed. He was a sceptic, none prouder of
the name; he had no horror at command, whether
for crimes or vices, but beheld and embraced the
world, with an immoral approbation, the frequent
consequence of youth and health. At the same
time he felt convinced that he dwelt under the
same roof with secret malefactors; and the un-
regenerate instinct of the chase impelled him to
severity. The bottle had run low; the summer
sun had finally withdrawn; and at the same moment, night and the pangs of hunger recalled him
from his dreams.

He went forth, and dined in the Criterion: a
dinner in consonance, not so much with his purse,
as with the admirable wine he had discussed. What

with one thing and another, it was long past midnight when he returned home. A cab was at the door; and entering the hall, Somerset found himself face to face with one of the most regular of the few who visited Mr. Jones: a man of powerful figure, strong lineaments, and a chin-beard in the American fashion. This person was carrying on one shoulder a black portmanteau, seemingly of considerable weight. That he should find a visitor removing baggage in the dead of night, recalled some odd stories to the young man's memory; he had heard of lodgers who thus gradually drained away, not only their own effects, but the very furniture and fittings of the house that sheltered them; and now, in a mood between pleasantry and suspicion, and aping the manner of a drunkard, he roughly bumped against the man with the chin-beard and knocked the portmanteau from his shoulder to the floor. With a face struck suddenly as white as paper, the man with the chin-beard called lamentably on the name of his maker, and fell in a mere heap on the mat at the foot of the stairs. At the same time, though only for a single instant, the heads of the sick lodger and the Irish nurse popped out like rabbits over the banisters of the first floor; and on both the same scare and pallor were apparent.

The sight of this incredible emotion turned Somerset to stone, and he continued speechless, while the man gathered himself together, and with the help of the handrail and audibly thanking God, scrambled once more upon his feet.

" What in Heaven's name ails you? " gasped
the young man as soon as he could find words
and utterance.

" Have you a drop of brandy? " returned the
other. " I am sick."

Somerset administered two drams, one after the
other, to the man with the chin-beard; who then,
somewhat restored, began to confound himself in
apologies for what he called his miserable nervousness, the result, he said, of a long course of
dumb ague; and having taken leave with a hand
that still sweated and trembled, he gingerly resumed his burthen and departed.

Somerset retired to bed but not to sleep. What,
he asked himself, had been the contents of the
black portmanteau? Stolen goods? the carcase of
one murdered? or — and at the thought he sat
upright in bed — an infernal machine? He took
a solemn vow that he would set these doubts at
rest; and with the next morning, installed himself beside the dining-room window, vigilant with
eye and ear, to await and profit by the earliest
opportunity.

The hours went heavily by. Within the house
there was no circumstance of novelty; unless it
might be that the nurse more frequently made
little journeys round the corner of the square, and
before afternoon was somewhat loose of speech
and gait. A little after six, however, there came
round the corner of the gardens a very handsome
and elegantly dressed young woman, who paused
a little way off, and for some time, and with fre-

quent sighs, contemplated the front of the Superfluous Mansion. It was not the first time that
she had thus stood afar and looked upon it, like
our common parents at the gates of Eden; and
the young man had already had occasion to remark the lively slimness of her carriage, and had
already been the butt of a chance arrow from her
eye. He hailed her coming, then, with pleasant
feelings, and moved a little nearer to the window
to enjoy the sight. What was his surprise, however, when, as if with a sensible effort, she drew
near, mounted the steps and tapped discreetly at
the door! He made haste to get before the Irish
nurse, who was not improbably asleep, and had
the satisfaction to receive this gracious visitor in
person.

She inquired for Mr. Jones; and then, without
transition, asked the young man if he were the
person of the house (and at the words, he thought
he could perceive her to be smiling), "because,"
she added, "if you are, I should like to see some
of the other rooms."

Somerset told her he was under an engagement
to receive no lodgers; but she assured him that
would be no matter, as these were friends of Mr.
Jones's. "And," she continued, moving suddenly
to the dining-room door, "let us begin here."
Somerset was too late to prevent her entering,
and perhaps he lacked the courage to essay.
"Ah!" she cried, "how changed it is!"

"Madam," cried the young man, "since your
entrance, it is I who have the right to say so."

She received this inane compliment with a demure and conscious droop of the eyelids, and gracefully steering her dress among the mingled litter, now with a smile, now with a sigh, reviewed the wonders of the two apartments. She gazed upon the cartoons with sparkling eyes, and a heightened colour, and in a somewhat breathless voice expressed a high opinion of their merits. She praised the effective disposition of the rockery, and in the bedroom, of which Somerset had vainly endeavoured to defend the entry, she fairly broke forth in admiration. "How simple and manly!" she cried: "none of that effeminacy of neatness, which is so detestable in a man!" Hard upon this, telling him, before he had time to reply, that she very well knew her way, and would trouble him no further, she took her leave with an engaging smile, and ascended the staircase alone.

For more than an hour, the young lady remained closeted with Mr. Jones; and at the end of that time, the night being now come completely, they left the house in company. This was the first time since the arrival of his lodger, that Somerset had found himself alone with the Irish widow; and without the loss of any more time than was required by decency, he stepped to the foot of the stairs and hailed her by her name. She came instantly, wreathed in weak smiles and with a nodding head; and when the young man politely offered to introduce her to the treasures of his art, she swore that nothing could afford her greater pleasure, for, though she had never crossed the threshold, she had frequently observed his beautiful pictures through the door. On entering the dining-room, the sight of a bottle and two glasses prepared her to be a gentle critic; and as soon as the pictures had been viewed and praised, she was easily persuaded to join the painter in a single glass. " Here," she said, " are my respects; and a pleasure it is, in this horrible house, to see a gentleman like yourself, so affable and free, and a very nice painter, I am sure." One glass so agreeably prefaced, was sure to lead to the acceptance of a second; at the third, Somerset was free to cease from the affectation of keeping her company; and as for the fourth, she asked it of her own accord. " For indeed," said she, " what with all these clocks and chemicals, without a drop of the creature life would be impossible entirely. And you seen yourself that even M'Guire was glad to beg for it. And even himself, when he is downhearted with all these cruel disappointments, though as temperate a man as any child, will be sometimes crying for a glass of it. And I 'll thank you for a thimbleful to settle what I got." Soon after, she began with tears to narrate the deathbed dispositions and lament the trifling assets of her husband. Then she declared she heard " the master " calling her, rose to her feet, made but one lurch of it into the still-life rockery, and with her head upon the lobster, fell into stertorous slumbers.

Somerset mounted at once to the first story, and opened the door of the drawing-room, which was brilliantly lighted by several lamps. It was a great apartment; looking on the square with three tall windows, and joined by a pair of ample folding-doors to the next room; elegant in proportion, papered in sea-green, furnished in velvet of a delicate blue, and adorned with a majestic mantelpiece of variously tinted marbles. Such was the room that Somerset remembered; that which he now beheld was changed in almost every feature: the furniture covered with a figured chintz; the walls hung with a rhubarb-coloured paper, and diversified by the curtained recesses for no less than seven windows. It seemed to himself that he must have entered, without observing the transition, into the adjoining house. Presently from these more specious changes, his eye condescended to the many curious objects with which the floor was littered. Here were the locks of dismounted pistols; clocks and clockwork in every stage of demolition, some still busily ticking, some reduced to their dainty elements; a great company of carboys, jars, and bottles; a carpenter's bench and a laboratory-table.

The back drawing-room, to which Somerset proceeded, had likewise undergone a change. It was transformed to the exact appearance of a common lodging-house bedroom; a bed with green curtains occupied one corner; and the window was blocked by the regulation table and mirror. The door of a small closet here attracted the young man's attention; and striking a vesta, he opened it and entered. On a table several wigs and

beards were lying spread; about the walls hung
an incongruous display of suits and overcoats; and
conspicuous among the last the young man observed a large overall of the most costly sealskin.
In a flash his mind reverted to the advertisement
in the *Standard* newspaper. The great height of
his lodger, the disproportionate breadth of his
shoulders, and the strange particulars of his in-
stalment, all pointed to the same conclusion.

The vesta had now burned to his fingers; and
taking the coat upon his arm, Somerset hastily
returned to the lighted drawing-room. There,
with a mixture of fear and admiration, he pored
upon its goodly proportions and the regularity
and softness of the pile. The sight of a large
pier-glass put another fancy in his head. He
donned the fur-coat; and standing before the
mirror in an attitude suggestive of a Russian
prince, he thrust his hands into the ample pockets.
There his fingers encountered a folded journal.
He drew it out, and recognised the type and
paper of the *Standard;* and at the same instant,
his eyes alighted on the offer of two hundred
pounds. Plainly then, his lodger, now no longer
mysterious, had laid aside his coat on the very
day of the appearance of the advertisement.

He was thus standing, the tell-tale coat upon his
back, the incriminating paper in his hand, when
the door opened and the tall lodger, with a firm
but somewhat pallid face, stepped into the room
and closed the door behind him. For some time,
the two looked upon each other in perfect silence;

then Mr. Jones moved forward to the table, took a seat, and, still without once changing the direction of his eyes, addressed the young man.

"You are right," he said. "It is for me the blood-money is offered. And now what will you do?"

It was a question to which Somerset was far from being able to reply. Taken as he was at unawares, masquerading in the man's own coat, and surrounded by a whole arsenal of diabolical explosives, the keeper of the lodging-house was silenced.

"Yes," resumed the other, "I am he. I am that man, whom with impotent hate and fear, they still hunt from den to den, from disguise to disguise. Yes, my landlord, you have it in your power, if you be poor, to lay the basis of your fortune; if you be unknown, to capture honour at one snatch. You have hocussed an innocent widow; and I find you here in my apartment, for whose use I pay you in stamped money, searching my wardrobe, and your hand — shame, sir! — your hand in my very pocket. You can now complete the cycle of your ignominious acts, by what will be at once the simplest, the safest, and most remunerative." The speaker paused as if to emphasise his words; and then, with a great change of tone and manner, thus resumed: "And yet, sir, when I look upon your face, I feel certain that I cannot be deceived: certain that in spite of all, I have the honour and pleasure of speaking to a gentleman. Take off my coat, sir —

which but cumbers you. Divest yourself of this confusion: that which is but thought upon, thank God, need be no burden to the conscience; we have all harboured guilty thoughts; and if it flashed into your mind to sell my flesh and blood, my anguish in the dock, and the sweat of my death agony — it was a thought, dear sir, you were as incapable of acting on, as I of any further question of your honour." At these words, the speaker, with a very open, smiling countenance, like a forgiving father, offered Somerset his hand.

It was not in the young man's nature to refuse forgiveness or dissect generosity. He instantly, and almost without thought, accepted the proffered grasp.

"And now," resumed the lodger, "now that I hold in mine your loyal hand, I lay by my apprehensions, I dismiss suspicion, I go further — by an effort of will, I banish the memory of what is past. How you came here, I care not: enough that you are here — as my guest. Sit ye down; and let us, with your good permission, improve acquaintance over a glass of excellent whisky."

So speaking, he produced glasses and a bottle; and the pair pledged each other in silence.

"Confess," observed the smiling host, "you were surprised at the appearance of the room."

"I was indeed," said Somerset; "nor can I imagine the purpose of these changes."

"These," replied the conspirator, "are the devices by which I continue to exist. Conceive me now, accused before one of your unjust tribunals; conceive the various witnesses appearing, and the singular variety of their reports! One will have visited me in this drawing-room as it originally stood; a second finds it as it is to-night; and to-morrow or next day, all may have been changed. If you love romance (as artists do), few lives are more romantic than that of the obscure individual now addressing you. Obscure yet famous. Mine is an anonymous, infernal glory. By infamous means, I work toward my bright purpose. I found the liberty and peace of a poor country desperately abused; the future smiles upon that land; yet, in the meantime, I lead the existence of a hunted brute, work toward appalling ends, and practise hell's dexterities."

Somerset, glass in hand, contemplated the strange fanatic before him, and listened to his heated rhapsody with indescribable bewilderment. He looked him in the face with curious particularity; saw there the marks of education; and wondered the more profoundly.

"Sir," he said — "for I know not whether I should still address you as Mr. Jones —— "

"Jones, Breitman, Higginbotham, Pumpernickel, Daviot, Henderland, by all or any of these you may address me," said the plotter; "for all I have at some time borne. Yet that which I most prize, that which is most feared, hated, and obeyed, is not a name to be found in your directories; it is not a name current in post-offices or banks; and indeed, like the celebrated

clan M'Gregor, I may justly describe myself as
being nameless by day. But," he continued, rising to his feet, "by night, and among my desperate followers, I am the redoubted Zero."

Somerset was unacquainted with the name; but
he politely expressed surprise and gratification. " I
am to understand," he continued, " that, under this
alias, you follow the profession of a dynamiter? " [1]

The plotter had resumed his seat and now re-
plenished the glasses.

" I do," he said. " In this dark period of time,
a star — the star of dynamite — has risen for the
oppressed; and among those who practise its use,
so thick beset with dangers and attended by such
incredible difficulties and disappointments, few have
been more assiduous, and not many —— " He
paused, and a shade of embarrassment appeared
upon his face — " not many have been more successful than myself."

" I can imagine," observed Somerset, " that,
from the sweeping consequences looked for, the
career is not devoid of interest. You have, besides, some of the entertainment of the game of
hide and seek. But it would still seem to me —
I speak as a layman — that nothing could be

[1] The Arabian author of the original has here a long passage
conceived in a style too oriental for the English reader. We sub-
join a specimen, and it seems doubtful whether it should be printed
as prose or verse: " Any writard who writes dynamitard shall find
in me a never-resting fightard "; and he goes on (if we correctly
gather his meaning) to object to such elegant and obviously correct spellings as lamp-lightard, corn-dealard, apple-filchard (clearly
justified by the parallel — pilchard), and opera dancard. " Dyna-
mitist," he adds, " I could understand."

simpler or safer than to deposit an infernal machine and retire to an adjacent county to await
the painful consequences."

"You speak, indeed," returned the plotter, with
some evidence of warmth, "you speak, indeed,
most ignorantly. Do you make nothing, then, of
such a peril as we share this moment? Do you
think it nothing to occupy a house like this one,
mined, menaced, and, in a word, literally tottering to its fall?"

"Good God!" ejaculated Somerset.

"And when you speak of ease," pursued Zero,
"in this age of scientific studies, you fill me with
surprise. Are you not aware that chemicals are
proverbially as fickle as woman, and clockwork as
capricious as the very devil? Do you see on my
brow these furrows of anxiety? do you observe
the silver threads that mingle with my hair?
Clockwork, clockwork has stamped them on my
brow — chemicals have sprinkled them upon my
locks! No, Mr. Somerset," he resumed, after a
moment's pause, his voice still quivering with
sensibility, "you must not suppose the dynamiter's
life to be all gold. On the contrary: you cannot picture to yourself the bloodshot vigils and
the staggering disappointments of a life like mine.
I have toiled (let us say) for months, up early
and down late; my bag is ready, my clock set;
a daring agent has hurried with white face to
deposit the instrument of ruin; we await the fall
of England, the massacre of thousands, the yell of
fear and execration; and lo! a snap like that

of a child's pistol, an offensive smell, and the
entire loss of so much time and plant! If," he
continued, musingly, "we had been merely able
to recover the lost bags, I believe with but a
touch or two, I could have remedied the peccant
engine. But what with the loss of plant and the
almost insuperable scientific difficulties of the task,
our friends in France are almost ready to desert
the chosen medium. They propose, instead, to
break up the drainage system of cities and sweep
off whole populations with the devastating typhoid
pestilence: a tempting and a scientific project: a
process, indiscriminate indeed, but of idyllical simplicity. I recognise its elegance; but, sir, I have
something of the poet in my nature; something,
possibly, of the tribune. And, for my small part,
I shall remain devoted to that more emphatic, more
striking, and (if you please) more popular method,
of the explosive bomb. Yes," he cried, with unshaken hope, "I will still continue, and I feel it
in my bosom I shall yet succeed."

"Two things I remark," said Somerset. "The
first somewhat staggers me. Have you, then — in
all this course of life, which you have sketched
so vividly — have you not once succeeded?"

"Pardon me," said Zero. "I have had one
success. You behold in me the author of the
outrage of Red Lion Court."

"But if I remember right," objected Somerset,
"the thing was a *fiasco*. A scavenger's barrow
and some copies of the ' Weekly Budget ' — these
were the only victims."

"You will pardon me again," returned Zero with positive asperity; "a child was injured."

"And that fitly brings me to my second point," said Somerset. "For I observed you to employ the word 'indiscriminate.' Now, surely, a scavenger's barrow and a child (if child there was) represent the very acme and top pin-point of indiscriminate, and, pardon me, of ineffectual reprisal."

"Did I employ the word?" asked Zero. "Well, I will not defend it. But for efficiency, you touch on graver matters; and before entering upon so vast a subject, permit me once more to fill our glasses. Disputation is dry work," he added, with a charming gaiety of manner.

Once more accordingly the pair pledged each other in a stalwart grog; and Zero, leaning back with an air of some complacency, proceeded more largely to develop his opinions.

"The indiscriminate," he began. "War, my dear sir, is indiscriminate. War spares not the child; it spares not the barrow of the harmless scavenger. No more," he concluded, beaming, "no more do I. Whatever may strike fear, whatever may confound or paralyse the activities of the guilty nation, barrow or child, imperial Parliament or excursion steamer, is welcome to my simple plans. You are not," he inquired, with a shade of sympathetic interest, "you are not, I trust, a believer?"

"Sir, I believe in nothing," said the young man.

"You are then," replied Zero, "in position to

grasp my argument. We agree that humanity is
the object, the glorious triumph of humanity; and
being pledged to labour for that end, and face
to face with the banded opposition of kings,
parliaments, churches, and the members of the
force, who am I — who are we, dear sir — to
affect a nicety about the tools employed? You
might, perhaps, expect us to attack the Queen,
the sinister Gladstone, the rigid Derby, or the
dexterous Granville; but there you would be
in error. Our appeal is to the body of the
people; it is these that we would touch and interest. Now, sir, have you observed the English
housemaid?"

"I should think I had," cried Somerset.

"From a man of taste and a votary of art, I
had expected it," returned the conspirator politely.
"A type apart; a very charming figure; and
thoroughly adapted to our ends. The neat cap,
the clean print, the comely person, the engaging
manner; her position between classes, parents in
one, employers in another; the probability that
she will have at least one sweetheart, whose feelings we shall address: — yes, I have a leaning —
call it, if you will, a weakness — for the housemaid. Not that I would be understood to despise
the nurse. For the child is a very interesting
feature: I have long since marked out the child
as the sensitive point in society." He wagged
his head, with a wise, pensive smile. "And
talking, sir, of children and of the perils of our
trade, let me now narrate to you a little in-

cident of an explosive bomb, that fell out some
weeks ago under my own observation. It fell out
thus."

And Zero, leaning back in his chair, narrated
the following simple tale.

ZERO'S TALE OF THE EXPLOSIVE BOMB [1]

I DINED by appointment with one of our most trusted agents, in a private chamber at St. James's Hall. You have seen the man: it was M'Guire, the most chivalrous of creatures, but not himself expert in our contrivances. Hence the necessity of our meeting; for I need not remind you what enormous issues depend upon the nice adjustment of the engine. I set our little petard for half an hour, the scene of action being hard by; and the better to avert miscarriage, employed a device, a recent invention of my own, by which the opening of the Gladstone bag in which the bomb was carried, should instantly determine the explosion. M'Guire was somewhat dashed by this arrangement, which was new to him; and pointed out, with excellent, clear good sense, that should he be arrested, it would probably involve him in the fall of our opponents. But I was not to be moved, made a strong appeal to his patriotism, gave him a good

---

[1] The Arabian author, with that quaint particularity of touch which our translation usually prætermits, here registers a somewhat interesting detail. Zero pronounced the word "boom"; and the reader, if but for the nonce, will possibly consent to follow him.

glass of whisky, and despatched him on his glorious errand.

Our objective was the effigy of Shakespeare in Leicester Square: a spot, I think, admirably chosen; not only for the sake of the dramatist, still very foolishly claimed as a glory by the English race, in spite of his disgusting political opinions; but from the fact that the seats in the immediate neighbourhood are often thronged by children, errand-boys, unfortunate young ladies of the poorer class and infirm old men — all classes making a direct appeal to public pity, and therefore suitable with our designs. As M'Guire drew near his heart was inflamed by the most noble sentiment of triumph. Never had he seen the garden so crowded; children, still stumbling in the impotence of youth, ran to and fro, shouting and playing, round the pedestal; an old, sick pensioner sat upon the nearest bench, a medal on his breast, a stick with which he walked (for he was disabled by wounds) reclining on his knee. Guilty England would thus be stabbed in the most delicate quarters; the moment had, indeed, been well selected; and M'Guire, with a radiant prevision of the event, drew merrily nearer. Suddenly his eye alighted on the burly form of a policeman, standing hard by the effigy in an attitude of watch. My bold companion paused; he looked about him closely; here and there, at different points of the inclosure, other men stood or loitered, affecting an abstraction, feigning to gaze upon the shrubs, feigning to talk, feigning to be weary and to rest upon the benches. M'Guire was no child in these affairs; he instantly divined one of the plots of the Machiavellian Gladstone.

A chief difficulty with which we have to deal, is a certain nervousness in the subaltern branches of the corps; as the hour of some design draws near, these chicken-souled conspirators appear to suffer some revulsion of intent: and frequently despatch to the authorities, not indeed specific denunciations, but vague anonymous warnings. But for this purely accidental circumstance, England had long ago been an historical expression. On the receipt of such a letter, the Government lay a trap for their adversaries, and surround the threatened spot with hirelings. My blood sometimes boils in my veins, when I consider the case of those who sell themselves for money in such a cause. True, thanks to the generosity of our supporters, we patriots receive a very comfortable stipend; I, myself, of course, touch a salary which puts me quite beyond the reach of any peddling, mercenary thoughts; M'Guire, again, ere he joined our ranks, was on the brink of starving, and now, thank God! receives a decent income. That is as it should be; the patriot must not be diverted from his task by any base consideration; and the distinction between our position and that of the police is too obvious to be stated.

Plainly, however, our Leicester Square design had been divulged; the Government had craftily filled the place with minions; even the pensioner

was not improbably a hireling in disguise; and
our emissary, without other aid or protection than
the simple apparatus in his bag, found himself
confronted by force; brutal force; that strong
hand which was a character of the ages of oppression.   Should he venture to deposit the machine, it was almost certain that he would be
observed and arrested; a cry would arise; and
there was just a fear that the police might not
be present in sufficient force to protect him from
the savagery of the mob.   The scheme must be
delayed. He stood with his bag on his arm, pretending to survey the front of the Alhambra, when
there flashed into his mind a thought to appall
the bravest. The machine was set; at the appointed hour it must explode; and how, in the
interval, was he to be rid of it?

Put yourself, I beseech you, into the body of
that patriot.   There he was, friendless and helpless; a man in the very flower of life, for he is
not yet forty; with long years of happiness before
him; and now condemned, in one moment, to a
cruel and revolting death by dynamite!   The
square, he said, went round him like a thauma-
trope; he saw the Alhambra leap into the air
like a balloon; and reeled against the railing.   It
is probable he fainted.

When he came to himself, a constable had him
by the arm.

" My God! " he cried.

" You seem to be unwell, sir," said the hireling.

" I feel better now," cried poor M'Guire; and

with uneven steps, for the pavement of the square seemed to lurch and reel under his footing, he fled from the scene of this disaster. Fled? Alas, from what was he fleeing? Did he not carry that from which he fled, along with him? and had he the wings of the eagle, had he the swiftness of the ocean winds, could he have been rapt into the uttermost quarters of the earth, how should he escape the ruin that he carried? We have heard of living men who have been fettered to the dead; the grievance, soberly considered, is no more than sentimental; the case is but a flea-bite to that of him who was linked, like poor M'Guire, to an explosive bomb.

A thought struck him in Green Street, like a dart through his liver; suppose it were the hour already. He stopped as though he had been shot, and plucked his watch out. There was a howling in his ears, as loud as a winter tempest; his sight was now obscured as if by a cloud, now, as by a lightning flash, would show him the very dust upon the street. But so brief were these intervals of vision, and so violently did the watch vibrate in his hands, that it was impossible to distinguish the numbers on the dial. He covered his eyes for a few seconds; and in that space, it seemed to him that he had fallen to be a man of ninety. When he looked again, the watch-plate had grown legible: he had twenty minutes. Twenty minutes, and no plan!

Green Street, at that time, was very empty; and he now observed a little girl of about six drawing near to him and, as she came, kicking in front of her, as children will, a piece of wood. She sang, too; and something in her accent recalling him to the past, produced a sudden clearness in his mind. Here was a God-sent opportunity!

"My dear," said he, "would you like a present of a pretty bag?"

The child cried aloud with joy and put out her hands to take it. She had looked first at the bag, like a true child; but most unfortunately, before she had yet received the fatal gift, her eyes fell directly on M'Guire; and no sooner had she seen the poor gentleman's face, than she screamed out and leaped backward, as though she had seen the devil. Almost at the same moment, a woman appeared upon the threshold of a neighbouring shop, and called upon the child in anger. "Come here, colleen," she said, "and don't be plaguing the poor old gentleman!" With that she re-entered the house, and the child followed her, sobbing aloud.

With the loss of this hope M'Guire's reason swooned within him. When next he awoke to consciousness, he was standing before St. Martin's-in-the-Fields, wavering like a drunken man; the passers-by regarding him with eyes in which he read, as in a glass, an image of the terror and horror that dwelt within his own.

"I am afraid you are very ill, sir," observed a woman, stopping and gazing hard in his face. "Can I do anything to help you?"

"Ill?" said M'Guire. "O God!" And then,

recovering some shadow of his self-command, " Chronic, madam," said he; " a long course of the dumb ague. But since you are so compassionate — an errand that I lack the strength to carry out," he gasped — " this bag to Portman Square. O compassionate woman, as you hope to be saved, as you are a mother, in the name of your babies that wait to welcome you at home, oh take this bag to Portman Square! I have a mother, too," he added, with a broken voice. " Number 19, Portman Square."

I suppose he had expressed himself with too much energy of voice; for the woman was plainly taken with a certain fear of him. " Poor gentleman!" said she. " If I were you, I would go home." And she left him standing there in his distress.

" Home!" thought M'Guire, " what a derision!" What home was there for him, the victim of philanthropy? He thought of his old mother, of his happy youth; of the hideous, rending pang of the explosion; of the possibility that he might not be killed, that he might be cruelly mangled, crippled for life, condemned to life-long pains, blinded perhaps, and almost surely deafened. Ah, you spoke lightly of the dynamiter's peril; but even waiving death, have you realised what it is for a fine, brave young man of forty, to be smitten suddenly with deafness, cut off from all the music of life, and from the voice of friendship and love? How little do we realise the sufferings of others! Even your brutal Government, in the heyday of its lust for cruelty, though it scruples not to hound the patriot with spies, to pack the corrupt jury, to bribe the hangman, and to erect the infamous gallows, would hesitate to inflict so horrible a doom: not, I am well aware, from virtue, not from philanthropy, but with the fear before it of the withering scorn of the good.

But I wander from M'Guire. From this dread glance into the past and future, his thoughts returned at a bound upon the present. How had he wandered there? and how long — O heavens! how long had he been about it? He pulled out his watch; and found that but three minutes had elapsed. It seemed too bright a thing to be believed. He glanced at the church clock; and sure enough, it marked an hour four minutes faster than the watch.

Of all that he endured, M'Guire declares that pang was the most desolate. Till then he had had one friend, one counsellor, in whom he plenarily trusted; by whose advertisement he numbered the minutes that remained to him of life; on whose sure testimony he could tell when the time was come to risk the last adventure, to cast the bag away from him, and take to flight. And now in what was he to place reliance? His watch was slow; it might be losing time; if so, in what degree? What limit could he set to its derangement? and how much was it possible for a watch to lose in thirty minutes? Five? ten? fifteen? It might be so; already it seemed years since he had left St. James's Hall on this so promising enterprise; at any moment, then, the blow was to be looked for.

In the face of this new distress, the wild disorder of his pulses settled down; and a broken weariness succeeded, as though he had lived for centuries and for centuries been dead. The buildings and the people in the street became incredibly small, and far-away, and bright; London sounded in his ears stilly, like a whisper; and the rattle of the cab that nearly charged him down, was like a sound from Africa. Meanwhile, he was conscious of a strange abstraction from himself; and heard and felt his footfalls on the ground, as those of a very old, small, debile, and tragically fortuned man, whom he sincerely pitied.

As he was thus moving forward past the National Gallery, in a medium, it seemed, of greater rarity and quiet than ordinary air, there slipped into his mind the recollection of a certain entry in Whitcomb Street hard by, where he might perhaps lay down his tragic cargo unremarked. Thither, then, he bent his steps, seeming, as he went, to float above the pavement; and there, in the mouth of the entry, he found a man in a sleeved waistcoat, gravely chewing a straw. He passed him by, and twice patrolled the entry, scouting for the barest chance; but the man had faced about and continued to observe him curiously.

Another hope was gone. M'Guire reissued from the entry, still followed by the wondering eyes of the man in the sleeved waistcoat. He once more consulted his watch: there was but fourteen minutes left to him. At that, it seemed as if a sudden, genial heat were spread about his brain; for a second or two, he saw the world as red as blood; and thereafter entered into a complete possession of himself, with an incredible cheerfulness of spirits, prompting him to sing and chuckle as he walked. And yet this mirth seemed to belong to things external; and within like a black and leaden-heavy kernel, he was conscious of the weight upon his soul.

> I care for nobody, no, not I,
> And nobody cares for me,

he sang, and laughed at the appropriate burthen, so that the passengers stared upon him on the street. And still the warmth seemed to increase and to become more genial. What was life? he considered, and what he, M'Guire? What even Erin, our green Erin? All seemed so incalculably little that he smiled as he looked down upon it. He would have given years, had he possessed them, for a glass of spirits; but time failed, and he must deny himself this last indulgence.

At the corner of the Haymarket, he very jauntily hailed a hansom cab; jumped in; bade the fellow drive him to a part of the Embankment, which he named; and as soon as the vehicle was in motion, concealed the bag as completely as he could under the vantage of the apron, and once more drew out his watch. So he rode for five interminable minutes, his heart in his mouth at every jolt, scarce able to possess his terrors, yet fearing to wake the attention of the driver by too obvious a change of plan, and willing, if possible, to leave him time to forget the Gladstone bag.

At length, at the head of some stairs on the Embankment, he hailed; the cab was stopped, and he alighted — with how glad a heart! He thrust his hand into his pocket. All was now over; he had saved his life; nor that alone, but he had engineered a striking act of dynamite; for what could be more pictorial, what more effective, than the explosion of a hansom cab as it sped rapidly along the streets of London. He felt in one pocket, then in another. The most crushing seizure of despair descended on his soul, and struck into abject dumbness, he stared upon the driver. He had not one penny.

" Hillo," said the driver; " don't seem well."

" Lost my money," said M'Guire, in tones so faint and strange that they surprised his hearing.

The man looked through the trap. " I dessay," said he; " you 've left your bag."

M'Guire half unconsciously fetched it out, and looking on that black continent at arm's length, withered inwardly and felt his features sharpen as with mortal sickness.

" This is not mine," said he. " Your last fare must have left it. You had better take it to the station."

" Now look here," returned the cabman, " are you off your chump? or am I ? "

" Well, then, I 'll tell you what," exclaimed M'Guire, " you take it for your fare."

" Oh, I dessay," replied the driver. " Anything

else? What's *in* your bag? Open it and let me see."

"No, no," returned M'Guire. "Oh, no, not that. It's a surprise; it's prepared expressly; a surprise for honest cabmen."

"No, you don't," said the man, alighting from his perch, and coming very close to the unhappy patriot. "You're either going to pay my fare, or get in again and drive to the office."

It was at this supreme hour of his distress that M'Guire spied the stout figure of one Godall, a tobacconist of Rupert Street, drawing near along the Embankment. The man was not unknown to him; he had bought of his wares, and heard him quoted for the soul of liberality; and such was now the nearness of his peril that even at such a straw of hope he clutched with gratitude.

"Thank God!" he cried. "Here comes a friend of mine. I'll borrow." And he dashed to meet the tradesman. "Sir," said he, "Mr. Godall, I have dealt with you — you doubtless know my face — calamities for which I cannot blame myself have overwhelmed me. Oh, sir, for the love of innocence, for the sake of the bonds of humanity, and as you hope for mercy at the throne of grace, lend me two-and-six!"

"I do not recognise your face," replied Mr. Godall; "but I remember the cut of your beard, which I have the misfortune to dislike. Here, sir, is a sovereign, which I very willingly advance to you on the single condition that you shave your chin."

M'Guire grasped the coin without a word, cast it to the cabman, calling out to him to keep the change; bounded down the steps, flung the bag far forth into the river, and fell headlong after it.   He was plucked from a watery grave, it is believed, by the hands of Mr. Godall.   Even as he was being hoisted, dripping, to the shore, a dull and choked explosion shook the solid masonry of the Embankment, and far out in the river a momentary fountain rose and disappeared.

THE SUPERFLUOUS MANSION
(*continued*)

SOMERSET in vain strove to attach a meaning to these words. He had in the meanwhile applied himself assiduously to the flagon; the plotter began to melt in twain, and seemed to expand and hover on his seat, and with a vague sense of nightmare, the young man rose unsteadily to his feet, and, refusing the proffer of a third grog, insisted that the hour was late and he must positively go to bed.

"Dear me," observed Zero, "I find you very temperate. But I will not be oppressive. Suffice it that we are now fast friends; and, my dear landlord, *au revoir!*"

So saying the plotter once more shook hands; and with the politest ceremonies, and some necessary guidance, conducted the bewildered young gentleman to the top of the stair.

Precisely how he got to bed was a point on which Somerset remained in utter darkness; but the next morning when, at a blow, he started broad awake, there fell upon his mind a perfect hurricane of horror and wonder. That he should have suffered himself to be led into the semblance of intimacy with such a man as his abominable lodger, appeared, in the cold light of day, a mys-

tery of human weakness.   True, he was caught
in a situation that might have tested the aplomb
of Talleyrand.   That was perhaps a palliation;
but it was no excuse.   For so wholesale a capitu-
lation of principle, for such a fall into criminal
familiarity, no excuse indeed was possible; nor
any remedy, but to withdraw at once from the
relation.

As soon as he was dressed, he hurried up-stairs,
determined on a rupture.   Zero hailed him with
the warmth of an old friend.

"Come in," he cried, "dear Mr. Somerset!
Come in, sit down, and without ceremony, join
me at my morning meal."

"Sir," said Somerset, "you must permit me
first to disengage my honour.   Last night I was
surprised into a certain appearance of complicity;
but once for all, let me inform you that I regard
you and your machinations with unmingled horror
and disgust, and I will leave no stone unturned
to crush your vile conspiracy."

"My dear fellow," replied Zero, with an air of
some complacency, "I am well accustomed to these
human weaknesses.   Disgust?   I have felt it myself; it speedily wears off.   I think none the worse,
I think the more of you for this engaging frankness.   And in the meanwhile, what are you to do?
You find yourself, if I interpret rightly, in very
much the same situation as Charles the Second
(possibly the least degraded of your British sovereigns) when he was taken into the confidence
of the thief.   To denounce me, is out of the ques-

tion; and what else can you attempt? No, dear
Mr. Somerset, your hands are tied; and you find
yourself condemned, under pain of behaving like
a cad, to be that same charming and intellectual
companion who delighted me last night."

"At least," cried Somerset, "I can and do order
you to leave this house."

"Ah!" cried the plotter, "but there I fail to
follow you. You may, if you choose, enact the
part of Judas; but if, as I suppose, you recoil
from that extremity of meanness, I am, on my
side, far too intelligent to leave these lodgings,
in which I please myself exceedingly, and from
which you lack the power to drive me. No,
no, dear sir; here I am, and here I propose to
stay."

"I repeat," cried Somerset, beside himself with
a sense of his own weakness, "I repeat that I
give you warning. I am master of this house;
and I emphatically give you warning."

"A week's warning?" said the imperturbable
conspirator. "Very well; we will talk of it a
week from now. That is arranged; and in the
meanwhile, I observe my breakfast growing cold.
Do, dear Mr. Somerset, since you find yourself
condemned, for a week at least, to the society of
a very interesting character, display some of that
open favour, some of that interest in life's obscurer
sides, which stamp the character of the true artist.
Hang me, if you will, to-morrow; but to-day show
yourself divested of the scruples of the burgess,
and sit down pleasantly to share my meal."

" Man ! " cried Somerset, " do you understand
my sentiments ? "

" Certainly," replied Zero; " and I respect them !
Would you be outdone in such a contest? will you
alone be partial? and in this nineteenth century,
cannot two gentlemen of education agree to differ
on a point of politics? Come, sir; all your hard
words have left me smiling; judge then, which
of us is the philosopher ! "

Somerset was a young man of a very tolerant
disposition and by nature easily amenable to soph-
istry. He threw up his hands with a gesture of
despair, and took the seat to which the conspirator invited him. The meal was excellent; the
host not only affable, but primed with curious information. He seemed, indeed, like one who had
too long endured the torture of silence, to exult
in the most wholesale disclosures. The interest
of what he had to tell was great; his character,
besides, developed step by step; and Somerset, as
the time fled, not only outgrew some of the discomfort of his false position, but began to regard
the conspirator with a familiarity that verged upon
contempt. In any circumstances, he had a singular inability to leave the society in which he found
himself; company, even if distasteful, held him
captive like a limed sparrow; and on this occasion, he suffered hour to follow hour, was easily
persuaded to sit down once more to table, and did
not even attempt to withdraw, till on the approach
of evening, Zero, with many apologies, dismissed
his guest. His fellow-conspirators, the dynamiter

handsomely explained, as they were unacquainted
with the sterling qualities of the young man, would
be alarmed at the sight of a strange face.

As soon as he was alone, Somerset fell back
upon the humour of the morning. He raged at
the thought of his facility; he paced the dining-
room, forming the sternest resolutions for the
future; he wrung the hand which had been dishonoured by the touch of an assassin; and among
all these whirling thoughts, there flashed in, from
time to time, and ever with a chill of fear, the
thought of the confounded ingredients with which
the house was stored. A powder-magazine seemed
a secure smoking-room alongside of the Superfluous Mansion.

He sought refuge in flight, in locomotion, in the
flowing bowl. As long as the bars were open, he
travelled from one to another, seeking light, safety,
and the companionship of human faces; when these
resources failed him, he fell back on the belated
baked-potato man; and at length, still pacing the
streets, he was goaded to fraternise with the police.
Alas, with what a sense of guilt he conversed with
these guardians of the law; how gladly had he
wept upon their ample bosoms; and how the secret
fluttered to his lips and was still denied an exit!
Fatigue began at last to triumph over remorse;
and about the hour of the first milkman, he returned to the door of the mansion; looked at it
with a horrid expectation, as though it should
have burst that instant into flames; drew out his
key, and when his foot already rested on the steps,

once more lost heart and fled for repose to the grisly shelter of a coffee-shop.

It was on the stroke of noon when he awoke. Dismally searching in his pockets, he found himself reduced to half a crown; and when he had paid the price of his distasteful couch, saw himself obliged to return to the Superfluous Mansion. He sneaked into the hall, and stole on tiptoe to the cupboard where he kept his money. Yet half a minute, he told himself, and he would be free for days from his obseding lodger, and might decide at leisure on the course he should pursue. But fate had otherwise designed; there came a tap at the door and Zero entered.

"Have I caught you?" he cried, with innocent gaiety. "Dear fellow, I was growing quite impatient." And on the speaker's somewhat stolid face, there came a glow of genuine affection. "I am so long unused to have a friend," he continued, "that I begin to be afraid I may prove jealous." And he wrung the hand of his landlord.

Somerset was, of all men, least fit to deal with such a greeting. To reject these kind advances was beyond his strength. That he could not return cordiality for cordiality, was already almost more than he could carry. That inequality between kind sentiments, which, to generous characters, will always seem to be a sort of guilt, oppressed him to the ground; and he stammered vague and lying words.

"That is all right," cried Zero — "that is as it should be — say no more! I had a vague alarm;

I feared you had deserted me; but I now own
that fear to have been unworthy, and apologise.
To doubt of your forgiveness were to repeat my
sin. Come, then; dinner waits; join me again
and tell me your adventures of the night."

Kindness still sealed the lips of Somerset; and
he suffered himself once more to be set down to
table with his innocent and criminal acquaintance.
Once more, the plotter plunged up to the neck in
damaging disclosures: now it would be the name
and biography of an individual, now the address
of some important centre, that rose, as if by accident, upon his lips; and each word was like
another turn of the thumbscrew to his unhappy
guest. Finally, the course of Zero's bland mono-
logue led him to the young lady of two days ago:
that young lady, who had flashed on Somerset for
so brief awhile but with so conquering a charm;
and whose engaging grace, communicative eyes,
and admirable conduct of the sweeping skirt, remained imprinted on his memory.

" You saw her? " said Zero. " Beautiful, is she
not? She, too, is one of ours: a true enthusiast:
nervous, perhaps, in presence of the chemicals;
but in matters of intrigue, the very soul of skill
and daring. Lake, Fonblanque, de Marly, Valdevia, such are some of the names that she em-
ploys; her true name — but there, perhaps, I go
too far. Suffice it, that it is to her I owe my
present lodging and, dear Somerset, the pleasure
of your acquaintance. It appears she knew the
house. You see, dear fellow, I make no conceal-

ment: all that you can care to hear, I tell you openly."

"For God's sake," cried the wretched Somerset, "hold your tongue! You cannot imagine how you torture me!"

A shade of serious discomposure crossed the open countenance of Zero.

"There are times," he said, "when I begin to fancy that you do not like me. Why, why, dear Somerset, this lack of cordiality? I am depressed; the touchstone of my life draws near; and if I fail " — he gloomily nodded — " from all the height of my ambitious schemes, I fall, dear boy, into contempt. These are grave thoughts, and you may judge my need of your delightful company. Innocent prattler, you relieve the weight of my concerns. And yet . . . and yet . . ." The speaker pushed away his plate, and rose from table. "Follow me," said he, "follow me. My mood is on; I must have air, I must behold the plain of battle."

So saying, he led the way hurriedly to the top flat of the mansion, and thence, by ladder and trap, to a certain leaded platform, sheltered at one end by a great stalk of chimneys and occupying the actual summit of the roof. On both sides, it bordered, without parapet or rail, on the incline of slates; and, northward above all, commanded an extensive view of housetops, and rising through the smoke, the distant spires of churches.

"Here," cried Zero, "you behold this field of city, rich, crowded, laughing with the spoil of

continents; but soon, how soon, to be laid low!
Some day, some night, from this coign of vantage, you shall perhaps be startled by the detonation of the judgment gun — not sharp and empty
like the crack of cannon, but deep-mouthed and
unctuously solemn. Instantly thereafter, you shall
behold the flames break forth. Ay," he cried,
stretching forth his hand, " ay, that will be a day
of retribution. Then shall the pallid constable flee
side by side with the detected thief. Blaze!" he
cried, " blaze, derided city! Fall, flatulent mon-
archy, fall like Dagon!"

With these words his foot slipped upon the lead;
and but for Somerset's quickness, he had been instantly precipitated into space. Pale as a sheet,
and limp as a pocket-handkerchief, he was dragged
from the edge of downfall by one arm; helped,
or rather carried, down the ladder; and deposited
in safety on the attic landing. Here he began to
come to himself, wiped his brow, and at length,
seizing Somerset's hand in both of his, began to
utter his acknowledgments.

" This seals it," said he. " Ours is a life and
death connection. You have plucked me from the
jaws of death; and if I were before attracted by
your character, judge now of the ardour of my
gratitude and love? But I perceive I am still
greatly shaken. Lend me, I beseech you, lend me
your arm as far as my apartment."

A dram of spirits restored the plotter to something of his customary self-possession; and he was
standing, glass in hand and genially convalescent,

13

when his eye was attracted by the dejection of the unfortunate young man.

"Good heavens, dear Somerset," he cried, "what ails you? Let me offer you a touch of spirits."

But Somerset had fallen below the reach of this material comfort.

"Let me be," he said, "I am lost; you have caught me in the toils. Up to this moment I have lived all my life in the most reckless manner, and done exactly what I pleased, with the most perfect innocence. And now — what am I? Are you so blind and wooden that you do not see the loathing you inspire me with? Is it possible you can suppose me willing to continue to exist upon such terms? To think," he cried, "that a young man, guilty of no fault on earth but amiability, should find himself involved in such a damned imbroglio!" and placing his knuckles in his eyes, Somerset rolled upon the sofa.

"My God," said Zero, "is this possible? And I so filled with tenderness and interest! Can it be, dear Somerset, that you are under the empire of these outworn scruples? or that you judge a patriot by the morality of the religious tract? I thought you were a good agnostic."

"Mr. Jones," said Somerset, "it is in vain to argue. I boast myself a total disbeliever not only in revealed religion, but in the data, method, and conclusions of the whole of ethics. Well! what matters it? what signifies a form of words? I regard you as a reptile, whom I would rejoice, whom I long, to stamp under my heel. You

would blow up others? Well then, understand:
I want, with every circumstance of infamy and
agony, to blow up you!"

"Somerset, Somerset!" said Zero, turning very
pale, "this is wrong; this is very wrong. You
pain, you wound me, Somerset."

"Give me a match!" cried Somerset wildly.
"Let me set fire to this incomparable monster!
Let me perish with him in his fall!"

"For God's sake," cried Zero, clutching hold
of the young man, "for God's sake command
yourself! We stand upon the brink; death yawns
around us; a man — a stranger in this foreign
land — one whom you have called your friend — "

"Silence!" cried Somerset, "you are no friend,
no friend of mine. I look on you with loathing,
like a toad: my flesh creeps with physical repulsion; my soul revolts against the sight of you."

Zero burst into tears. "Alas!" he sobbed, "this
snaps the last link that bound me to humanity.
My friend disowns — he insults me. I am indeed
accursed."

Somerset stood for an instant staggered by this
sudden change of front. The next moment, with
a despairing gesture, he fled from the room and
from the house. The first dash of his escape carried him hard upon half-way to the next police
office; but presently he began to droop; and before he reached the house of lawful intervention,
he fell once more among doubtful counsels. Was
he an agnostic? had he a right to act? Away
with such nonsense, and let Zero perish! ran his

thoughts. And then again: had he not promised,
had he not shaken hands and broken bread? and
that with open eyes? and if so how could he
take action, and not forfeit honour? But honour!
what was honour? A figment, which, in the hot
pursuit of crime he ought to dash aside. Ay, but
crime? A figment, too, which his enfranchised
intellect discarded. All day he wandered in the
parks, a prey to whirling thoughts; all night,
patrolled the city; and at the peep of day he sat
down by the wayside in the neighbourhood of
Peckham and bitterly wept. His gods had fallen.
He who had chosen the broad, daylighted, unen-
cumbered paths of universal scepticism, found himself still the bond slave of honour. He who had
accepted life from a point of view as lofty as the
predatory eagle's, though with no design to prey;
he who had clearly recognised the common moral
basis of war, of commercial competition, and of
crime; he who was prepared to help the escaping
murderer or to embrace the impenitent thief, found,
to the overthrow of all his logic, that he objected
to the use of dynamite. The dawn crept among
the sleeping villas and over the smokeless fields
of city; and still the unfortunate sceptic sobbed
over his fall from consistency.

At length, he rose and took the rising sun to
witness. "There is no question as to fact," he
cried; " right and wrong are but figments and the
shadow of a word; but for all that, there are
certain things that I cannot do, and there are certain others that I will not stand." Thereupon he

decided to return, to make one last effort of persuasion, and, if he could not prevail on Zero to desist from his infernal trade, throw delicacy to the winds, give the plotter an hour's start, and denounce him to the police. Fast as he went, being winged by this resolution, it was already well on in the morning, when he came in sight of the Superfluous Mansion. Tripping down the steps, was the young lady of the various aliases; and he was surprised to see upon her countenance the marks of anger and concern.

"Madam," he began, yielding to impulse and with no clear knowledge of what he was to add.

But at the sound of his voice she seemed to experience a shock of fear or horror; started back; lowered her veil with a sudden movement; and fled, without turning, from the square.

Here then, we step aside a moment from following the fortunes of Somerset, and proceed to relate the strange and romantic episode of THE BROWN BOX.

DESBOROUGH'S ADVENTURE: THE BROWN BOX

MR. HARRY DESBOROUGH lodged in the fine and grave old quarter of Bloomsbury, roared about on every side by the high tides of London, but itself rejoicing in romantic silence and city peace. It was in Queen Square that he had pitched his tent, next door to the Children's Hospital, on your left hand as you go north: Queen Square, sacred to humane and liberal arts, whence homes were made beautiful, where the poor were taught, where the sparrows were plentiful and loud, and where groups of patient little ones would hover all day long before the hospital, if by chance they might kiss their hand or speak a word to their sick brother at the window. Desborough's room was on the first floor and fronted to the square; but he enjoyed besides, a right by which he often profited, to sit and smoke upon a terrace at the back, which looked down upon a fine forest of back gardens, and was in turn commanded by the windows of an empty room.

On the afternoon of a warm day, Desborough sauntered forth upon this terrace, somewhat out of hope and heart, for he had been now some weeks on the vain quest of situations, and prepared for melancholy and tobacco. Here, at least, he told himself that he would be alone; for, like most youths, who are neither rich, nor witty, nor successful, he rather shunned than courted the society of other men. Even as he expressed the thought his eye alighted on the window of the room that looked upon the terrace; and to his surprise and annoyance, he beheld it curtained with a silken hanging. It was like his luck, he thought; his privacy was gone, he could no longer brood and sigh unwatched, he could no longer suffer his discouragement to find a vent in words or soothe himself with sentimental whistling; and in the irritation of the moment he struck his pipe upon the rail with unnecessary force. It was an old, sweet, seasoned brier-root, glossy and dark with long employment and justly dear to his fancy. What, then, was his chagrin, when the head snapped from the stem, leaped airily in space, and fell and disappeared among the lilacs of the garden?

He threw himself savagely into the garden chair, pulled out the story-paper which he had brought with him to read, tore off a fragment of the last sheet, which contains only the answers to correspondents, and set himself to roll a cigarette. He was no master of the art; again and again, the paper broke between his fingers and the tobacco showered upon the ground; and he was already on the point of angry resignation, when the window swung slowly inward, the silken curtain was thrust aside, and a lady, somewhat strangely attired, stepped forth upon the terrace.

" Señorito," said she, and there was a rich thrill in her voice, like an organ note, " Señorito, you are in difficulties. Suffer me to come to your assistance."

With the words, she took the paper and tobacco from his unresisting hands; and with a facility that, in Desborough's eyes, seemed magical, rolled and presented him a cigarette. He took it, still without a word; staring with all his eyes upon that apparition. Her face was warm and rich in colour; in shape, it was the kitten face, that piquant triangle, so mysterious, so pleasingly attractive, so rare in our more northern climates; her eyes were large, starry, and visited by changing lights; her hair was partly covered by a lace mantilla, through which her arms, bare to the shoulder, gleamed white; her figure, full and soft in all the womanly contours, was yet alive and active, light with excess of life, and slender by grace of some divine proportion.

" You do not like my cigarrito, Señor? " she asked. " Yet it is better made than yours." At that she laughed, and her laughter trilled in his ear like music; but the next moment her face fell. " I see," she cried. " It is my manner that repels you. I am too constrained, too cold. I am not," she added, with a more engaging air, " I am not the simple English maiden I appear."

" Oh! " murmured Harry, filled with inexpressible thoughts.

" In my own dear land," she pursued, " things
are differently ordered. There, I must own, a
girl is bound by many and rigorous restrictions;
little is permitted her; she learns to be distant,
she learns to appear forbidding. But here, in
free England — O glorious liberty," she cried, and
threw up her arms with a gesture of inimitable
grace — " here there are no fetters; here the
woman may dare to be herself entirely, and the
men, the chivalrous men — is it not written on
the very shield of your nation, *honi soit?* Ah,
it is hard for me to learn, hard for me to dare
to be myself. You must not judge me yet awhile;
I shall end by conquering this stiffness, I shall
end by growing English. Do I speak the language well? "

" Perfectly — oh, perfectly! " said Harry, with a
fervency of conviction worthy of a graver subject.

" Ah, then," she said, " I shall soon learn; English blood ran in my father's veins; and I have
had the advantage of some training in your expressive tongue. If I speak already without accent,
with my thorough English appearance, there is
nothing left to change except my manners."

" Oh no," said Desborough. " Oh pray not! I
— madam —— "

" I am," interrupted the lady, " the Señorita
Teresa Valdevia. The evening air grows chill.
Adios, Señorito." And before Harry could stam-
mer out a word, she had disappeared into her
room.

He stood transfixed, the cigarette still unlighted

in his hand. His thoughts had soared above tobacco, and still recalled and beautified the image
of his new acquaintance. Her voice re-echoed in
his memory; her eyes, of which he could not tell
the colour, haunted his soul. The clouds had risen
at her coming, and he beheld a new-created world.
What she was, he could not fancy, but he adored
her. Her age, he durst not estimate; fearing to
find her older than himself, and thinking sacrilege
to couple that fair favour with the thought of
mortal changes. As for her character, beauty to
the young is always good. So the poor lad lingered late upon the terrace, stealing timid glances
at the curtained window, sighing to the gold
laburnums, rapt into the country of romance; and
when at length he entered and sat down to dine,
on cold boiled mutton and a pint of ale, he feasted
on the food of gods.

Next day when he returned to the terrace, the
window was a little ajar and he enjoyed a view
of the lady's shoulder, as she sat patiently sewing
and all unconscious of his presence. On the next,
he had scarce appeared when the window opened,
and the Señorita tripped forth into the sunlight,
in a morning disorder, delicately neat, and yet
somehow foreign, tropical, and strange. In one
hand she held a packet.

"Will you try," she said, "some of my father's
tobacco — from dear Cuba? There, as I suppose
you know, all smoke, ladies as well as gentlemen.
So you need not fear to annoy me. The fragrance
will remind me of home. My home, Señor, was

by the sea." And as she uttered these few words, Desborough, for the first time in his life, realised the poetry of the great deep. "Awake or asleep, I dream of it; dear home, dear Cuba!"

"But some day," said Desborough, with an inward pang, "some day you will return?"

"Never!" she cried; "ah, never, in Heaven's name!"

"Are you then resident for life in England?" he inquired, with a strange lightening of spirit.

"You ask too much, for you ask more than I know," she answered, sadly; and then, resuming her gaiety of manner: "But you have not tried my Cuban tobacco," she said.

"Señorita," said he, shyly abashed by some shadow of coquetry in her manner, "whatever comes to me — you — I mean," he concluded, deeply flushing, "that I have no doubt the tobacco is delightful."

"Ah, Señor," she said, with almost mournful gravity, "you seemed so simple and good, and already you are trying to pay compliments — and besides," she added, brightening, with a quick, upward glance, into a smile, "you do it, oh, so badly! English gentlemen, I used to hear, could be fast friends, respectful, honest friends; could be companions, comforters, if the need arose, or champions, and yet never encroach. Do not seek to please me by copying the graces of my countrymen. Be yourself; the frank, kindly, honest English gentleman that I have heard of since my childhood and still long to meet."

Harry, much bewildered, and far from clear as
to the manners of the Cuban gentleman, strenu-
ously disclaimed the thought of plagiarism.

"Your national seriousness of bearing best becomes you, Señor," said the lady. "See!" mark-
ing a line with her dainty, slippered foot, "thus
far it shall be common ground; there, at my
window-sill, begins the scientific frontier. If you
choose, you may drive me to my forts; but if,
on the other hand, we are to be real English
friends, I may join you here when I am not too
sad; or, when I am yet more graciously inclined,
you may draw your chair beside the window and
teach me English customs, while I work. You
will find me an apt scholar, for my heart is in the
task." She laid her hand lightly upon Harry's
arm, and looked into his eyes. "Do you know,"
said she, "I am emboldened to believe that I have
already caught something of your English aplomb?
Do you not perceive a change, Señor? Slight,
perhaps, but still a change? Is my deportment
not more open, more free, more like that of the
dear 'British Miss,' than when you saw me first?"
She gave a radiant smile; withdrew her hand from
Harry's arm; and before the young man could
formulate in words the eloquent emotions that ran
riot through his brain — with an "Adios, Señor:
good-night, my English friend," she vanished from
his sight behind the curtain.

The next day, Harry consumed an ounce of
tobacco in vain upon the neutral terrace; neither
sight nor sound rewarded him, and the dinner-

hour summoned him at length from the scene of
disappointment. On the next, it rained; but nothing, neither business nor weather, neither prospec-
tive poverty nor present hardship, could now divert
the young man from the service of his lady; and
wrapped in a long ulster, with the collar raised,
he took his stand against the balustrade, awaiting
fortune, the picture of damp and discomfort to
the eye, but glowing inwardly with tender and
delightful ardours. Presently the window opened;
and the fair Cuban, with a smile imperfectly dis-
sembled, appeared upon the sill.

"Come here," she said, "here, beside my window. The small veranda gives a belt of shelter."
And she graciously handed him a folding-chair.

As he sat down, visibly aglow with shyness and
delight, a certain bulkiness in his pocket reminded
him that he was not come empty-handed.

"I have taken the liberty," said he, "of bringing you a little book. I thought of you, when I
observed it on the stall, because I saw it was in
Spanish. The man assured me it was by one of
the best authors, and quite proper." As he spoke,
he placed a little volume in her hand. Her eyes
fell as she turned the pages, and a flush rose and
died again upon her cheeks, as deep as it was fleet-
ing. "You are angry," he cried in agony. "I
have presumed!"

"No, Señor, it is not that," returned the lady.
"I"—and a flood of colour once more mounted
to her brow—"I am confused and ashamed because I have deceived you. Spanish," she began,

and paused — " Spanish is of course my native
tongue," she resumed, as though suddenly taking
courage; " and this should certainly put the highest value on your thoughtful present; but alas,
sir, of what use is it to me? And how shall I
confess to you the truth — the humiliating truth
— that I cannot read? "

As Harry's eyes met hers in undisguised amazement, the fair Cuban seemed to shrink before his
gaze. " Read? " repeated Harry. " You? "

She pushed the window still more widely open
with a large and noble gesture. " Enter, Señor,"
said she. " The time has come to which I have
long looked forward, not without alarm; when I
must either fear to lose your friendship, or tell
you without disguise the story of my life."

It was with a sentiment bordering on devotion,
that Harry passed the window. A semi-barbarous
delight in form and colour had presided over the
studied disorder of the room in which he found
himself. It was filled with dainty stuffs, furs and
rugs and scarves of brilliant hues, and set with
elegant and curious trifles — fans on the mantel-
shelf, an antique lamp upon a bracket, and on the
table a silver-mounted bowl of cocoa-nut about
half full of unset jewels. The fair Cuban, herself a gem of colour and the fit masterpiece for
that rich frame, motioned Harry to a seat, and
sinking herself into another, thus began her
history.

STORY OF THE FAIR CUBAN

I AM not what I seem. My father drew his descent, on the one hand, from grandees of Spain, and on the other, through the maternal line, from the patriot Bruce. My mother, too, was the descendant of a line of kings; but, alas! these kings were African. She was fair as the day: fairer than I, for I inherited a darker strain of blood from the veins of my European father; her mind was noble, her manners queenly and accomplished; and seeing her more than the equal of her neighbours and surrounded by the most considerate affection and respect, I grew up to adore her, and when the time came, received her last sigh upon my lips, still ignorant that she was a slave and, alas! my father's mistress. Her death, which befell me in my sixteenth year, was the first sorrow I had known: it left our home bereaved of its attractions, cast a shade of melancholy on my youth, and wrought in my father a tragic and durable change. Months went by; with the elasticity of my years, I regained some of the simple mirth that had before distinguished me; the plantation smiled with fresh crops; the negroes on the estate had already forgotten my mother and transferred their simple obedience to myself; but still the cloud only darkened on the

brows of Señor Valdevia. His absences from
home had been frequent even in the old days, for
he did business in precious gems in the city of
Havana; they now became almost continuous; and
when he returned, it was but for the night and
with the manner of a man crushed down by ad-
verse fortune.

The place where I was born and passed my days
was an isle set in the Caribbean Sea, some half-
hour's rowing from the coast of Cuba. It was
steep, rugged, and, except for my father's family
and plantation, uninhabited and left to nature. The
house, a low building surrounded by spacious ve-
randas, stood upon a rise of ground and looked
across the sea to Cuba. The breezes blew about
it gratefully, fanned us as we lay swinging in
our silken hammocks, and tossed the boughs and
flowers of the magnolia. Behind and to the left,
the quarter of the negroes and the waving fields
of the plantation covered an eighth part of the
surface of the isle. On the right and closely
bordering on the garden lay a vast and deadly
swamp, densely covered with wood, breathing
fever, dotted with profound sloughs, and inhabited by poisonous oysters, man-eating crabs,
snakes, alligators, and sickly fishes. In the recesses of that jungle none could penetrate but
those of African descent; an invisible, unconquerable foe lay there in wait for the European;
and the air was death.

One morning (from which I must date the beginning of my ruinous misfortune) I left my room

a little after day, for in that warm climate all are early risers, and found not a servant to attend upon my wants. I made the circuit of the house, still calling: and my surprise had almost changed into alarm, when coming at last into a large verandaed court, I found it thronged with negroes. Even then, even when I was amongst them, not one turned or paid the least regard to my arrival. They had eyes and ears for but one person: a woman richly and tastefully attired; of elegant carriage, and a musical speech; not so much old in years, as worn and marred by self-indulgence: her face, which was still attractive, stamped with the most cruel passions, her eye burning with the greed of evil. It was not from her appearance, I believe, but from some emanation of her soul, that I recoiled in a kind of fainting terror; as we hear of plants that blight and snakes that fascinate, the woman shocked and daunted me. But I was of a brave nature; trod the weakness down; and forcing my way through the slaves, who fell back before me in embarrassment, as though in the presence of rival mistresses, I asked, in imperious tones: " Who is this person? "

A girl slave, to whom I had been kind, whispered in my ear to have a care, for that was Madam Mendizabal; but the name was new to me.

In the meanwhile the woman, applying a pair of glasses to her eyes, studied me with insolent particularity from head to foot.

" Young woman," said she, at last, " I have had a great experience in refractory servants, and take a pride in breaking them. You really tempt me; and if I had not other affairs, and these of more importance, on my hand, I should certainly buy you at your father's sale."

"Madam — " I began, but my voice failed me.

"Is it possible that you do not know your position?" she returned with a hateful laugh. "How comical! Positively, I must buy her. Accomplishments, I suppose?" she added, turning to the servants.

Several assured her that the young mistress had been brought up like any lady, for so it seemed in their inexperience.

"She would do very well for my place of business in Havana," said the Señora Mendizabal, once more studying me through her glasses; "and I should take a pleasure," she pursued, more directly addressing myself, "in bringing you acquainted with a whip." And she smiled at me with a savoury lust of cruelty upon her face.

At this I found expression. Calling by name upon the servants, I bade them turn this woman from the house, fetch her to the boat, and set her back upon the mainland. But with one voice, they protested that they durst not obey, coming close about me, pleading and beseeching me to be more wise; and when I insisted, rising higher in passion and speaking of this foul intruder in the terms she had deserved, they fell back from me as from one who had blasphemed. A superstitious reverence plainly encircled the stranger; I could read it in their changed demeanour, and in the paleness that prevailed upon the natural colour of their faces; and their fear perhaps reacted on myself. I looked again at Madam Mendizabal. She stood perfectly composed, watching my face through her glasses with a smile of scorn; and at the sight of her assured superiority to all my threats, a cry broke from my lips, a cry of rage, fear, and despair, and I fled from the veranda and the house.

I ran I knew not where, but it was toward the beach. As I went, my head whirled; so strange, so sudden, were these events and insults. Who was she? what in Heaven's name the power she wielded over my obedient negroes? Why had she addressed me as a slave? why spoken of my father's sale? To all these tumultuary questions I could find no answer; and in the turmoil of my mind, nothing was plain except the hateful, leering image of the woman.

I was still running, mad with fear and anger, when I saw my father coming to meet me from the landing-place; and with a cry that I thought would have killed me, leaped into his arms and broke into a passion of sobs and tears upon his bosom. He made me sit down below a tall palmetto that grew not far off, comforted me, but with some abstraction in his voice, and as soon as I regained the least command upon my feelings, asked me, not without harshness, what this grief betokened. I was surprised by his tone into a still greater measure of composure; and in firm tones, though still interrupted by sobs, I told him there was a stranger in the island, at which I thought he started and turned pale; that the servants would not obey me; that the stranger's name was Madam Mendizabal, and at that he seemed to me both troubled and relieved; that she had insulted me, treated me as a slave (and here my father's brow began to darken), threatened to buy me at a sale, and questioned my own servants before my face; and that, at last, finding myself quite helpless and exposed to these intolerable liberties, I had fled from the house in terror, indignation, and amazement.

"Teresa," said my father, with singular gravity of voice, "I must make to-day a call upon your courage; much must be told you, there is much that you must do to help me; and my daughter must prove herself a woman by her spirit. As for this Mendizabal, what shall I say? or how am I to tell you what she is? Twenty years ago she was the loveliest of slaves; to-day she is what you see her — prematurely old, disgraced by the practice of every vice and every nefarious industry, but free, rich, married, they say, to some reputable man, whom may Heaven assist! and exercising among her ancient mates, the slaves of Cuba, an influence as unbounded as its reason is mysterious. Horrible rites, it is supposed, cement her empire: the rites of Hoodoo. Be that as it may, I would have you dismiss the thought of this incomparable witch; it is not from her that danger threatens us, and into her hands, I make bold to promise, you shall never fall."

"Father!" I cried. "Fall? Was there any truth, then, in her words? Am I — oh, father, tell me plain; I can bear anything but this suspense."

"I will tell you," he replied, "with merciful bluntness. Your mother was a slave; it was my design, so soon as I had saved a competence, to sail to the free land of Britain, where the law would suffer me to marry her: a design too long procrastinated; for death at the last moment intervened. You will now understand the heaviness with which your mother's memory hangs about my neck."

I cried out aloud, in pity for my parents; and in seeking to console the survivor, I forgot myself.

"It matters not," resumed my father. "What I have left undone can never be repaired, and I must bear the penalty of my remorse. But, Teresa, with so cutting a reminder of the evils of delay, I set myself at once to do what was still possible: to liberate yourself."

I began to break forth in thanks, but he checked me with a sombre roughness.

"Your mother's illness," he resumed, "had engaged too great a portion of my time; my business in the city had lain too long at the mercy of ignorant underlings; my head, my taste, my unequalled knowledge of the more precious stones, that art by which I can distinguish, even on the darkest night, a sapphire from a ruby, and tell at a glance in what quarter of the earth a gem was disinterred — all these had been too long ab-

sent from the conduct of affairs. Teresa, I was
insolvent."

"What matters that?" I cried. "What matters poverty, if we be left together with our love
and sacred memories?"

"You do not comprehend," he said gloomily.
"Slave, as you are, young — alas! scarce more
than child! — accomplished, beautiful with the
most touching beauty, innocent as an angel — all
these qualities that should disarm the very wolves
and crocodiles, are, in the eyes of those to whom
I stand indebted, commodities to buy and sell.
You are a chattel; a marketable thing; and worth
— heavens, that I should say such words! — worth
money. Do you begin to see? If I were to give
you freedom, I should defraud my creditors; the
manumission would be certainly annulled; you
would be still a slave, and I a criminal."

I caught his hand in mine, kissed it, and moaned
in pity for myself, in sympathy for my father.

"How I have toiled," he continued, "how I
have dared and striven to repair my losses, Heaven
has beheld and will remember. Its blessing was
denied to my endeavours, or, as I please myself
by thinking, but delayed to descend upon my
daughter's head. At length, all hope was at an
end; I was ruined beyond retrieve; a heavy debt
fell due upon the morrow, which I could not
meet; I should be declared a bankrupt, and my
goods, my lands, my jewels that I so much loved,
my slaves whom I have spoiled and rendered
happy, and oh! tenfold worse, you, my beloved

daughter, would be sold and pass into the hands of ignorant and greedy traffickers. Too long, I saw, had I accepted and profited by this great crime of slavery; but was my daughter, my innocent, unsullied daughter, was *she* to pay the price? I cried out — no! — I took Heaven to witness my temptation; I caught up this bag and fled. Close upon my track are the pursuers; perhaps to-morrow, they will land upon this isle, sacred to the memory of the dear soul that bore you, to consign your father to an ignominious prison, and yourself to slavery and dishonour. We have not many hours before us. Off the north coast of our isle, by strange good fortune, an English yacht has for some days been hovering. It belongs to Sir George Greville, whom I slightly know, to whom ere now I have rendered unusual services, and who will not refuse to help in our escape. Or if he did, if his gratitude were in default, I have the power to force him. For what does it mean, my child — what means this Englishman, who hangs for years upon the shores of Cuba, and returns from every trip with new and valuable gems!"

"He may have found a mine," I hazarded.

"So he declares," returned my father; "but the strange gift I have received from nature, easily transpierced the fable. He brought me diamonds only, which I bought, at first, in innocence; at a second glance, I started; for of these stones, my child, some had first seen the day in Africa, some in Brazil; while others, from their peculiar water

and rude workmanship, I divined to be the spoil
of ancient temples. Thus put upon the scent, I
made inquiries: oh, he is cunning, but I was cun-
ninger than he. He visited, I found, the shop of
every jeweller in town; to one he came with rubies,
to one with emeralds, to one with precious beryl;
to all, with this same story of the mine. But in
what mine, what rich epitome of the earth's surface, were there conjoined the rubies of Ispahan,
the pearls of Coromandel, and the diamonds of
Golconda? No, child, that man, for all his yacht
and title, that man must fear and must obey me.
To-night, then, as soon as it is dark, we must
take our way through the swamp by the path
which I shall presently show you; thence, across
the highlands of the isle, a track is blazed, which
shall conduct us to the haven on the north; and
close by the yacht is riding. Should my pursuers
come before the hour at which I look to see them,
they will still arrive too late; a trusty man at-
tends on the mainland; as soon as they appear,
we shall behold, if it be dark, the redness of a
fire, if it be day, a pillar of smoke, on the oppos-
ing headland; and thus warned, we shall have
time to put the swamp between ourselves and
danger. Meantime, I would conceal this bag; I
would, before all things, be seen to arrive at the
house with empty hands; a blabbing slave might
else undo us. For see!" he added; and holding
up the bag, which he had already shown me, he
poured into my lap a shower of unmounted jewels,
brighter than flowers, of every size and colour,

and catching, as they fell, upon a million dainty facets, the ardour of the sun.

I could not restrain a cry of admiration.

"Even in your ignorant eyes," pursued my father, "they command respect. Yet what are they but pebbles, passive to the tool, cold as death? Ingrate!" he cried. "Each one of these — miracles of nature's patience, conceived out of the dust in centuries of microscopical activity — each one is, for you and me, a year of life, liberty, and mutual affection. How, then, should I cherish them? and why do I delay to place them beyond reach? Teresa, follow me."

He rose to his feet and led me to the borders of the great jungle, where they overhung, in a wall of poisonous and dusky foliage, the declivity of the hill on which my father's house stood planted. For some while he skirted, with attentive eyes, the margin of the thicket. Then, seeming to recognise some mark, for his countenance became immediately lightened of thought, he paused and addressed me.

"Here," said he, "is the entrance of the secret path that I have mentioned, and here you shall await me. I but pass some hundreds of yards into the swamp to bury my poor treasure; as soon as that is safe, I will return."

It was in vain that I sought to dissuade him, urging the dangers of the place; in vain that I begged to be allowed to follow, pleading the black blood that I now knew to circulate in my veins. To all my appeals he turned a deaf ear, and, bending back a portion of the screen of bushes, disappeared into the pestilential silence of the swamp.

At the end of a full hour the bushes were once more thrust aside, and my father stepped from out the thicket and paused and almost staggered in the first shock of the blinding sunlight. His face was of a singular dusky red; and yet for all the heat of the tropical noon, he did not seem to sweat.

" You are tired," I cried, springing to meet him. " You are ill."

" I am tired," he replied; " the air in that jungle stifles one; my eyes, besides, have grown accustomed to its gloom, and the strong sunshine pierces them like knives. A moment, Teresa, give me but a moment. All shall yet be well. I have buried the hoard under a cypress, immediately beyond the bayou, on the left-hand margin of the path; beautiful, bright things, they now lie whelmed in slime; you shall find them there, if needful. But come, let us to the house; it is time to eat against our journey of the night; to eat and then to sleep, my poor Teresa; then to sleep." And he looked upon me out of bloodshot eyes, shaking his head as if in pity.

We went hurriedly, for he kept murmuring that he had been gone too long and that the servants might suspect; passed through the airy stretch of the veranda, and came at length into the grateful twilight of the shuttered house. The meal was spread; the house servants, already informed by the boatmen of the master's return, were all back at their posts, and terrified, as I could see, to face me. My father still murmuring of haste with weary and feverish pertinacity, I hurried at once to take my place at table; but I had no sooner left his arm than he paused and thrust forth both his hands with a strange gesture of groping. " How is this? " he cried, in a sharp, inhuman voice. " Am I blind? " I ran to him and tried to lead him to the table; but he resisted and stood stiffly where he was, opening and shutting his jaws, as if in a painful effort after breath. Then suddenly he raised both hands to his temples, cried out, " My head, my head! " and reeled and fell against the wall.

I knew too well what it must be. I turned and begged the servants to relieve him. But they, with one accord, denied the possibility of hope; the master had gone into the swamp, they said, the master must die; all help was idle. Why should I dwell upon his sufferings? I had him carried to a bed, and watched beside him. He lay still, and at times ground his teeth, and talked at times unintelligibly, only that one word of hurry, hurry, coming distinctly to my ears, and telling me that, even in the last struggle with the powers of death, his mind was still tortured by his daughter's peril. The sun had gone down, the darkness had fallen, when I perceived that I was alone on this unhappy earth. What thought had I of flight, of safety, of the impending dangers of my situation? Beside the body of my last friend, I had forgotten all except the natural pangs of my bereavement.

The sun was some four hours above the eastern line, when I was called to a knowledge of the things of earth, by the entrance of the slave-girl to whom I have already referred. The poor soul was indeed devotedly attached to me; and it was with streaming tears that she broke to me the import of her coming. With the first light of dawn a boat had reached our landing-place, and set on shore upon our isle (till now so fortunate) a party of officers bearing a warrant to arrest my father's person, and a man of a gross body and low manners, who declared the island, the plantation, and all its human chattels, to be now his own. " I think," said my slave-girl, " he must be a politician or some very powerful sorcerer; for Madam Mendizabal had no sooner seen them coming, than she took to the woods."

" Fool," said I, " it was the officers she feared; and at any rate why does that beldam still dare to pollute the island with her presence? And oh, Cora," I exclaimed, remembering my grief, " what matter all these troubles to an orphan? "

" Mistress," said she, " I must remind you of two things. Never speak as you do now of Madam Mendizabal; or never to a person of colour; for she is the most powerful woman in this world, and her real name even, if one durst pronounce it, were a spell to raise the dead. And whatever you do, speak no more of her to your unhappy Cora; for though it is possible she may be afraid of the police (and indeed I think that I have heard that she is in hiding) and though I know that you will laugh and not believe, yet it is true, and proved, and known that she hears every word that people utter in this whole, vast world; and your poor Cora is already deep enough in her black books. She looks at me, mistress, till my blood turns ice. That is the first I had to say; and now for the second: do, pray, for Heaven's sake, bear in mind that you are no longer the poor Señor's daughter. He is gone, dear gentleman; and now you are no more than a common slave-girl like myself. The man to whom you belong calls for you; oh, my dear mistress, go at once! With your youth and beauty, you may still, if you are winning and obedient, secure yourself an easy life."

For a moment I looked on the creature with the indignation you may conceive; the next it was gone: she did but speak after her kind, as the bird sings or cattle bellow. "Go," said I. "Go, Cora. I thank you for your kind intentions. Leave me alone one moment with my dead father; and tell this man that I will come at once."

She went; and I, turning to the bed of death, addressed to those deaf ears the last appeal and defence of my beleaguered innocence. "Father," I said, "it was your last thought, even in the pangs of dissolution, that your daughter should escape disgrace. Here, at your side, I swear to you that purpose shall be carried out; by what means, I know not; by crime, if need be; and Heaven forgive both you and me and our oppressors, and Heaven help my helplessness!" There-

upon I felt strengthened as by long repose; stepped
to the mirror, ay, even in that chamber of the
dead; hastily arranged my hair, refreshed my tear-
worn eyes, breathed a dumb farewell to the origi-
nator of my days and sorrows; and composing
my features to a smile, went forth to meet my
master.

He was in a great, hot bustle, reviewing that
house, once ours, to which he had but now succeeded; a corpulent, sanguine man of middle age,
sensual, vulgar, humourous, and, if I judged
rightly, not ill disposed by nature. But the sparkle
that came into his eye as he observed me enter,
warned me to expect the worst.

"Is this your late mistress?" he inquired of the
slaves; and when he had learned it was so, instantly dismissed them. "Now, my dear," said
he, "I am a plain man: none of your damned
Spaniards, but a true blue, hard-working, honest
Englishman. My name is Caulder."

"Thank you, sir," said I, and curtseyed very
smartly as I had seen the servants.

"Come," said he, "this is better than I had
expected; and if you choose to be dutiful in the
station to which it has pleased God to call you,
you will find me a very kind old fellow. I like
your looks," he added, calling me by my name,
which he scandalously mispronounced. "Is your
hair all your own?" he then inquired with a certain sharpness, and coming up to me, as though
I were a horse, he grossly satisfied his doubts. I
was all one flame from head to foot, but I con-

tained my righteous anger and submitted. " That is very well," he continued, chucking me good-humouredly under the chin. " You will have no cause to regret coming to old Caulder, eh? But that is by the way. What is more to the point is this: your late master was a most dishonest rogue and levanted with some valuable property that belonged of rights to me. Now, considering your relation to him, I regard you as the likeliest person to know what has become of it; and I warn you, before you answer, that my whole future kindness will depend upon your honesty. I am an honest man myself, and expect the same in my servants."

" Do you mean the jewels?" said I, sinking my voice into a whisper.

" That is just precisely what I do," said he, and chuckled.

" Hush!" said I.

" Hush?" he repeated. " And why hush? I am on my own place, I would have you to know, and surrounded by my own lawful servants."

" Are the officers gone?" I asked; and oh, how my hopes hung upon the answer!

" They are," said he, looking somewhat discon-certed. " Why do you ask?"

" I wish you had kept them," I answered, sol-emnly enough, although my heart at that same moment leaped with exultation. " Master, I must not conceal from you the truth. The servants on this estate are in a dangerous condition, and mu-tiny has long been brewing."

"Why," he cried, "I never saw a milder-looking lot of niggers in my life." But for all that he turned somewhat pale.

"Did they tell you," I continued, "that Madam Mendizabal is on the island? that, since her coming, they obey none but her? that if, this morning, they have received you with even decent civility, it was only by her orders — issued with what after-thought I leave you to consider?"

"Madam Jezebel?" said he. "Well, she is a dangerous devil; the police are after her, besides, for a whole series of murders; but after all, what then? To be sure, she has a great influence with you coloured folk. But what in fortune's name can be her errand here?"

"The jewels," I replied. "Ah, sir, had you seen that treasure, sapphire and emerald and opal, and the golden topaz, and rubies, red as the sunset — of what incalculable worth, of what un-equalled beauty to the eye! — had you seen it, as I have, and alas! as *she* has — you would un-derstand and tremble at your danger."

"She has seen them!" he cried, and I could see, by his face, that my audacity was justified by its success.

I caught his hand in mine. "My master," said I, "I am now yours; it is my duty, it should be my pleasure, to defend your interests and life. Hear my advice then; and, I conjure you, be guided by prudence. Follow me privily; let none see where we are going; I will lead you to the place where the treasure has been buried; that once disinterred, let us make straight for the boat, escape to the mainland, and not return to this dangerous isle without the countenance of soldiers."

What free man in a free land would have credited so sudden a devotion? But this oppressor, through the very arts and sophistries he had abused, to quiet the rebellion of his conscience and to convince himself that slavery was natural, fell like a child into the trap I laid for him. He praised and thanked me; told me I had all the qualities he valued in a servant; and when he had questioned me further as to the nature and value of the treasure, and I had once more artfully inflamed his greed, bade me without delay proceed to carry out my plan of action.

From a shed in the garden, I took a pick and a shovel; and thence, by devious paths among the magnolias, led my master to the entrance of the swamp. I walked first, carrying, as I was now in duty bound, the tools, and glancing continually behind me, lest we should be spied upon and followed. When we were come as far as the beginning of the path, it flashed into my mind I had forgotten meat; and leaving Mr. Caulder in the shadow of a tree, I returned alone to the house for a basket of provisions. Were they for him? I asked myself. And a voice within me answered, No. While we were face to face, while I still saw before my eyes the man to whom I belonged as the hand belongs to the body, my indignation held me bravely up. But now that I was alone, I conceived a sickness at myself and my designs that I could scarce endure; I longed to throw myself at his feet, avow my intended treachery, and warn him from that pestilential swamp, to which I was decoying him to die; but my vow to my dead father, my duty to my innocent youth, prevailed against these scruples; and though my face was pale and must have reflected the horror that oppressed my spirits, it was with a firm step that I returned to the borders of the swamp, and with smiling lips bade him rise and follow me.

The path on which we now entered was cut like a tunnel, through the living jungle. On either hand and overhead, the mass of foliage was continuously joined; the day sparingly filtered through the depth of superimpending wood; and the air was hot like steam, and heavy with vegetable odours, and lay like a load upon the lungs and brain. Underfoot, a great depth of mould received our silent footprints; on each side mimosas, as tall as a man, shrank from my passing skirts with a continuous hissing rustle; and but for these sentient vegetables, all in that den of pestilence was motionless and noiseless.

We had gone but a little way in, when Mr. Caulder was seized with sudden nausea, and must sit down a moment on the path. My heart yearned, as I beheld him; and I seriously begged the doomed mortal to return upon his steps. What were a few jewels in the scales with life? I asked. But no, he said; that witch Madam Jezebel would find them out; he was an honest man, and would not stand to be defrauded, and so forth, panting, the

while, like a sick dog. Presently he got to his
feet again, protesting he had conquered his uneasiness; but as we again began to go forward,
I saw in his changed countenance the first approach of death.

"Master," said I, "you look pale, deathly pale;
your pallor fills me with dread. Your eyes are
bloodshot; they are red like the rubies that we
seek."

"Wench," he cried, "look before you; look
at your steps. I declare to Heaven, if you annoy
me once again by looking back, I shall remind
you of the change in your position."

A little after, I observed a worm upon the
ground, and told, in a whisper, that its touch
was death. Presently a great green serpent, vivid
as the grass in spring, wound rapidly across the
path; and once again I paused and looked back
at my companion with a horror in my eyes. "The
coffin snake," said I, "the snake that dogs its
victim like a hound."

But he was not to be dissuaded. "I am an old
traveller," said he. "This is a foul jungle indeed;
but we shall soon be at an end."

"Ay," said I, looking at him with a strange
smile, "what end?"

Thereupon he laughed again and again, but not
very heartily; and then, perceiving that the path
began to widen and grow higher, "There!" said
he. "What did I tell you? We are past the
worst."

Indeed, we had now come to the bayou, which

was in that place very narrow and bridged across by a fallen trunk; but on either hand we could see it broaden out, under a cavern of great arms of trees and hanging creepers; sluggish, putrid, of a horrible and sickly stench, floated on by the flat heads of alligators, and its banks alive with scarlet crabs.

"If we fall from that unsteady bridge," said I, "see, where the cayman lies ready to devour us! If, by the least divergence from the path, we should be snared in a morass, see, where those myriads of scarlet vermin scour the border of the thicket! Once helpless, how they would swarm together to the assault! What could a man do against a thousand of such mailed assailants? And what a death were that, to perish alive under their claws!"

"Are you mad, girl?" he cried. "I bid you be silent and lead on."

Again I looked upon him, half relenting; and at that he raised the stick that was in his hand and cruelly struck me on the face. "Lead on!" he cried again. "Must I be all day, catching my death in this vile slough, and all for a prating slave-girl?"

I took the blow in silence, I took it smiling; but the blood welled back upon my heart. Something, I know not what, fell at that moment with a dull plunge in the waters of the lagoon, and I told myself that it was my pity that had fallen.

On the further side, to which we now hastily

scrambled, the wood was not so dense, the web
of creepers not so solidly convolved. It was possible, here and there, to mark a patch of somewhat
brighter daylight, or to distinguish, through the
lighter web of parasites, the proportions of some
soaring tree. The cypress on the left stood very
visibly forth upon the edge of such a clearing;
the path in that place widened broadly; and there
was a patch of open ground, beset with horrible
ant-heaps, thick with their artificers. I laid down
the tools and basket by the cypress root, where
they were instantly blackened over with the
crawling ants; and looked once more in the
face of my unconscious victim. Mosquitoes and
foul flies wove so close a veil between us that
his features were obscured; and the sound of
their flight was like the turning of a mighty
wheel.

"Here," I said, "is the spot. I cannot dig, for
I have not learned to use such instruments; but, for
your own sake, I beseech you to be swift in what
you do."

He had sunk once more upon the ground, panting like a fish; and I saw rising in his face the same
dusky flush that had mantled on my father's. "I
feel ill," he gasped, "horribly ill; the swamp turns
around me; the drone of these carrion flies con-
founds me. Have you not wine?"

I gave him a glass, and he drank greedily. "It is
for you to think," said I, "if you should further
persevere. The swamp has an ill name." And at
the word I ominously nodded.

" Give me the pick," said he. " Where are the jewels buried? "

I told him vaguely; and in the sweltering heat and closeness, and dim twilight of the jungle, he began to wield the pickaxe, swinging it overhead with the vigour of a healthy man. At first, there broke forth upon him a strong sweat, that made his face to shine, and in which the reedy insects settled thickly.

" To sweat in such a place," said I. " Oh, master, is this wise? Fever is drunk in through open pores."

" What do you mean? " he screamed, pausing with the pick buried in the soil. " Do you seek to drive me mad? Do you think I do not understand the danger that I run? "

" That is all I want," said I; " I only wish you to be swift." And then, my mind flitting to my father's death-bed, I began to murmur, scarce above my breath, the same vain repetition of words, Hurry, hurry, hurry.

Presently, to my surprise, the treasure-seeker took them up; and while he still wielded the pick, but now with staggering and uncertain blows, repeated to himself, as it were the burden of a song, " Hurry, hurry, hurry "; and then again, " There is no time to lose; the marsh has an ill name, ill name "; and then back to " Hurry, hurry, hurry," with a dreadful, mechanical, hurried, and yet wearied utterance, as a sick man rolls upon his pillow. The sweat had disappeared; he was now dry, but all that I could see of him, of the same dull

brick red. Presently his pick unearthed the bag
of jewels; but he did not observe it, and continued
hewing the soil.

"Master," said I, "there is the treasure."

He seemed to waken from a dream. "Where?"
he cried; and then, seeing it before his eyes, "Can
this be possible?" he added. "I must be light-
headed. Girl," he cried suddenly, with the same
screaming tone of voice that I had once before observed, "what is wrong? is this swamp accursed?"

"It is a grave," I answered. "You will not go
out alive; and as for me, my life is in God's
hands."

He fell upon the ground like a man struck by a
blow, but whether from the effect of my words, or
from sudden seizure of the malady, I cannot tell.
Pretty soon, he raised his head. "You have
brought me here to die," he said; "at the risk of
your own days, you have condemned me. Why?"

"To save my honour," I replied. "Bear me out
that I have warned you. Greed of these pebbles,
and not I, has been your undoer."

He took out his revolver and handed it to me.
"You see," he said, "I could have killed you even
yet. But I am dying, as you say; nothing could
save me; and my bill is long enough already. Dear
me, dear me," he said, looking in my face with a
curious, puzzled, and pathetic look, like a dull child
at school, "if there be a judgment afterwards, my
bill is long enough."

At that, I broke into a passion of weeping,
crawled at his feet, kissed his hands, begged his

forgiveness, put the pistol back into his grasp and besought him to avenge his death; for indeed, if with my life I could have brought back his, I had not balanced at the cost. But he was determined, the poor soul, that I should yet more bitterly regret my act.

"I have nothing to forgive," said he. "Dear Heaven, what a thing is an old fool! I thought, upon my word, you had taken quite a fancy to me."

He was seized, at the same time, with a dreadful, swimming dizziness, clung to me like a child, and called upon the name of some woman. Presently this spasm, which I watched with choking tears, lessened and died away; and he came again to the full possession of his mind. "I must write my will," he said. "Get out my pocket-book." I did so, and he wrote hurriedly on one page with a pencil. "Do not let my son know," he said, "he is a cruel dog, is my son Philip; do not let him know how you have paid me out"; and then all of a sudden, "God," he cried, "I am blind," and clapped both hands before his eyes; and then again, and in a groaning whisper, "Don't leave me to the crabs!" I swore I would be true to him so long as a pulse stirred; and I redeemed my promise. I sat there and watched him, as I had watched my father, but with what different, with what appalling thoughts! Through the long afternoon he gradually sank. All that while I fought an up-hill battle to shield him from the swarms of ants and the clouds of mosquitoes: the prisoner of my crime. The night fell, the roar of insects instantly redoubled in the dark arcades of the swamp; and still I was not sure that he had breathed his last. At length, the flesh of his hand, which I yet held in mine, grew chill between my fingers, and I knew that I was free.

I took his pocket-book and the revolver, being resolved rather to die than to be captured, and laden besides with the basket and the bag of gems, set forward towards the north. The swamp, at that hour of the night, was filled with a continuous din; animals and insects of all kinds, and all inimical to life, contributing their parts. Yet in the midst of this turmoil of sound, I walked as though my eyes were bandaged, beholding nothing. The soil sank under my foot, with a horrid, slippery consistence, as though I were walking among toads; the touch of the thick wall of foliage, by which alone I guided myself, affrighted me like the touch of serpents; the darkness checked my breathing like a gag; indeed, I have never suffered such extremes of fear as during that nocturnal walk, nor have I ever known a more sensible relief than when I found the path beginning to mount and to grow firmer under foot, and saw, although still some way in front of me, the silver brightness of the moon.

Presently, I had crossed the last of the jungle, and come forth amongst noble and lofty woods, clean rock, the clean, dry dust, the aromatic smell of mountain plants that had been baked all day in sunlight, and the expressive silence of the night. My negro blood had carried me unhurt across that

reeking and pestiferous morass; by mere good fortune, I had escaped the crawling and stinging vermin with which it was alive; and I had now before
me the easier portion of my enterprise, to cross the
isle and to make good my arrival at the haven and
my acceptance on the English yacht. It was impossible by night to follow such a track as my
father had described; and I was casting about for
any landmark, and, in my ignorance, vainly consulting the disposition of the stars, when there fell
upon my ear, from somewhere far in front, the
sound of many voices hurriedly singing.

I scarce knew upon what grounds I acted; but
I shaped my steps in the direction of that sound;
and in a quarter of an hour's walking came unperceived to the margin of an open glade. It was
lighted by the strong moon and by the flames of
a fire. In the midst, there stood a little low and
rude building, surmounted by a cross: a chapel,
as I then remembered to have heard, long since desecrated and given over to the rites of Hoodoo.
Hard by the steps of entrance was a black mass,
continually agitated and stirring to and fro as if
with inarticulate life; and this I presently perceived to be a heap of cocks, hares, dogs, and other
birds and animals, still struggling, but helplessly
tethered and cruelly tossed one upon another.
Both the fire and the chapel were surrounded by a
ring of kneeling Africans, both men and women.
Now they would raise their palms half closed to
heaven, with a peculiar, passionate gesture of sup-
plication; now they would bow their heads and

spread their hands before them on the ground. As
the double movement passed and repassed along
the line, the heads kept rising and falling, like
waves upon the sea; and still, as if in time to these
gesticulations, the hurried chant continued. I
stood spell-bound, knowing that my life depended
by a hair, knowing that I had stumbled on a celebration of the rites of Hoodoo.

Presently, the door of the chapel opened and
there came forth a tall negro, entirely nude, and
bearing in his hand the sacrificial knife. He was
followed by an apparition still more strange and
shocking: Madam Mendizabal, naked also, and
carrying in both hands and raised to the level of
her face, an open basket of wicker. It was filled
with coiling snakes; and these, as she stood there
with the uplifted basket, shot through the osier
grating and curled about her arms. At the sight
of this, the fervour of the crowd seemed to swell
suddenly higher; and the chant rose in pitch and
grew more irregular in time and accent. Then, at
a sign from the tall negro, where he stood, motionless and smiling, in the moon and firelight, the
singing died away, and there began the second
stage of this barbarous and bloody celebration.
From different parts of the ring, one after another,
man or woman, ran forth into the midst; ducked,
with that same gesture of the thrown-up hand,
before the priestess and her snakes; and with
various adjurations, uttered aloud the blackest
wishes of the heart. Death and disease were the
favours usually invoked: the death or the disease

of enemies or rivals; some calling down these plagues upon the nearest of their own blood, and one, to whom I swear I had been never less than kind, invoking them upon myself. At each petition, the tall negro, still smiling, picked up some bird or animal from the heaving mass upon his left, slew it with the knife, and tossed its body on the ground. At length, it seemed, it reached the turn of the high-priestess. She set down the basket on the steps, moved into the centre of the ring, grovelled in the dust before the reptiles, and still grovelling lifted up her voice, between speech and singing, and with so great, with so insane fervour of excitement, as struck a sort of horror through my blood.

" Power," she began, " whose name we do not utter; power that is neither good nor evil, but below them both; stronger than good, greater than evil — all my life long I have adored and served thee. Who has shed blood upon thine altars? whose voice is broken with the singing of thy praises? whose limbs are faint before their age with leaping in thy revels? Who has slain the child of her body? I," she cried, " I, Metamnbogu! By my own name, I name myself. I tear away the veil. I would be served or perish. Hear me, slime of the fat swamp, blackness of the thunder, venom of the serpent's udder — hear or slay me! I would have two things, O shapeless one, O horror of emptiness — two things, or die! The blood of my white-faced husband; oh! give me that; he is the enemy of Hoodoo; give me his blood! And yet another, O racer of the blind winds, O germinator in the ruins of the dead, O root of life, root of corruption! I grow old, I grow hideous; I am known, I am hunted for my life: let thy servant then lay by this outworn body; let thy chief priestess turn again to the blossom of her days, and be a girl once more, and the desired of all men, even as in the past! And, O lord and master, as I here ask a marvel not yet wrought since we were torn from the old land, have I not prepared the sacrifice in which thy soul delighteth — the kid without the horns?"

Even as she uttered the words, there was a great rumour of joy through all the circle of the worshippers; it rose, and fell, and rose again; and swelled at last into rapture, when the tall negro, who had stepped an instant into the chapel, reappeared before the door, carrying in his arms the body of the slave-girl, Cora. I know not if I saw what followed. When next my mind awoke to a clear knowledge, Cora was laid upon the steps before the serpents; the negro with the knife stood over her; the knife rose, and at this I screamed out in my great horror, bidding them, in God's name, to pause.

A stillness fell upon the mob of cannibals. A moment more, and they must have thrown off this stupor, and I infallibly have perished. But Heaven had designed to save me. The silence of these wretched men was not yet broken, when there arose, in the empty night, a sound louder than the roar of any European tempest, swifter to travel

than the wings of any Eastern wind. Blackness
ingulfed the world: blackness, stabbed across from
every side by intricate and blinding lightning.
Almost in the same second, at one world-swallow-
ing stride, the heart of the tornado reached the
clearing. I heard an agonising crash, and the light
of my reason was overwhelmed.

When I recovered consciousness, the day was
come. I was unhurt; the trees close about me
had not lost a bough; and I might have thought
at first that the tornado was a feature in a dream.
It was otherwise indeed; for when I looked abroad,
I perceived I had escaped destruction by a hand's-
breadth. Right through the forest, which here
covered hill and dale, the storm had ploughed a
lane of ruin. On either hand, the trees waved
uninjured in the air of the morning; but in the
forthright course of its advance, the hurricane had
left no trophy standing. Everything, in that line
tree, man, or animal, the desecrated chapel and
the votaries of Hoodoo, had been subverted and
destroyed in that brief spasm of anger of the
powers of air. Everything, but a yard or two
beyond the line of its passage, humble flower,
lofty tree, and the poor vulnerable maid who now
kneeled to pay her gratitude to heaven, awoke
unharmed in the crystal purity and peace of the
new day.

To move by the path of the tornado was a thing
impossible to man, so wildly were the wrecks of
the tall forest piled together by that fugitive con-
vulsion. I crossed it indeed; with such labour

and patience, with so many dangerous slips and
falls, as left me, at the further side, bankrupt
alike of strength and courage.   There I sat down
awhile to recruit my forces; and as I ate (how
should I bless the kindliness of heaven!) my eyes,
flitting to and fro in the colonnade of the great
trees, alighted on a trunk that had been blazed.
Yes, by the directing hand of providence, I had
been conducted to the very track I was to follow.
With what a light heart I now set forth, and walking with how glad a step, traversed the uplands
of the isle!

It was hard upon the hour of noon when I came,
all tattered and wayworn, to the summit of a steep
descent, and looked below me on the sea.   About
all the coast, the surf, roused by the tornado of
the night, beat with a particular fury and made
a fringe of snow.   Close at my feet, I saw a haven,
set in precipitous and palm-crowned bluffs of rock.
Just outside, a ship was heaving on the surge, so
trimly sparred, so glossily painted, so elegant and
point-device in every feature, that my heart was
seized with admiration.   The English colours blew
from her masthead; and from my high station, I
caught glimpses of her snowy planking, as she
rolled on the uneven deep, and saw the sun glitter
on the brass of her deck furniture.   There, then,
was my ship of refuge; and of all my difficulties
only one remained: to get on board of her.

Half an hour later, I issued at last out of the
woods on the margin of a cove, into whose jaws
the tossing and blue billows entered, and along

whose shores they broke with a surprising loudness. A wooded promontory hid the yacht; and
I had walked some distance round the beach, in
what appeared to be a virgin solitude, when my
eye fell on a boat, drawn into a natural harbour,
where it rocked in safety, but deserted. I looked
about for those who should have manned her;
and presently, in the immediate entrance of the
wood, spied the red embers of a fire and, stretched
around in various attitudes, a party of slumber-
ing mariners. To these I drew near: most were
black, a few white; but all were dressed with the
conspicuous decency of yachtsmen; and one, from
his peaked cap and glittering buttons, I rightly
divined to be an officer. Him, then, I touched
upon the shoulder. He started up; the sharpness
of his movement woke the rest; and they all stared
upon me in surprise.

" What do you want? " inquired the officer.

" To go on board the yacht," I answered.

I thought they all seemed disconcerted at this;
and the officer, with something of sharpness, asked
me who I was. Now I had determined to conceal
my name until I met Sir George; and the first
name that rose to my lips was that of Señora
Mendizabal. At the word, there went a shock
about the little party of seamen; the negroes
stared at me with indescribable eagerness, the
whites themselves with something of a scared
surprise; and instantly the spirit of mischief
prompted me to add: " And if the name is new
to your ears, call me Metamnbogu."

I had never seen an effect so wonderful. The negroes threw their hands into the air, with the same gesture I remarked the night before about the Hoodoo camp-fire; first one, and then another, ran forward and kneeled down and kissed the skirts of my torn dress; and when the white officer broke out swearing and calling to know if they were mad, the coloured seamen took him by the shoulders, dragged him on one side till they were out of hearing, and surrounded him with open mouths and extravagant pantomime. The officer seemed to struggle hard; he laughed aloud, and I saw him make gestures of dissent and protest; but in the end, whether overcome by reason or simply weary of resistance, he gave in — approached me civilly enough, but with something of a sneering manner underneath — and touching his cap, " My lady," said he, " if that is what you are, the boat is ready."

My reception on board the *Nemorosa* (for so the yacht was named) partook of the same mingled nature. We were scarcely within hail of that great and elegant fabric, where she lay rolling gunwale under and churning the blue sea to snow, before the bulwarks were lined with the heads of a great crowd of seamen, black, white, and yellow; and these and the few who manned the boat began exchanging shouts in some *lingua franca* incomprehensible to me. All eyes were directed on the passenger, and once more I saw the negroes toss up their hands to heaven, but now as if with passionate wonder and delight.

16

At the head of the gangway I was received by another officer, a gentlemanly man with blond and bushy whiskers, and to whom I addressed my demand to see Sir George.

" But this is not —— " he cried, and paused.

" I know it," returned the other officer, who had brought me from the shore. " But what the devil can we do? Look at all the niggers! "

I followed his direction; and as my eye lighted upon each, the poor ignorant Africans ducked and bowed and threw their hands into the air, as though in the presence of a creature half divine. Apparently the officer with the whiskers had instantly come round to the opinion of his subaltern, for he now addressed me with every signal of respect.

" Sir George is at the island, my lady," said he, " for which, with your ladyship's permission, I shall immediately make all sail. The cabins are prepared. Steward, take Lady Greville below."

Under this new name, then, and so captivated by surprise that I could neither think nor speak, I was ushered into a spacious and airy cabin, hung about with weapons and surrounded by divans. The steward asked for my commands, but I was by this time so wearied, bewildered, and disturbed that I could only wave him to leave me to myself and sink upon a pile of cushions. Presently, by the changed motion of the ship, I knew her to be under way; my thoughts, so far from clarifying, grew the more distracted and confused; dreams began to mingle and confound them, and at length, by insensible transition, I sank into a dreamless slumber.

When I awoke the day and night had passed, and it was once more morning. The world on which I reopened my eyes swam strangely up and down; the jewels in the bag that lay beside me chinked together ceaselessly; the clock and the barometer wagged to and fro like pendulums, and overhead seamen were singing out at their work, and coils of rope clattering and thumping on the deck. Yet it was long before I had divined that I was at sea; long before I had recalled, one after another, the tragical, mysterious, and inexplicable events that had brought me where I was.

When I had done so, I thrust the jewels, which I was surprised to find had been respected, into the bosom of my dress, and seeing a silver bell hard by upon a table, rang it loudly. The steward instantly appeared; I asked for food, and he proceeded to lay the table, regarding me the while with a disquieting and pertinacious scrutiny. To relieve myself of my embarrassment, I asked him, with as fair a show of ease as I could muster, if it were usual for yachts to carry so numerous a crew?

" Madam," said he, " I know not who you are, nor what mad fancy has induced you to usurp a name and an appalling destiny that are not yours. I warn you from the soul. No sooner arrived at the island ——— "

At this moment he was interrupted by the whiskered officer, who had entered unperceived behind

him, and now laid a hand upon his shoulder. The
sudden pallor, the deadly and sick fear that was
imprinted on the steward's face, formed a startling
addition to his words.

"Parker!" said the officer, and pointed towards
the door.

"Yes, Mr. Kentish," said the steward. "For
God's sake, Mr. Kentish!" and vanished with a
white face from the cabin.

Thereupon the officer bade me sit down, and
began to help me, and join in the meal. "I fill
your ladyship's glass," said he, and handed me a
tumbler of neat rum.

"Sir," cried I, "do you expect me to drink
this?"

He laughed heartily. "Your ladyship is so
much changed," said he, "that I no longer expect
any one thing more than any other."

Immediately after, a white seaman entered the
cabin, saluted both Mr. Kentish and myself, and
informed the officer there was a sail in sight, which
was bound to pass us very close, and that Mr.
Harland was in doubt about the colours.

"Being so near the island?" asked Mr. Kentish.

"That was what Mr. Harland said, sir," returned the sailor, with a scrape.

"Better not, I think," said Mr. Kentish. "My
compliments to Mr. Harland; and if she seem a
lively boat, give her the stars and stripes; but if
she be dull, and we can easily outsail her, show
John Dutchman. That is always another word
for incivility at sea; so we can disregard a

hail or a flag of distress, without attracting notice."

As soon as the sailor had gone on deck, I turned to the officer in wonder. "Mr. Kentish, if that be your name," said I, "are you ashamed of your own colours?"

"Your ladyship refers to the 'Jolly Roger'?" he inquired, with perfect gravity; and immediately after, went into peals of laughter. "Pardon me," said he; "but here for the first time, I recognise your ladyship's impetuosity." Nor, try as I pleased, could I extract from him any explanation of this mystery, but only oily and commonplace evasion.

While we were thus occupied, the movement of the *Nemorosa* gradually became less violent; its speed at the same time diminished; and presently after, with a sullen plunge, the anchor was discharged into the sea. Kentish immediately rose, offered his arm and conducted me on deck; where I found we were lying in a roadstead among many low and rocky islets, hovered about by an innumerable cloud of sea-fowl. Immediately under our board, a somewhat larger isle was green with trees, set with a few low buildings and approached by a pier of very crazy workmanship; and a little inshore of us, a smaller vessel lay at anchor.

I had scarce time to glance to the four quarters, ere a boat was lowered. I was handed in, Kentish took place beside me, and we pulled briskly to the pier. A crowd of villainous, armed loiterers, both black and white, looked on upon our landing; and again the word passed about among the ne-

groes, and again I was received with prostrations
and the same gesture of the flung-up hand. By
this, what with the appearance of these men and
the lawless, sea-girt spot in which I found myself,
my courage began a little to decline, and clinging
to the arm of Mr. Kentish, I begged him to tell
me what it meant.

" Nay, madam," he returned, " *you* know." And
leading me smartly through the crowd, which continued to follow at a considerable distance, and
at which he still kept looking back, I thought, with
apprehension, he brought me to a low house that
stood alone in an encumbered yard, opened the
door, and begged me to enter.

" But why? " said I. " I demanded to see Sir
George."

" Madam," returned Mr. Kentish, looking suddenly as black as thunder, " to drop all fence, I
know neither who nor what you are, beyond the
fact that you are not the person whose name you
have assumed. But be what you please, spy, ghost,
devil, or most ill-judging jester, if you do not immediately enter that house, I will cut you to the
earth." And even as he spoke, he threw an uneasy glance behind him at the following crowd of
blacks.

I did not wait to be twice threatened; I obeyed
at once and with a palpitating heart; and the next
moment, the door was locked from outside and
the key withdrawn. The interior was long, low,
and quite unfurnished, but filled, almost from end
to end, with sugar-cane, tar barrels, old tarry rope,

and other incongruous and highly inflammable material; and not only was the door locked, but the solitary window barred with iron.

I was by this time so exceedingly bewildered and afraid, that I would have given years of my life to be once more the slave of Mr. Caulder. I still stood, with my hands clasped, the image of despair, looking about me on the lumber room or raising my eyes to heaven; when there appeared outside the window bars the face of a very black negro, who signed to me imperiously to draw near. I did so, and he instantly, and with every mark of fervour, addressed me a long speech in some unknown and barbarous tongue.

"I declare," I cried, clasping my brow, "I do not understand one syllable."

"Not?" he said in Spanish. "Great, great, are the powers of Hoodoo! Her very mind is changed! But, O chief priestess, why have you suffered yourself to be shut into this cage? why did you not call your slaves at once to your defence? Do you not see that all has been prepared to murder you? at a spark, this flimsy house will go in flames; and alas! who shall then be the chief priestess? and what shall be the profit of the miracle?"

"Heavens!" cried I, "can I not see Sir George? I must, I must, come by speech of him. Oh, bring me to Sir George!" And, my terror fairly mastering my courage, I fell upon my knees and began to pray to all the saints.

"Lordy!" cried the negro, "here they come!"

And his black head was instantly withdrawn from the window.

"I never heard such nonsense in my life," exclaimed a voice.

"Why, so we all say, Sir George," replied the voice of Mr. Kentish. "But put yourself in our place. The niggers were near two to one. And upon my word, if you'll excuse me, sir, considering the notion they have taken in their heads, I regard it as precious fortunate for all of us that the mistake occurred."

"This is no question of fortune, sir," returned Sir George. "It is a question of my orders, and you may take my word for it, Kentish, either Harland, or yourself, or Parker — or, by George! all three of you — shall swing for this affair. These are my sentiments. Give me the key and be off."

Immediately after, the key turned in the lock; and there appeared upon the threshold a gentleman, between forty and fifty, with a very open countenance and of a stout and personable figure.

"My dear young lady," said he, "who the devil may you be?"

I told him my story in a rush of words. He heard me, from the first, with an amazement you can scarcely picture, but when I came to the death of the Señora Mendizabal in the tornado, he fairly leaped into the air.

"My dear child," he cried, clasping me in his arms, "excuse a man who might be your father! This is the best news I have heard since I was born; for that hag of a mulatto was no less a per-

son than my wife." He sat down upon a tar-
barrel, as if unmanned by joy. "Dear me," said
he, "I declare this tempts me to believe in providence. And what," he added, "can I do for
you?"

"Sir George," said I, "I am already rich: all
that I ask is your protection."

"Understand one thing," he said, with great
energy: "I will never marry."

"I had not ventured to propose it," I exclaimed,
unable to restrain my mirth; "I only seek to be
conveyed to England, the natural home of the
escaped slave."

"Well," returned Sir George, "frankly I owe
you one for this exhilarating news; besides, your
father was of use to me. Now, I have made up a
small competence in business — a jewel mine, a
sort of naval agency, et cætera, and I am on the
point of breaking up my company, and retiring to
my place in Devonshire to pass a plain old age, un-
married. One good turn deserves another: if
you swear to hold your tongue about this island,
these little bonfire arrangements, and the whole
episode of my unfortunate marriage, why, I'll
carry you home aboard the *Nemorosa*."

I eagerly accepted his conditions.

"One thing more," said he. "My late wife was
some sort of a sorceress among the blacks; and
they are all persuaded she has come alive again
in your agreeable person. Now, you will have the
goodness to keep up that fancy, if you please; and
to swear to them, on the authority of Hoodoo or

whatever his name may be, that I am from this
moment quite a sacred character."

"I swear it," said I, "by my father's memory;
and that is a vow that I will never break."

"I have considerably better hold on you than
any oath," returned Sir George, with a chuckle;
"for you are not only an escaped slave, but have,
by your own account, a considerable amount of
stolen property."

I was struck dumb; I saw it was too true; in a
glance, I recognised that these jewels were no
longer mine; with similar quickness, I decided
they should be restored, ay, if it cost me the liberty
that I had just regained. Forgetful of all else,
forgetful of Sir George, who sat and watched me
with a smile, I drew out Mr. Caulder's pocket-book
and turned to the page on which the dying man
had scrawled his testament. How shall I describe
the agony of happiness and remorse with which
I read it! for my victim had not only set me free,
but bequeathed to me the bag of jewels.

My plain tale draws toward a close. Sir George
and I, in my character of his rejuvenated wife, displayed ourselves arm-in-arm among the negroes,
and were cheered and followed to the place of
embarkation. There, Sir George, turning about,
made a speech to his old companions, in which he
thanked and bade them farewell with a very manly
spirit; and toward the end of which, he fell on
some expressions which I still remember. "If
any of you gentry lose your money," he said,
"take care you do not come to me; for in the first

place, I shall do my best to have you murdered;
and if that fails, I hand you over to the law. Black-
mail won't do for me. I 'll rather risk all upon a
cast, than be pulled to pieces by degrees. I 'll
rather be found out and hang, than give a doit to
one man-jack of you." That same night we got
under way and crossed to the port of New Orleans,
whence, as a sacred trust, I sent the pocket-book
to Mr. Caulder's son. In a week's time, the
men were all paid off; new hands were shipped;
and the *Nemorosa* weighed her anchor for Old
England.

A more delightful voyage it were hard to fancy.
Sir George, of course, was not a conscientious
man; but he had an unaffected gaiety of character
that naturally endeared him to the young; and it
was interesting to hear him lay out his projects for
the future, when he should be returned to parliament, and place at the service of the nation his
experience of marine affairs. I asked him, if his
notion of piracy upon a private yacht were not
original. But he told me, no. "A yacht, Miss
Valdevia," he observed, "is a chartered nuisance.
Who smuggles? Who robs the salmon rivers of
the west of Scotland? Who cruelly beats the
keepers if they dare to intervene? The crews and
the proprietors of yachts. All I have done is to
extend the line a trifle; and if you ask me for my
unbiassed opinion, I do not suppose that I am in
the least alone."

In short we were the best of friends, and lived
like father and daughter; though I still withheld

from him, of course, that respect which is only due
to moral excellence.

We were still some days' sail from England,
when Sir George obtained, from an outward-
bound ship, a packet of newspapers; and from that
fatal hour my misfortunes recommenced. He sat,
the same evening, in the cabin, reading the news,
and making savoury comments on the decline of
England and the poor condition of the navy; when
I suddenly observed him to change countenance.

" Hullo! " said he, " this is bad; this is deuced
bad, Miss Valdevia. You would not listen to
sound sense, you would send that pocket-book to
that man Caulder's son."

" Sir George," said I, " it was my duty."

" You are prettily paid for it, at least," says
he; " and much as I regret it, I, for one, am done
with you. This fellow Caulder demands your
extradition."

" But a slave," I returned, " is safe in England."

" Yes, by George! " replied the baronet; " but
it 's not a slave, Miss Valdevia, it 's a thief that he
demands. He has quietly destroyed the will; and
now accuses you of robbing your father's bankrupt
estate of jewels to the value of a hundred thousand
pounds."

I was so much overcome by indignation at this
hateful charge and concern for my unhappy fate
that the genial baronet made haste to put me more
at ease.

" Do not be cast down," said he. " Of course, I
wash my hands of you, myself. A man in my

position — baronet, old family, and all that — cannot possibly be too particular about the company he keeps. But I am a deuced good-humoured old boy, let me tell you, when not ruffled, and I will do the best I can to put you right. I will lend you a trifle of ready money, give you the address of an excellent lawyer in London, and find a way to set you on shore unsuspected."

He was in every particular as good as his word. Four days later, the *Nemorosa* sounded her way, under the cloak of a dark night, into a certain haven of the coast of England; and a boat, rowing with muffled oars, set me ashore upon the beach within a stone's throw of a railway station. Thither, guided by Sir George's directions, I groped a devious way; and finding a bench upon the platform, sat me down, wrapped in a man's fur great-coat, to await the coming of the day. It was still dark when a light was struck behind one of the windows of the building; nor had the east begun to kindle to the warmer colours of the dawn, before a porter, carrying a lantern, issued from the door and found himself face to face with the unfortunate Teresa. He looked all about him; in the grey twilight of the dawn, the haven was seen to lie deserted, and the yacht had long since disappeared.

"Who are you?" he cried.

"I am a traveller," said I.

"And where do you come from?" he asked.

"I am going by the first train, to London," I replied.

In such manner, like a ghost or a new creation, was Teresa with her bag of jewels landed on the shores of England; in this silent fashion, without history or name, she took her place among the millions of a new country.

Since then, I have lived by the expedients of my lawyer, lying concealed in quiet lodgings, dogged by the spies of Cuba, and not knowing at what hour my liberty and honour may be lost.

THE BROWN BOX

(*concluded*)

THE effect of this tale on the mind of Harry Desborough was instant and convincing. The fair Cuban had been already the loveliest, she now became, in his eyes, the most romantic, the most innocent, and the most unhappy of her sex. He was bereft of words to utter what he felt: what pity, what admiration, what youthful envy of a career so vivid and adventurous. "Oh, madam!" he began; and finding no language adequate to that apostrophe, caught up her hand and wrung it in his own. "Count upon me," he added, with bewildered fervour; and getting somehow or other out of the apartment and from the circle of that radiant sorceress, he found himself in the strange out-of-doors, beholding dull houses, wondering at dull passers-by, a fallen angel. She had smiled upon him as he left, and with how significant, how beautiful a smile! The memory lingered in his heart; and when he found his way to a certain restaurant where music was performed, flutes (as it were of Paradise) accompanied his meal. The strings went to the melody of that parting smile; they paraphrased and glossed it in the sense that he desired; and for the first time in his plain and somewhat dreary life, he perceived himself to have a taste for music.

The next day, and the next, his meditations moved to that delectable air. Now he saw her and was favoured; now saw her not at all; now saw her and was put by. The fall of her foot upon the stair entranced him; the books that he sought out and read, were books on Cuba and spoke of her indirectly; nay, and in the very landlady's parlour, he found one that told of precisely such a hurricane, and, down to the smallest detail, confirmed (had confirmation been required) the truth of her recital. Presently he began to fall into that prettiest mood of a young love, in which the lover scorns himself for his presumption. Who was he, the dull one, the commonplace unemployed, the man without adventure, the impure, the untruthful, to aspire to such a creature made of fire and air, and hallowed and adorned by such incomparable passages of life? What should he do to be more worthy? By what devotion call down the notice of these eyes to so terrene a being as himself?

He betook himself, thereupon, to the rural privacy of the square, where, being a lad of a kind heart, he had made himself a circle of acquaintances among its shy frequenters, the half-domestic cats and the visitors that hung before the windows of the Children's Hospital. There he walked, considering the depth of his demerit and the height of the adored one's super-excellence; now lighting upon earth to say a pleasant word to the brother

of some infant invalid; now, with a great heave
of breath, remembering the queen of women, and
the sunshine of his life.

What was he to do? Teresa, he had observed,
was in the habit of leaving the house toward afternoon; she might, perchance, run danger from some
Cuban emissary, when the presence of a friend
might turn the balance in her favour: how, then,
if he should follow her? To offer his company
would seem like an intrusion; to dog her openly
were a manifest impertinence; he saw himself reduced to a more stealthy part, which, though in
some ways distasteful to his mind, he did not
doubt that he could practise with the skill of a
detective.

The next day he proceeded to put his plan in
action. At the corner of Tottenham Court Road,
however, the Señorita suddenly turned back, and
met him face to face, with every mark of pleasure
and surprise.

"Ah, Señor, I am sometimes fortunate!" she
cried. "I was looking for a messenger"; and with
the sweetest of smiles, she despatched him to the
east end of London, to an address which he was
unable to find. This was a bitter pill to the knight-
errant; but when he returned at night, worn out
with fruitless wandering and dismayed by his *fiasco,*
the lady received him with a friendly gaiety, protesting that all was for the best, since she had
changed her mind and long since repented of her
message.

Next day he resumed his labours, glowing with

pity and courage, and determined to protect Teresa
with his life.   But a painful shock awaited him.
In the narrow and silent Hanway Street, she turned
suddenly about and addressed him with a manner
and a light in her eyes, that were new to the young
man's experience.

"Do I understand that you follow me, Señor?"
she cried.   "Are these the manners of the English
gentleman?"

Harry confounded himself in the most abject
apologies and prayers to be forgiven, vowed to
offend no more, and was at length dismissed, crest-
fallen and heavy of heart.   The check was final;
he gave up that road to service; and began once
more to hang about the square or on the terrace,
filled with remorse and love, admirable and idiotic,
a fit object for the scorn and envy of older men.
In these idle hours, while he was courting fortune
for a sight of the beloved, it fell out naturally that
he should observe the manners and appearance of
such as came about the house.   One person alone
was the occasional visitor of the young lady; a
man of considerable stature and distinguished only
by the doubtful ornament of a chin-beard in the
style of an American deacon.   Something in his
appearance grated upon Harry; this distaste grew
upon him in the course of days; and when at
length he mustered courage to inquire of the fair
Cuban who this was, he was yet more dismayed
by her reply.

"That gentleman," said she, a smile struggling
to her face, "that gentleman, I will not attempt

to conceal from you, desires my hand in marriage, and presses me with the most respectful ardour. Alas, what am I to say? I, the forlorn Teresa, how shall I refuse or accept such protestations?"

Harry feared to say more; a horrid pang of jealousy transfixed him; and he had scarce the strength of mind to take his leave with decency. In the solitude of his own chamber, he gave way to every manifestation of despair. He passionately adored the Señorita; but it was not only the thought of her possible union with another that distressed his soul, it was the indefeasible conviction that her suitor was unworthy. To a duke, a bishop, a victorious general, or any man adorned with obvious qualities, he had resigned her with a sort of bitter joy; he saw himself follow the wedding-party from a great way off; he saw himself return to the poor house, then robbed of its jewel; and while he could have wept for his despair, he felt he could support it nobly. But this affair looked otherwise. The man was patently no gentleman; he had a startled, skulking, guilty bearing; his nails were black, his eyes evasive; his love perhaps was a pretext; he was, perhaps, under this deep disguise, a Cuban emissary! Harry swore that he would satisfy these doubts; and the next evening, about the hour of the usual visit, he posted himself at a spot whence his eye commanded the three issues of the square.

Presently after, a four-wheeler rumbled to the door; and the man with the chin-beard alighted, paid off the cabman, and was seen by Harry to enter the house with a brown box hoisted on his back. Half an hour later, he came forth again without the box, and struck eastward at a rapid walk; and Desborough, with the same skill and caution that he had displayed in following Teresa, proceeded to dog the steps of her admirer. The man began to loiter, studying with apparent interest the wares of the small fruiterer or tobacconist; twice he returned hurriedly upon his former course; and then, as though he had suddenly conquered a moment's hesitation, once more set forth with resolute and swift steps in the direction of Lincoln's Inn. At length, in a deserted by-street, he turned; and coming up to Harry with a countenance which seemed to have become older and whiter, inquired with some severity of speech if he had not had the pleasure of seeing the gentleman before.

" You have, sir," said Harry, somewhat abashed, but with a good show of stoutness; " and I will not deny that I was following you on purpose. Doubtless," he added, for he supposed that all men's minds must still be running on Teresa, " you can divine my reason."

At these words, the man with the chin-beard was seized with a palsied tremor. He seemed, for some seconds, to seek the utterance which his fear denied him; and then whipping sharply about, he took to his heels at the most furious speed of running.

Harry was at first so taken aback that he neglected to pursue; and by the time he had recovered his wits, his best expedition was only rewarded by a glimpse of the man with the chin-beard mounting into a hansom, which immediately after disappeared into the moving crowds of Holborn.

Puzzled and dismayed by this unusual behaviour, Harry returned to the house in Queen Square, and ventured for the first time to knock at the fair Cuban's door. She bade him enter, and he found her kneeling with rather a disconsolate air beside a brown wooden trunk.

"Señorita," he broke out, "I doubt whether that man's character is what he wishes you to believe. His manner, when he found, and indeed when I admitted that I was following him, was not the manner of an honest man."

"Oh!" she cried, throwing up her hands as in desperation, "Don Quixote, Don Quixote, have you again been tilting against windmills?" And then, with a laugh, "Poor soul!" she added, "how you must have terrified him! For know that the Cuban authorities are here, and your poor Teresa may soon be hunted down. Even yon humble clerk from my solicitor's office may find himself at any moment the quarry of armed spies."

"A humble clerk?" cried Harry; "why, you told me yourself that he wished to marry you!"

"I thought you English like what you call a joke," replied the lady, calmly. "As a matter of fact he is my lawyer's clerk, and has been here to-night charged with disastrous news. I am in sore straits, Señor Harry. Will you help me?"

At this most welcomed word, the young man's heart exulted; and in the hope, pride, and self-esteem that kindled with the very thought of service, he forgot to dwell upon the lady's jest. "Can you ask?" he cried. "What is there that I can do? Only tell me that."

With signs of an emotion that was certainly unfeigned, the fair Cuban laid her hand upon the box. "This box," she said, "contains my jewels, papers, and clothes; all, in a word, that still connects me with Cuba and my dreadful past. They must now be smuggled out of England; or, by the opinion of my lawyer, I am lost beyond remedy. To-morrow, on board the Irish packet, a sure hand awaits the box; the problem still unsolved, is to find some one to carry it as far as Holyhead, to see it placed on board the steamer, and instantly return to town. Will you be he? Will you leave to-morrow by the first train, punctually obey orders, bear still in mind that you are surrounded by Cuban spies; and without so much as a look behind you, or a single movement to betray your interest, leave the box where you have put it and come straight on shore? Will you do this, and so save your friend?"

"I do not clearly understand——" began Harry.

"No more do I," replied the Cuban. "It is not necessary that we should, so long as we obey the lawyer's orders."

"Señorita," returned Harry, gravely, "I think this, of course, a very little thing to do for you, when I would willingly do all. But suffer me to say one word. If London is unsafe for your treasures, it cannot long be safe for you; and indeed, if I at all fathom the plan of your solicitor, I fear I may find you already fled on my return. I am not considered clever, and can only speak out plainly what is in my heart: that I love you, and that I cannot bear to lose all knowledge of you. I hope no more than to be your servant; I ask no more than just that I shall hear of you. Oh, promise me so much!"

"You shall," she said, after a pause. "I promise you, you shall." But though she spoke with earnestness, the marks of great embarrassment and a strong conflict of emotions appeared upon her face.

"I wish to tell you," resumed Desborough, "in case of accidents . . ."

"Accidents!" she cried; "why do you say that?"

"I do not know," said he; "you may be gone before my return, and we may not meet again for long. And so I wished you to know this: That since the day you gave me the cigarette, you have never once, not once, been absent from my mind; and if it will in any way serve you, you may crumple me up like that piece of paper, and throw me on the fire. I would love to die for you."

"Go!" she said. "Go now at once! My brain is in a whirl. I scarce know what we are talking. Go; and good-night; and oh, may you come safe!"

Once back in his own room a fearful joy possessed the young man's mind; and as he recalled her face struck suddenly white and the broken utterance of her last words, his heart at once exulted and misgave him. Love had indeed looked upon him with a tragic mask; and yet what mattered, since at least it was love — since at least she was commoved at their division? He got to bed with these parti-coloured thoughts; passed from one dream to another all night long, the white face of Teresa still haunting him, wrung with unspoken thoughts; and in the grey of the dawn, leaped suddenly out of bed, in a kind of horror. It was already time for him to rise. He dressed, made his breakfast on cold food that had been laid for him the night before; and went down to the room of his idol for the box. The door was open; a strange disorder reigned within; the furniture all pushed aside, and the centre of the room left bare of impediment, as though for the pacing of a creature with a tortured mind. There lay the box, however, and upon the lid a paper with these words: " Harry, I hope to be back before you go. Teresa."

He sat down to wait, laying his watch before him on the table. She had called him Harry: that should be enough, he thought, to fill the day with sunshine; and yet somehow the sight of that disordered room still poisoned his enjoyment. The door of the bedchamber stood gaping open; and though he turned aside his eyes as from a sacrilege, he could not but observe the bed had not

been slept in. He was still pondering what this
should mean, still trying to convince himself that
all was well, when the moving needle of his watch
summoned him to set forth without delay. He
was before all things a man of his word; ran
round to Southampton Row to fetch a cab; and
taking the box on the front seat, drove off toward
the terminus.

The streets were scarcely awake; there was little
to amuse the eye; and the young man's attention
centred on the dumb companion of his drive. A
card was nailed upon one side, bearing the super-
scription: " Miss Doolan, passenger to Dublin.
Glass. With care." He thought with a sentimental shock that the fair idol of his heart was
perhaps driven to adopt the name of Doolan; and
as he still studied the card, he was aware of a
deadly, black depression settling steadily upon his
spirits. It was in vain for him to contend against
the tide; in vain that he shook himself or tried to
whistle: the sense of some impending blow was
not to be averted. He looked out; in the long,
empty streets, the cab pursued its way without a
trace of any follower. He gave ear; and over and
above the jolting of the wheels upon the road, he
was conscious of a certain regular and quiet sound
that seemed to issue from the box. He put his ear
to the cover; at one moment, he seemed to perceive
a delicate ticking: the next, the sound was gone,
nor could his closest hearkening recapture it. He
laughed at himself; but still the gloom continued;
and it was with more than the common relief of an

arrival that he leaped from the cab before the
station.

Probably enough on purpose, Teresa had named
an hour some thirty minutes earlier than needful;
and when Harry had given the box into the charge
of a porter, who set it on a truck, he proceeded
briskly to pace the platform. Presently the book-
stall opened; and the young man was looking at
the books when he was seized by the arm. He
turned, and, though she was closely veiled, at once
recognised the fair Cuban.

"Where is it?" she asked; and the sound of
her voice surprised him.

"It?" he said. "What?"

"The box. Have it put on a cab instantly. I
am in fearful haste."

He hurried to obey, marvelling at these changes
but not daring to trouble her with questions; and
when the cab had been brought round, and the box
mounted on the front, she passed a little way off
upon the pavement and beckoned him to follow.

"Now," said she, still in those mechanical and
hushed tones that had at first affected him, "you
must go on to Holyhead alone; go on board the
steamer; and if you see a man in tartan trousers
and a pink scarf, say to him that all has been put
off: if not," she added, with a sobbing sigh, "it
does not matter. So, good-bye."

"Teresa," said Harry, "get into your cab, and
I will go along with you. You are in some distress, perhaps some danger; and till I know the
whole, not even you can make me leave you."

"You will not?" she asked. "Oh, Harry, it were better!"

"I will not," said Harry, stoutly.

She looked at him for a moment through her veil; took his hand suddenly and sharply, but more as if in fear than tenderness; and still holding him, walked to the cab-door.

"Where are we to drive?" asked Harry.

"Home, quickly," she answered; "double fare!" And as soon as they had both mounted to their places, the vehicle crazily trundled from the station.

Teresa leaned back in a corner. The whole way Harry could perceive her tears to flow under her veil; but she vouchsafed no explanation. At the door of the house in Queen Square both alighted; and the cabman lowered the box, which Harry, glad to display his strength, received upon his shoulders.

"Let the man take it," she whispered. "Let the man take it."

"I will do no such thing," said Harry cheerfully; and having paid the fare, he followed Teresa through the door which she had opened with her key. The landlady and maid were gone upon their morning errands; the house was empty and still; and as the rattling of the cab died away down Gloucester Street, and Harry continued to ascend the stair with his burthen, he heard close against his shoulders the same faint and muffled ticking as before. The lady, still preceding him, opened the door of her room, and helped him to lower the box tenderly in the corner by the window.

"And now," said Harry, "what is wrong?"

"You will not go away?" she cried, with a sudden break in her voice and beating her hands together in the very agony of impatience. "Oh! Harry, Harry, go away! Oh! go, and leave me to the fate that I deserve!"

"The fate?" repeated Harry. "What is this?"

"No fate," she resumed. "I do not know what I am saying. But I wish to be alone. You may come back this evening, Harry; come again when you like; but leave me now, only leave me now!" And then suddenly, "I have an errand," she exclaimed; "you cannot refuse me that."

"No," replied Harry, "you have no errand. You are in grief or danger. Lift your veil and tell me what it is."

"Then," she said, with a sudden composure, "you leave but one course open to me." And raising the veil, she showed him a countenance from which every trace of colour had fled, eyes marred with weeping, and a brow on which resolve had conquered fear. "Harry," she began, "I am not what I seem."

"You have told me that before," said Harry, "several times."

"Oh! Harry, Harry," she cried, "how you shame me! But this is the God's truth. I am a dangerous and wicked girl. My name is Clara Luxmore. I was never nearer Cuba than Penzance. From first to last I have cheated and played with you. And what I am I dare not even name to you in words. Indeed, until to-day, until the sleepless watches of last night, I never grasped the depth and foulness of my guilt."

The young man looked upon her aghast. Then a generous current poured along his veins. " That is all one," he said. " If you be all you say, you have the greater need of me."

" Is it possible," she exclaimed, " that I have schemed in vain? And will nothing drive you from this house of death? "

" Of death? " he echoed.

" Death! " she cried; " death! In that box that you have dragged about London and carried on your defenceless shoulders, sleep, at the trigger's mercy, the destroying energies of dynamite."

" My God! " cried Harry.

" Ah! " she continued wildly, " will you flee now? At any moment you may hear the click that sounds the ruin of this building. I was sure M'Guire was wrong; this morning, before day, I flew to Zero; he confirmed my fears; I beheld you, my beloved Harry, fall a victim to my own contrivances. I knew then I loved you — Harry, will you go now? Will you not spare me this unwilling crime? "

Harry remained speechless, his eyes fixed upon the box: at last he turned to her.

" Is it," he asked hoarsely, " an infernal machine? "

Her lips formed the word " yes "; which her voice refused to utter.

With fearful curiosity, he drew near and bent above the box: in that still chamber, the ticking was distinctly audible; and at the measured sound, the blood flowed back upon his heart.

" For whom? " he asked.

" What matters it? " she cried, seizing him by the arm. " If you may still be saved, what matter questions? "

" God in heaven! " cried Harry. " And the children's hospital! At whatever cost, this damned contrivance must be stopped! "

" It cannot," she gasped. " The power of man cannot avert the blow. But you, Harry — you, my beloved — you may still —— "

And then from the box that lay so quietly in the corner, a sudden catch was audible, like the catch of a clock before it strikes the hour. For one second, the two stared at each other with lifted brows and stony eyes. Then Harry, throwing one arm over his face, with the other clutched the girl to his breast and staggered against the wall.

A dull and startling thud resounded through the room; their eyes blinked against the coming horror; and still clinging together like drowning people, they fell to the floor. Then followed a prolonged and strident hissing as from the indignant pit; an offensive stench seized them by the throat; the room was filled with dense and choking fumes.

Presently these began a little to disperse; and when at length they drew themselves, all limp and shaken, to a sitting posture, the first object that greeted their vision was the box reposing uninjured in its corner, but still leaking little wreaths of vapour round the lid.

"Oh, poor Zero!" cried the girl with a strange sobbing laugh. "Alas, poor Zero! This will break his heart!"

THE SUPERFLUOUS MANSION

(concluded)

SOMERSET ran straight up-stairs; the door of the drawing-room, contrary to all custom, was unlocked; and bursting in, the young man found Zero seated on a sofa in an attitude of singular dejection. Close beside him stood an untasted grog, the mark of strong preoccupation. The room besides was in confusion; boxes had been tumbled to and fro; the floor was strewn with keys and other implements; and in the midst of this disorder, lay a lady's glove.

"I have come," cried Somerset, "to make an end of this. Either you will instantly abandon all your schemes, or (cost what it may) I will denounce you to the police."

"Ah!" replied Zero, slowly shaking his head. "You are too late, dear fellow! I am already at the end of all my hopes and fallen to be a laughing-stock and mockery. My reading," he added, with a gentle despondency of manner, "has not been much among romances; yet I recall from one a phrase that depicts my present state with critical exactitude; and you behold me sitting here 'like a burst drum.'"

"What has befallen you?" cried Somerset.

"My last batch," returned the plotter, wearily,

"like all the others, is a hollow mockery and a fraud. In vain do I combine the elements; in vain adjust the springs; and I have now arrived at such a pitch of disconsideration that (except yourself, dear fellow) I do not know a soul that I can face. My subordinates themselves have turned upon me. What language have I heard to-day, what illiberality of sentiment, what pungency of expression! She came once; I could have pardoned that, for she was moved; but she returned, returned to announce to me this crushing blow; and, Somerset, she was very inhumane. Yes, dear fellow, I have drunk a bitter cup; the speech of females is remarkable for . . . well, well! Denounce me, if you will, you but denounce the dead. I am extinct. It is strange how, at this supreme crisis of my life, I should be haunted by quotations from works of an inexact and even fanciful description; but here," he added, "is another: 'Othello's occupation's gone.' Yes, dear Somerset, it is gone; I am no more a dynamiter; and how, I ask you, after having tasted of these joys, am I to condescend to a less glorious life?"

"I cannot describe how you relieve me," returned Somerset, sitting down on one of the several boxes that had been drawn out into the middle of the floor. "I had conceived a sort of maudlin toleration for your character; I have a great distaste, besides, for anything in the nature of a duty; and upon both grounds, your news delights me. But I seem to perceive," he added, "a certain sound of ticking in this box."

18

"Yes," replied Zero, with the same slow weariness of manner, "I have set several of them going."

"My God!" cried Somerset, bounding to his feet. "Machines?"

"Machines!" returned the plotter, bitterly. "Machines indeed! I blush to be their author. Alas!" he said, burying his face in his hands, "that I should live to say it!"

"Madman!" cried Somerset, shaking him by the arm. "What am I to understand? Have you, indeed, set these diabolical contrivances in motion, and do we stay here to be blown up?"

"'Hoist with his own petard'?" returned the plotter musingly. "One more quotation: strange! But indeed my brain is struck with numbness. Yes, dear boy, I have, as you say, put my contrivance in motion. The one on which you are sitting, I have timed for half an hour. Yon other——"

"Half an hour!" echoed Somerset, dancing with trepidation. "Merciful heavens, in half an hour!"

"Dear fellow, why so much excitement?" inquired Zero. "My dynamite is not more dangerous than toffy; had I an only child I would give it him to play with. You see this brick?" he continued, lifting a cake of the infernal compound from the laboratory table; "at a touch it should explode, and that with such unconquerable energy as should bestrew the square with ruins. Well, now, behold! I dash it on the floor.'

Somerset sprang forward, and with the strength of the very ecstasy of terror, wrested the brick from his possession. " Heavens! " he cried, wiping his brow, and then with more care than ever mother handled her firstborn withal, gingerly transported the explosive to the far end of the apartment, the plotter, his arms once more fallen to his side, dispiritedly watching him.

" It was entirely harmless," he sighed. " They describe it as burning like tobacco."

" In the name of fortune," cried Somerset, " what have I done to you, or what have you done to yourself, that you should persist in this insane behaviour? If not for your own sake, then for mine, let us depart from this doomed house, where I profess I have not the heart to leave you; and then, if you will take my advice, and if your determination be sincere, you will instantly quit this city, where no further occupation can detain you."

" Such, dear fellow, was my own design," replied the plotter. " I have, as you observe, no further business here, and once I have packed a little bag I shall ask you to share a frugal meal, to go with me as far as to the station and see the last of a broken-hearted man. And yet," he added, looking on the boxes with a lingering regret, " I should have liked to make quite certain. I cannot but suspect my underlings of some mismanagement; it may be fond, but yet I cherish that idea: it may be the weakness of a man of science, but yet," he cried, rising into some energy, " I

will never, I cannot if I try, believe that my poor
dynamite has had fair usage!"

"Five minutes!" said Somerset, glancing with
horror at the timepiece. "If you do not instantly
buckle to your bag, I leave you."

"A few necessaries," returned Zero, "only a
few necessaries, dear Somerset, and you behold
me ready."

He passed into the bedroom, and after an interval which seemed to draw out into eternity for
his unfortunate companion, he returned, bearing
in his hand an open Gladstone bag. His movements were still horribly deliberate, and his eyes
lingered gloatingly on his dear boxes, as he moved
to and fro about the drawing-room, gathering a
few small trifles. Last of all, he lifted one of the
squares of dynamite.

"Put that down!" cried Somerset. "If what
you say be true, you have no call to load yourself
with that ungodly contraband."

"Merely a curiosity, dear boy," he said persua-
sively, and slipped the brick into his bag; "merely
a memento of the past — ah, happy past, bright
past! You will not take a touch of spirits? no?
I find you very abstemious. Well," he added,
'if you have really no curiosity to await the
event ——"

"I!" cried Somerset. "My blood boils to get
away."

"Well, then," said Zero, "I am ready; I would
I could say, willing; but thus to leave the scene
of my sublime endeavours ——"

Without further parley, Somerset seized him by
the arm, and dragged him down-stairs; the hall-
door shut with a clang on the deserted mansion;
and still towing his laggardly companion, the
young man sped across the square in the Oxford
Street direction.   They had not yet passed the
corner of the garden, when they were arrested by
a dull thud of an extraordinary amplitude of sound,
accompanied and followed by a shattering *fracas.*
Somerset turned in time to see the mansion rend
in twain, vomit forth flames and smoke, and instantly collapse into its cellars.   At the same moment, he was thrown violently to the ground.   His
first glance was towards Zero.   The plotter had
but reeled against the garden rail; he stood there,
the Gladstone bag clasped tight upon his heart, his
whole face radiant with relief and gratitude; and
the young man heard him murmur to himself:
" *Nunc dimittis, nunc dimittis!* "

The consternation of the populace was indescribable; the whole of Golden Square was alive
with men, women, and children, running wildly
to and fro, and like rabbits in a warren, dashing
in and out of the house doors.   And under favour
of this confusion, Somerset dragged away the lingering plotter.

" It was grand," he continued to murmur: " it
was indescribably grand.   Ah, green Erin, green
Erin, what a day of glory! and oh, my calum-
niated dynamite, how triumphantly hast thou
prevailed! "

Suddenly a shade crossed his face; and paus-

ing in the middle of the footway, he consulted
the dial of his watch.

"Good God!" he cried, "how mortifying! seven
minutes too early! The dynamite surpassed my
hopes; but the clockwork, fickle clockwork, has
once more betrayed me. Alas, can there be no
success unmixed with failure? and must even this
red-letter day be checkered by a shadow?"

"Incomparable ass!" said Somerset, "what
have you done? Blown up the house of an un-
offending old lady, and the whole property of the
only person who is fool enough to befriend you!"

"You do not understand these matters," replied
Zero, with an air of great dignity. "This will
shake England to the heart. Gladstone, the trucu-
lent old man, will quail before the pointing finger
of revenge. And now that my dynamite is proved
effective —— "

"Heavens, you remind me!" ejaculated Somerset. "That brick in your bag must be instantly
disposed of. But how? If we could throw it in
the river —— "

"A torpedo," cried Zero, brightening, "a torpedo in the Thames! Superb, dear fellow! I
recognise in you the marks of an accomplished
anarch."

"True!" returned Somerset. "It cannot so be
done; and there is no help but you must carry it
away with you. Come on, then, and let me at
once consign you to a train."

"Nay, nay, dear boy," protested Zero. "There
is now no call for me to leave. My character is

now reinstated; my fame brightens; this is the best thing I have done yet; and I see from here the ovations that await the author of the Golden Square Atrocity."

" My young friend," returned the other, " I give you your choice. I will either see you safe on board a train or safe in gaol."

" Somerset, this is unlike you!" said the chymist. " You surprise me, Somerset."

" I shall considerably more surprise you at the next police office," returned Somerset, with something bordering on rage. " For on one point my mind is settled: either I see you packed off to America, brick and all, or else you dine in prison."

" You have perhaps neglected one point," returned the unoffended Zero: " for, speaking as a philosopher, I fail to see what means you can employ to force me. They will, my dear fellow —— "

" Now, see here," interrupted Somerset. " You are ignorant of anything but science, which I can never regard as being truly knowledge; I, sir, have studied life; and allow me to inform you that I have but to raise my hand and voice — here in this street — and the mob —— "

" Good God in heaven, Somerset!" cried Zero, turning deadly white and stopping in his walk, " great God in heaven, what words are these! Oh, not in jest, not even in jest, should they be used! The brutal mob, the savage passions . . . Somerset, for God's sake, a public-house!"

Somerset considered him with freshly awakened

curiosity. "This is very interesting," said he. "You recoil from such a death?"

"Who would not?" asked the plotter.

"And to be blown up by dynamite," inquired the young man, "doubtless strikes you as a form of euthanasia?"

"Pardon me," returned Zero: "I own, and since I have braved it daily in my professional career, I own it even with pride: it is a death unusually distasteful to the mind of man."

"One more question," said Somerset: "you object to Lynch Law? why?"

"It is assassination," said the plotter calmly; but with eyebrows a little lifted, as in wonder at the question.

"Shake hands with me," cried Somerset. "Thank God, I have now no ill-feeling left; and though you cannot conceive how I burn to see you on the gallows, I can quite contentedly assist at your departure."

"I do not very clearly take your meaning," said Zero, "but I am sure you mean kindly. As to my departure, there is another point to be considered. I have neglected to supply myself with funds; my little all has perished in what history will love to relate under the name of the Golden Square Atrocity; and without what is coarsely if vigorously called stamps, you must be well aware it is impossible for me to pass the ocean."

"For me," said Somerset, "you have now ceased to be a man. You have no more claim upon me than a door-scraper; but the touching confusion of your mind disarms me from extremities. Until to-day, I always thought stupidity was funny; I now know otherwise; and when I look upon your idiot face, laughter rises within me like a deadly sickness, and the tears spring up into my eyes as bitter as blood. What should this portend? I begin to doubt; I am losing faith in scepticism. Is it possible," he cried, in a kind of horror of himself — " is it conceivable that I believe in right and wrong? Already I have found myself, with incredulous surprise, to be the victim of a prejudice of personal honour. And must this change proceed? Have you robbed me of my youth? Must I fall, at my time of life, into the Common Banker? But why should I address that head of wood? Let this suffice. I dare not let you stay among women and children; I lack the courage to denounce you, if by any means I may avoid it; you have no money: well then, take mine, and go; and if ever I behold your face after to-day, that day will be your last."

"Under the circumstances," replied Zero, " I scarce see my way to refuse your offer. Your expressions may pain, they cannot surprise me; I am aware our point of view requires a little training, a little moral hygiene, if I may so express it; and one of the points that has always charmed me in your character, is this delightful frankness. As for the small advance, it shall be remitted you from Philadelphia."

" It shall not," said Somerset.

" Dear fellow, you do not understand," returned

the plotter. "I shall now be received with fresh confidence by my superiors; and my experiments will be no longer hampered by pitiful conditions of the purse."

"What I am now about, sir, is a crime," replied Somerset; "and were you to roll in wealth like Vanderbilt, I should scorn to be reimbursed of money I had so scandalously misapplied. Take it, and keep it. By George, sir, three days of you have transformed me to an ancient Roman."

With these words, Somerset hailed a passing hansom; and the pair were driven rapidly to the railway terminus. There, an oath having been exacted, the money changed hands.

"And now," said Somerset, "I have bought back my honour with every penny I possess. And I thank God, though there is nothing before me but starvation, I am free from all entanglement with Mr. Zero Pumpernickel Jones."

"To starve!" cried Zero. "Dear fellow, I cannot endure the thought."

"Take your ticket!" returned Somerset.

"I think you display temper," said Zero.

"Take your ticket," reiterated the young man.

"Well," said the plotter, as he returned, ticket in hand, "your attitude is so strange and painful, that I scarce know if I should ask you to shake hands."

"As a man, no," replied Somerset; "but I have no objection to shake hands with you, as I might with a pump-well that ran poison or hell-fire."

"This is a very cold parting," sighed the dynamiter; and still followed by Somerset, he began to descend the platform. This was now bustling with passengers; the train for Liverpool was just about to start, another had but recently arrived; and the double tide made movement difficult. As the pair reached the neighbourhood of the book-stall, however, they came into an open space; and here the attention of the plotter was attracted by a *Standard* broadside bearing the words: " Second Edition: Explosion in Golden Square." His eye lighted; groping in his pocket for the necessary coin, he sprang forward — his bag knocked sharply on the corner of the stall — and instantly, with a formidable report, the dynamite exploded. When the smoke cleared away the stall was seen much shattered, and the stall-keeper running forth in terror from the ruins; but of the Irish patriot or the Gladstone bag no adequate remains were to be found.

In the first scramble of the alarm, Somerset made good his escape, and came out upon the Euston Road, his head spinning, his body sick with hunger, and his pockets destitute of coin. Yet, as he continued to walk the pavements, he wondered to find in his heart a sort of peaceful exultation, a great content, a sense, as it were, of divine presence and the kindliness of fate; and he was able to tell himself that even if the worst befell, he could now starve with a certain comfort since Zero was expunged.

Late in the afternoon, he found himself at the door of Mr. Godall's shop; and being quite unmanned by his long fast, and scarce considering what he did, he opened the glass door and entered.

"Ha!" said Mr. Godall, "Mr. Somerset! Well, have you met with an adventure? Have you the promised story? Sit down, if you please; suffer me to choose you a cigar of my own special brand, and reward me with a narrative in your best style."

"I must not take a cigar," said Somerset.

"Indeed!" said Mr. Godall. "But now I come to look at you more closely, I perceive that you are changed. My poor boy, I hope there is nothing wrong?"

Somerset burst into tears.

EPILOGUE OF THE CIGAR DIVAN

ON a certain day of lashing rain in the December of last year, and between the hours of nine and ten in the morning, Mr. Edward Challoner pioneered himself under an umbrella to the door of the Cigar Divan in Rupert Street. It was a place he had visited but once before: the memory of what had followed on that visit and the fear of Somerset, having prevented his return. Even now, he looked in before he entered; but the shop was free of customers.

The young man behind the counter was so intently writing in a penny-version book, that he paid no heed to Challoner's arrival. On a second glance, it seemed to the latter that he recognised him.

" By Jove," he thought, " unquestionably Somerset! "

And though this was the very man he had been so sedulously careful to avoid, his unexplained position at the receipt of custom changed distaste to curiosity.

" ' Or opulent rotunda strike the sky,' " said the shopman to himself, in the tone of one considering a verse. " I suppose it would be too much to say ' orotunda,' and yet how noble it were! ' Or

opulent orotunda strike the sky.' But that is the
bitterness of arts; you see a good effect and some
nonsense about sense continually intervenes."

"Somerset, my dear fellow," said Challoner, "is
this a masquerade?"

"What? Challoner!" cried the shopman. "I
am delighted to see you. One moment, till I finish
the octave of my sonnet: only the octave." And
with a friendly waggle of the hand, he once more
buried himself in the commerce of the Muses. "I
say," he said presently, looking up, "you seem in
wonderful preservation: how about the hundred
pounds?"

"I have made a small inheritance from a great-
aunt in Wales," replied Challoner modestly.

"Ah," said Somerset, "I very much doubt the
legitimacy of inheritance. The State, in my view,
should collar it. I am now going through a stage
of socialism and poetry," he added apologetically,
as one who spoke of a course of medicinal waters.

"And are you really the person of the — establishment?" inquired Challoner, deftly evading the
word "shop."

"A vendor, sir, a vendor," returned the other,
pocketing his poesy. "I help old Happy and
Glorious. Can I offer you a weed?"

"Well, I scarcely like . . . " began Challoner.

"Nonsense, my dear fellow," cried the shopman.
"We are very proud of the business; and the old
man, let me inform you, besides being the most
egregious of created beings from the point of view
of ethics, is literally sprung from the loins of kings.

' *De Godall je suis le fervent.*' There is only one Godall. — By the way," he added, as Challoner lit his cigar, " how did you get on with the detective trade? "

" I did not try," said Challoner curtly.

" Ah, well, I did," returned Somerset, " and made the most incomparable mess of it: lost all my money and fairly covered myself with odium and ridicule. There is more in that business, Challoner, than meets the eye; there is more, in fact, in all businesses. You must believe in them, or get up the belief that you believe. Hence," he added, " the recognised inferiority of the plumber, for no one could believe in plumbing."

" *A propos,*" asked Challoner, " do you still paint? "

" Not now," replied Paul; " but I think of taking up the violin."

Challoner's eye, which had been somewhat restless since the trade of the detective had been named, now rested for a moment on the columns of the morning paper, where it lay spread upon the counter.

" By Jove," he cried, " that's odd! "

" What is odd? " asked Paul.

" Oh, nothing," returned the other: " only I once met a person called M'Guire."

" So did I! " cried Somerset. " Is there anything about him? "

Challoner read as follows: " *Mysterious death in Stepney.* An inquest was held yesterday on the body of Patrick M'Guire, described as a carpenter.

Dr. Dovering stated that he had for some time treated the deceased as a dispensary patient, for sleeplessness, loss of appetite, and nervous depression. There was no cause of death to be found. He would say the deceased had sunk. Deceased was not a temperate man, which doubtless accelerated death. Deceased complained of dumb ague, but witness had never been able to detect any positive disease. He did not know that he had any family. He regarded him as a person of unsound intellect, who believed himself a member and the victim of some secret society. If he were to hazard an opinion, he would say deceased had died of fear."

" And the doctor would be right," cried Somerset ; " and, my dear Challoner, I am so relieved to hear of his demise, that I will —— Well, after all," he added, " poor devil, he was well served."

The door at this moment opened, and Desborough appeared upon the threshold. He was wrapped in a long waterproof, imperfectly supplied with buttons ; his boots were full of water, his hat greasy with service ; and yet he wore the air of one exceedingly well content with life. He was hailed by the two others with exclamations of surprise and welcome.

" And did you try the detective business ? " inquired Paul.

" No," returned Harry. " Oh yes, by the way, I did though ; twice, and got caught out both times. But I thought I should find my — my wife here ! " he added, with a kind of proud confusion.

" What! are you married? " cried Somerset.

" Oh yes," said Harry, " quite a long time: a month at least."

" Money? " asked Challoner.

" That 's the worst of it," Desborough admitted. " We are deadly hard up. But the Pri — Mr. Godall is going to do something for us. That is what brings us here."

" Who was Mrs. Desborough? " said Challoner, in the tone of a man of society.

" She was a Miss Luxmore," returned Harry. " You fellows will be sure to like her, for she is much cleverer than I. She tells wonderful stories, too; better than a book."

And just then the door opened, and Mrs. Desborough entered. Somerset cried out aloud to recognise the young lady of the Superfluous Mansion, and Challoner fell back a step and dropped his cigar as he beheld the sorceress of Chelsea.

" What! " cried Harry, " do you both know my wife? "

" I believe I have seen her," said Somerset, a little wildly.

" I think I have met the gentleman," said Mrs. Desborough, sweetly; " but I cannot imagine where it was."

" Oh no," cried Somerset fervently: " I have no notion — I cannot conceive — where it could have been. Indeed," he continued, growing in emphasis, " I think it highly probable that it 's a mistake."

"And you, Challoner?" asked Harry, "you seemed to recognise her, too."

"These are both friends of yours, Harry?" said the lady. "Delighted, I am sure. I do not remember to have met Mr. Challoner."

Challoner was very red in the face, perhaps from having groped after his cigar. "I do not remember to have had the pleasure," he responded huskily.

"Well, and Mr. Godall?" asked Mrs. Desborough.

"Are you the lady that has an appointment with old . . ." began Somerset, and paused blushing. "Because if so," he resumed, "I was to announce you at once."

And the shopman raised a curtain, opened the door, and passed into a small pavilion which had been added to the back of the house. On the roof the rain resounded musically. The walls were lined with maps and prints and a few works of reference. Upon a table was a large-scale map of Egypt and the Soudan, and another of Tonkin, on which, by the aid of coloured pins, the progress of the different wars was being followed day by day. A light, refreshing odour of the most delicate tobacco hung upon the air; and a fire, not of foul coal, but of clear-flaming resinous billets, chattered upon silver dogs. In this elegant and plain apartment, Mr. Godall sat in a morning muse, placidly gazing at the fire and hearkening to the rain upon the roof.

"Ha, my dear Mr. Somerset," said he, "and

have you since last night adopted any fresh political principle?"

"The lady, sir," said Somerset, with another blush.

"You have seen her, I believe?" returned Mr. Godall; and on Somerset's replying in the affirmative: "You will excuse me, my dear sir," he resumed, "if I offer you a hint. I think it not improbable this lady may desire entirely to forget the past. From one gentleman to another, no more words are necessary."

A moment after, he had received Mrs. Desborough with that grave and touching urbanity that so well became him.

"I am pleased, madam, to welcome you to my poor house," he said; "and shall be still more so, if what were else a barren courtesy and a pleasure personal to myself, shall prove to be of serious benefit to you and Mr. Desborough."

"Your Highness," replied Clara, "I must begin with thanks; it is like what I have heard of you, that you should thus take up the case of the unfortunate; and as for my Harry, he is worthy of all that you can do." She paused.

"But for yourself?" suggested Mr. Godall — "it was thus you were about to continue, I believe."

"You take the words out of my mouth," she said. "For myself it is different."

"I am not here to be a judge of men," replied the Prince; "still less of women. I am now a private person like yourself and many million others; but I am one who still fights upon the side of quiet.

Now, madam, you know better than I, and God
better than you, what you have done to mankind
in the past; I pause not to inquire; it is with the
future I concern myself, it is for the future I demand security. I would not willingly put arms
into the hands of a disloyal combatant; and I dare
not restore to wealth one of the leviers of a private
and a barbarous war. I speak with some severity,
and yet I pick my terms. I tell myself continually
that you are a woman; and a voice continually
reminds me of the children whose lives and limbs
you have endangered. A woman," he repeated
solemnly — " and children. Possibly, madam,
when you are yourself a mother, you will feel the
bite of that antithesis: possibly when you kneel at
night beside a cradle, a fear will fall upon you,
heavier than any shame; and when your child lies
in the pain and danger of disease, you shall hesitate
to kneel before your Maker."

" You look at the fault," she said, " and not at
the excuse. Has your own heart never leaped
within you at some story of oppression? But, alas,
no! for you were born upon a throne."

" I was born of woman," said the Prince; " I
came forth from my mother's agony, helpless as a
wren, like other nurslings. This, which you forgot, I have still faithfully remembered. Is it not
one of your English poets that looked abroad upon
the earth and saw vast circumvallations, innumerable troops manœuvring, war-ships at sea, and a
great dust of battles on shore; and casting anx-
iously about for what should be the cause of so

many and painful preparations, spied at last, in the centre of all, a mother and her babe? These, madam, are my politics; and the verses, which are by Mr. Coventry Patmore, I have caused to be translated into the Bohemian tongue. Yes, these are my politics: to change what we can; to better what we can; but still to bear in mind that man is but a devil weakly fettered by some generous beliefs and impositions; and for no word however nobly sounding, and no cause however just and pious, to relax the stricture of these bonds."

There was a silence of a moment.

"I fear, madam," resumed the Prince, "that I but weary you. My views are formal like myself, and like myself, they also begin to grow old. But I must still trouble you for some reply."

"I can say but one thing," said Mrs. Desborough: "I love my husband."

"It is a good answer," returned the Prince; "and you name a good influence, but one that need not be conterminous with life."

"I will not play at pride with such a man as you," she answered. "What do you ask of me? not protestations, I am sure. What shall I say? I have done much that I cannot defend and that I would not do again. Can I say more? Yes: I can say this: I never abused myself with the muddle-headed fairy tales of politics. I was at least prepared to meet reprisals. While I was levying war myself — or levying murder if you choose the plainer term — I never accused my adversaries of assassination. I never felt or feigned a righteous horror, when a price was put upon my life by those whom I attacked. I never called the policeman a hireling. I may have been a criminal, in short; but never was a fool."

"Enough, madam," returned the Prince: "more than enough! Your words are most reviving to my spirits; for in this age, when even the assassin is a sentimentalist, there is no virtue greater in my eyes than intellectual clarity. Suffer me then to ask you to retire; for by the signal of that bell, I perceive my old friend, your mother, to be close at hand. With her I promise you to do my utmost."

And as Mrs. Desborough returned to the Divan, the Prince, opening a door upon the other side, admitted Mrs. Luxmore.

"Madam and my very good friend," said he, "is my face so much changed that you no longer recognise Prince Florizel in Mr. Godall?"

"To be sure!" she cried, looking at him through her glasses. "I have always regarded your Highness as a perfect man; and in your altered circumstances, of which I have already heard with deep regret, I will beg you to consider my respect increased instead of lessened."

"I have found it so," returned the Prince, "with every class of my acquaintance. But, madam, I pray you to be seated. My business is of a delicate order and regards your daughter."

"In that case," said Mrs. Luxmore, "you may save yourself the trouble of speaking, for I have fully made up my mind to have nothing to do with her. I will not hear one word in her defence; but as I value nothing so particularly as the virtue of justice, I think it my duty to explain to you the grounds of my complaint. She deserted me, her natural protector; for years she has consorted with the most disreputable persons; and to fill the cup of her offence, she has recently married. I refuse to see her, or the being to whom she has linked herself. One hundred and twenty pounds a year, I have always offered her: I offer it again. It is what I had myself when I was her age."

"Very well, madam," said the Prince, "and be that so! But to touch upon another: what was the income of the Reverend Bernard Fanshawe?"

"My father?" asked the spirited old lady. "I believe he had seven hundred pounds in the year."

"You were one, I think, of several?" pursued the Prince.

"Of four," was the reply. "We were four daughters; and painful as the admission is to make, a more detestable family could scarce be found in England."

"Dear me!" said the Prince. "And you, madam, have an income of eight thousand?"

"Not more than five," returned the old lady; "but where on earth are you conducting me?"

"To an allowance of one thousand pounds a year," replied Florizel, smiling. "For I must not suffer you to take your father for a rule. He was poor, you are rich. He had many calls upon his poverty; there are none upon your wealth. And indeed, madam, if you will let me touch this matter with a needle, there is but one point in common to your two positions: that each had a daughter more remarkable for liveliness than duty."

"I have been entrapped into this house," said the old lady, getting to her feet. "But it shall not avail. Not all the tobacconists in Europe . . ."

"Ah, madam," interrupted Florizel, "before what is referred to as my fall, you had not used such language! And since you so much object to the simple industry by which I live, let me give you a friendly hint. If you will not consent to support your daughter, I shall be constrained to place that lady behind my counter, where I doubt not she would prove a great attraction; and your son-in-law shall have a livery and run the errands. With such young blood my business might be doubled, and I might be bound, in common gratitude, to place the name of Luxmore beside that of Godall."

"Your Highness," said the old lady, "I have been very rude, and you are very cunning. I suppose the minx is on the premises. Produce her."

"Let us rather observe them unperceived," said the Prince; and so saying, he rose and quietly drew back the curtain.

Mrs. Desborough sat with her back to them on a chair; Somerset and Harry were hanging on her words with extraordinary interest; Challoner, alleging some affair, had long ago withdrawn from the detested neighbourhood of the enchantress.

"At that moment," Mrs. Desborough was saying, "Mr. Gladstone detected the features of his cowardly assailant. A cry rose to his lips: a cry of mingled triumph . . ."

" That is Mr. Somerset!" interrupted the spirited old lady, in the highest note of her register. " Mr. Somerset, what have you done with my house-property? "

" Madam," said the Prince, " let it be mine to give the explanation; and in the meanwhile welcome your daughter."

" Well, Clara, how do you do? " said Mrs. Luxmore. " It appears I am to give you an allowance. So much the better for you. As for Mr. Somerset, I am very ready to have an explanation; for the whole affair, though costly, was eminently humourous. And at any rate," she added, nodding to Paul, " he is a young gentleman for whom I have a great affection, and his pictures were the funniest I ever saw."

" I have ordered a collation," said the Prince. " Mr. Somerset, as these are all your friends, I propose, if you please, that you should join them at table. I will take the shop."